This was insane, I thought.

Sitting in a cold car—a rusty station wagon, no less—listening to songs from my high school years with the same yearning in my heart that I'd felt then. "Abby," I whispered into the icy air, "you picked a great time to have a midlife crisis."

I drove home, hauled the packages into the house and went into the living room.

Natalie looked up from her magazine. "Ma, the kids keep asking me when you're going to decorate for Christmas. As their grandmother, and since it is your house, it's your responsibility."

You know that saying "I saw red"? Well, it's true. I saw red. And we're not talking twinkling lights here.

I remembered a story I'd heard. If a man could go on strike against his wife for lack of affection, why couldn't a woman go on strike against her family for lack of cooperation?

"As of this moment, all of you are on your own. I. Am. On. Strike."

Nikki Rivers

When she was twelve years old, Nikki Rivers knew she wanted to be a writer. Unfortunately, due to many forks in the road of life, she didn't start writing seriously until several decades later. She considers herself an observer in life, and often warns family and friends that anything they say or do could end up on the pages of a novel. She lives in Milwaukee, Wisconsin, with her husband—and best friend—Ron, and her feisty cairn terrier, Sir Hairy Scruffles. Her daughter Jennifer—friend, critic, shopping accomplice and constant source of grist for the mill—lives just down the street.

Nikki loves to hear from her readers. E-mail her at nikkiriverswrites@yahoo.com.

Nikki Rivers
The Christmas Strike

THE CHRISTMAS STRIKE

copyright © 2006 by Sharon Edwin

isbn-13:978-0-373-88121-5

isbn-10:   0-373-88121-5

TheNextNovel.com

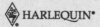 HARLEQUIN®

PRINTED IN U.S.A.

From the Author

Dear Reader,

Ah, the holidays. Don't you just love them? I do. Really. At the first sign of winter I'm all set to jingle the bells and put out the gumdrop tree I inherited from my grandmother. But who among us, if we're totally honest, hasn't at one time or another thought of chucking it all in. Let someone else hang the tinsel and wrap the presents for a change!

One of the pleasures of being a writer is that you get to create people who do the things you only occasionally dream about. Abby Blake is just such a character. She is an everywoman who discovers that her dreams haven't yet completely died. I hope how Abby sets out to reclaim herself and accidentally winds up in Paris will make you laugh during even the worst of the holiday chaos.

But this Christmas, I also wanted to bring you the kind of hero who is a guilty pleasure for us all. The alpha male. Cole Hudson—and Paris—are my Christmas gifts to you!

Happy holidays to you all, and may you all soar in the New Year! After all, if you hang on to your dreams, anything is possible.

Nikki Rivers

This book is dedicated to my mother, Shirley Olsen,
who always knew how to make
the holidays special—no matter what.

I'd also like to thank Dane Jenning, president of
Tandava Aviation, who was so generous in sharing
his time and his expertise in private aviation for
the research for this book.

And a special thanks to my sister, Judy, for teaching
me the right way to do tequila shots!

I pulled up the hood of my baby-blue parka as I hurried down Main Street on my way to Dempsey's Diner. It was unseasonably cold even for a waning December afternoon in Willow Creek, Wisconsin. The weatherman on the radio that morning had forecast snow. The steely sky above me and the wetness of the wind on my face made me think he'd gotten it right for a change. I waved at Ivan Mueller as I passed Mueller the Jeweler. While hanging a Christmas wreath in the window, he paused long enough to wave back. The entire downtown—all two blocks of it—was decked out for the holiday, which was only two weeks away. My own Christmas spirit was woefully lacking this year, making me almost resent the festive candy cane wreath on the door at the diner.

Just as I reached for the knob on the diner's front door, it was pushed open from inside, nearly knocking me off my feet. A gaggle of teenagers spilled onto the sidewalk, laughing and hooting. I smiled slightly at their antics. I'd been young once myself—I think.

They hadn't bothered to hold the door for me, so I pulled it open and went inside. The aroma of freshly brewing coffee and frying donuts embraced me right down to my chilled bones.

"Will you look at this?" Joanne Dempsey demanded as she

shook her head at the mound of salt on the counter in front of her. "I bet those rotten kids that were just in here loosened every damned salt shaker in the place."

I shook my head. "Remember when we used to do that?"

"If that's your polite way of telling me that paybacks are a bitch, forget it. It is not lost on me that I am now the Old Mrs. Dempsey down at the diner that the kids from junior high get to harass for the price of a Coke."

I slid into one of the booths by the window and shrugged out of my parka. "Trust me, you're nothing like your mother-in-law was."

"Maybe not to you, since you're now a middle-aged curmudgeon, too. But to those young hoodlums—"

"You know," I interrupted, "using those kinds of words isn't helping the image."

"What kinds of words?" Iris Johnson asked as she entered the diner along with a burst of arctic air. "I hope I didn't miss anything vulgar," she said as she teetered over to the booth on four-inch heeled boots.

"Jo just called me a middle-aged curmudgeon," I told her.

Iris, glaring at Jo, slipped off her full-length white fake fur, revealing tight black leather jeans and a gold metallic ruffled shirt, and tossed the coat toward the empty booth nearby. "Fifty-two is *not* middle-aged," she emphatically insisted as she sat down across from me. "And what the hell is a curmudgeon? It sounds like something from *The Wizard of Oz*."

"Those are Munchkins," I corrected. Iris never had any kids.

"My mother-in-law, may she rest in peace," Jo explained, "was a curmudgeon."

Iris shrugged. "If you mean old bitch, say old bitch." She lit a cigarette and we both glared at her. She, as usual, ignored us. "It's true that you can be bitchy, Jo, honey, but you're certainly not an *old* bitch. We are," she said before pausing to blow smoke toward the hammered tin ceiling, "the same age."

"Thank you," Jo said.

"She's upset because some kids loosened the tops on the salt shakers," I explained.

"We used to do that," Iris said.

"Exactly," Jo exclaimed as she came over with three mugs, a carafe of coffee and a basket of hot donuts. "The postpubescent are now doing to me what we used to do to Mike's mother. In other words, I've crossed over to the other side. Next thing you know they'll be throwing snowballs at me hoping I fall on my ass."

Iris took another drag then put the cigarette out. Her current program to quit smoking involved taking only two drags per cigarette. It was costing her a small fortune. The nicotine withdrawal wasn't helping her mood, either. "Keep those donuts away from me," she griped as she waved off the basket Jo was holding out to her. "I had a hard enough time zipping these jeans this morning."

Jo pulled the basket closer to our side of the booth and we both dug in with gusto.

"Look," Iris complained, "having coffee with you two every Friday afternoon is supposed to cheer me up. Get a clue. This conversation isn't doing it. And the sight of you two scarfing down donuts like it's the day before Armageddon isn't helping." She sighed. "Neither is the fact that that guy I met in Milwaukee last weekend still hasn't called."

Jo and I made sympathetic noises, but we couldn't relate. Jo had been married to Mike Dempsey, her high school sweetheart, since the age of nineteen and even though I'd been widowed for over twenty years, I'd never put myself back on the market. When you have lived in a town of less than five thousand people nearly all your life, you pretty much know why every eligible man is still eligible. The reason was never good. Which is why Iris had started fishing in a bigger pond.

She examined her nails, then started to play with the ends of her hair—auburn this week. Iris was a huge fan of the current resurgence of big hair. As owner of Iris's House of Beauty, she had half the women in town looking like they should be living in Texas. Luckily, I wore my graying blond hair too short for one of her makeovers. It didn't keep her from trying to talk me into it, though. So far, Jo, who still wore her brown hair like she had in high school—short bob with full bangs—had also resisted.

Mike came out of the kitchen with a rack of clean glasses and noisily set them on the counter. "You taking another break?" he asked.

"Friday afternoon coffee klatch, remember?"

"You know, you can be replaced," Mike quipped.

"I'd like to see you try," Jo shot back.

It was their usual banter. Mike, who was still built like the linebacker he'd been in high school and still had that mop of wavy brown hair and a pair of dimples that could kill, was crazy about Jo and we all knew it, even when he gave her a hard time.

"You know," Mike said, "I just saw something on the news about a man who went on strike against his wife because she wasn't giving him enough affection."

We all laughed.

"Go ahead, laugh. But I'm serious, ladies. It was on CNN."

"Don't worry, Mike, I've got you penciled in for some affection later tonight," Jo assured him.

He shook his head. "Not good enough. I want indelible ink or nothing."

Jo smiled. "You got it, babe. Now get back in that kitchen and start frying some more donuts before the after-work crowd gets here."

He gave her a look. "Boy, that better be a lot of affection I'm gonna get."

Mike disappeared into the kitchen and I thought about how lucky Jo was not to have to sleep alone at night.

"Look at that," Iris said as she jerked her chin toward the window. "Old man Kilbourn at the drugstore has been putting those same decorations in his windows since the Beatles made their first record." She sighed. "Nothing ever changes in this town. How the hell did the three of us end up back here?"

Although it was a question one of us asked periodically, no one really ever bothered to answer. We each had our reasons. Certainly, none of us had intended to live out our lives here. As far as we were concerned the whole point of growing up in Willow Creek was to get out of Willow Creek. My two much older siblings, a brother and sister, had moved to the west coast long before I'd graduated from high school. I'd made my escape at the age of nineteen when I'd moved to Milwaukee and enrolled in night courses in accounting while working as a secretary during the day at an accounting firm. That was where I'd met my husband, Charlie.

Nat and Gwen were babies and Charlie and I were looking for our first house when my father became terminally ill. I moved back to Willow Creek with the kids to help my mother take care of my father. Charlie came down on weekends. After my father died, it was clear my aging mother could no longer live alone. We didn't want to have just a weekend marriage, so Charlie moved into my mother's house with me and the kids, and opened an accounting office in Willow Creek. Neither of us considered the move a permanent one, though. We figured it was only a matter of time before we'd pick up our lives in the city where we'd left off.

Then came the car accident and in the blink of an eye, I became the Widow of Willow Creek. With two toddlers tugging at my jeans and an increasingly needy mother to take care of, I closed Charlie's office and opened a bookkeeping and tax preparation service that I ran out of the house. By the time my mother had passed on, the girls were entering their teens with social lives of their own and I figured I was meant to be born, live and die in Willow Creek.

I looked at my watch. "I've got to keep an eye on the time."

"Fetching the grandkids from school again today?" Jo asked.

I nodded. "Natalie picked up an extra half shift out at the Mega-mart. They can use the money."

"Jeremy find anything yet?"

I sighed, refilled my mug and grabbed another donut. "My son-in-law has taken root on the sofa," I said with my mouth full. "I'm afraid I'm going to have to start watering him soon."

"Must be in the depression stage," Iris said. "Unemployment can put you through the same five stages as grief, you know."

Jo and I looked at each other, then back at Iris.

"Something you read in *Vogue*?" Jo asked with sweet sarcasm and a batting of her mascara-less lashes.

Iris shook her hair back. "I read other things, too, you know."

She sniffed. "Anyway, it's only common sense. You put a virile guy like Jeremy out of work and give him nothing to do and he's bound to start struggling with his ego."

"Believe me," I said dryly as I sipped my coffee, "I've given Jeremy plenty to do. Nice little list that looks as fresh as the day I gave it to him."

"See? Another symptom of depression is an inability to take action," Iris pointed out. "It's like you become frozen. Jeremy could even be on the verge of a nervous breakdown. I read just the other day—"

Iris was a magazine junkie. While you waited your turn at Iris's House of Beauty, you could read everything from *Psychology Today* and *Herbal Monthly* to *Vogue* and *Cosmo*. She claimed that since she could use the subscriptions as a business expense that ordering so many was just her way of sticking it to the government, but Jo and I knew she was addicted.

"All I want to know about a breakdown," I said as I struggled back into my parka, "is when is it going to be my turn to have one? I wouldn't mind lying on the sofa and watching old movies all day long in my pajamas." I slid out of the booth and headed for the door.

"Hey, wait a minute," Jo called. "We haven't decided on what the Prisoners of Willow Creek Enrichment Society is doing tomorrow. This is our Saturday, you know."

Iris groaned. "I've got a great idea. Let's sleep."

Jo gave her a look of reproach. We'd formed the Prisoners Enrichment Society several years ago when it became clear that none of us was likely to escape Willow Creek a second time. We may be stuck in Willow Creek but we didn't plan on becoming stagnant.

"Okay, okay." Iris gave in under Jo's look. "Just let's not go bowling again."

"If this snow keeps up, why don't we plan on a hike along the creek?" I suggested. "It'll be gorgeous."

"It'll be cold," Iris said.

"Besides, Iris doesn't own a pair of boots with heels under three inches," Jo pointed out. "Why don't we drive over to that new ceramics shop near Lake Geneva? They're having an introductory class. For ten bucks you get to paint your own latte cup."

"Yippeee," Iris drawled sarcastically as she lit another cigarette.

"That reminds me," I asked Jo, "how's the cappuccino war going?"

Jo was currently working on Mike to buy a cappuccino maker. She had dreams of turning the diner into a café. She felt it would give the town a little dash. We were in an area about halfway between Milwaukee and Chicago and surrounded by towns that had become weekend spots for the upper middle class from both cities. Willow Creek had remained just a small town while many of the neighboring ones had become favorites of tourists looking for a bucolic, small town experience but who didn't want to travel far from home.

Many in Willow Creek saw the town's anonymity as a victory and were happy with less intrusion from the outside world. Jo wasn't one of them. She was constantly battling with Mike to turn the diner into the kind of place that would pull in business from tourists. But I had a feeling that if she ever won we would all miss the geometric-patterned gray Formica countertops, the red fake-leather-covered booths and the old fashioned soda fountain behind the curved counter with its chrome and red stools that spun in place. We'd all been coming here since Mike's parents were probably younger than we were now—unsettling thought that that was. Most of the girls in town had done a stint as a waitress at Dempsey's. That's how Jo first fell in love with Mike.

"Mike still thinks the diner, like his mother, is perfect," Jo said. "He says why tamper with success. Which is exactly what his mother always said. But, frankly, with all three kids in college, we could use a little more success." She took a moment to make sure Mike was out of earshot. "I'm sneaking a pasta dish on the menu next week," she whispered. "And he doesn't know it yet, but I'm thinking about putting our Christmas club money into a new sign out on the highway."

"The assault begins," Iris pronounced.

"I don't care who wins," I said, "as long as you don't switch coffee suppliers or take the donuts off the menu."

The diner only offered one kind of donut—a plain cake one—but they were made fresh several times daily. The outsides were always just slightly crunchy while the insides were so tender they melted in your mouth. Nearly the entire town was addicted to them.

"So," I said as I zipped up my parka, "ceramics class tomorrow?"

We both looked at Iris. She took a second drag on the new cigarette then stamped it out in the black plastic ashtray in front of her.

"I can hardly wait," she said.

Face it, I wasn't exactly enthralled with the idea of painting flowers on a latte cup, either. But at least it would get me out of the house on a Saturday.

When we first formed the Prisoner's Enrichment Society, we'd had loftier goals than ceramics or bowling in mind. We'd even planned a trip to Europe once. Went so far as to get our passports. Then my daughter Natalie found out she was pregnant with her second child on the same day Jeremy got laid off from the auto plant two towns over. Suddenly my Europe fund had other, more important places to go. The farthest the Society had ever taken us was a weekend trip to Chicago two years ago. But at least we hadn't given up completely.

It was snowing lightly when I left the diner. Dark enough, in fact, on this December afternoon for the Christmas lights hanging from lampposts along Main Street to already be lit. I tried to muster up some Christmas spirit at the sight. Who knows? Maybe the snowfall put Jeremy in the mood and he'd gotten off the sofa long enough to put up our outdoor Christmas lights like he'd been promising to do since the day after Thanksgiving.

Luckily, the wind was at my back as I walked the few blocks to my car. I yanked open the door of my slightly rusting station wagon, wincing at the screech, and slid behind the wheel while I sent a silent wish into the frosty air that the wagon would start on the first try. It didn't. I resisted the urge to pump the gas and tried again. The engine caught and I smiled and patted the dashboard. "Good girl. Now just get us to the grade school then home and I'll tuck you in for the rest of the night."

I drove over to the school, contemplating what to fix for dinner. Natalie, my twenty-nine-year-old daughter, and her husband, Jeremy, had moved in nearly four months ago when Jeremy's unemployment ran out and the bank foreclosed on their house, but I still wasn't used to planning family meals again. I'd grown accustomed to just grabbing a bowl of cereal or heating up some soup. Now meals were a big, noisy, messy deal again. Not that I didn't love my grandkids. I loved them like crazy even when they made me crazy.

I pulled up behind a row of cars in front of the elementary school and waited. As usual, eight-year-old Tyler, dark haired and green eyed with a wrestler's body like his father's, was the first one to reach the car. "Shotgun!" he yelled while ten-year-old Matt, tall, lanky and sandy haired like his grandfather, tried to shove him out of the way.

"Knock it off, Matt," I said.

"No fair," Matt grumbled. "Tyler got shotgun yesterday."

"You're right. Tyler, get in the back, it's Matty's turn to ride up front."

"Aww—" Tyler groused as he gave in.

"Where's your sister?" I asked, craning my neck to get a look at the steady stream of kids coming out of the school.

"Probably giggling with those two morons she hangs around with," said Matt.

I was just about to send one of the boys to look for her when Ashley broke from the pack and started skipping toward the car, her long blunt-cut auburn hair swinging from beneath her winter hat.

"Hi, Grandma," she said as she got into the backseat. She threw her arms around my neck from behind and gave me a kiss on the cheek. She was the only one of my grandchildren who still showed me affection in public.

"Get on your own side of the car," Tyler yelled.

"Dork," Ashley said with all the indignity a six-year-old can muster.

"Ha! Dork? That the best you can do, loser?"

No doubt about it, Ashley sometimes had a tough time being the only girl.

"Hey," she squealed, "stop elbowing me!"

Matt turned around and threw his cap at Ashley. "Quit screaming in my ear, weirdo."

I stuck two fingers in my mouth and whistled. That got their attention. "The next one of you who says anything nasty or pokes, prods, elbows or otherwise harasses anyone gets to do the dishes tonight. All. By. Themselves."

There were moans of varying degrees, but the dishes deterrent never failed. The three of them settled down. I turned on the radio, perpetually set on an oldies station, and everyone started singing along to "Sweet Caroline." By the time we got home, we were mutilating the lyrics to "Brown Eyed Girl."

Home was still the two-story Victorian with a wraparound porch in perpetual need of painting that had once belonged to my parents. I had just gotten around to the idea of selling it when Nat and Jeremy lost their house almost four months ago. What could I do? They needed a roof over their heads and I was still the mom, a role that no longer suited me as much as it used to. I was the grandmother. I was supposed to get to do the fun things with my grandchildren. Instead, I'd become the one who wiped up the spilled milk and broke up the fights.

The kids tumbled out of the car while I checked for any sign of Christmas light activity on the bare branches of the barberry bushes lining the front porch. Not one string was strung. I didn't see any of the electric candles I'd asked him to put in the front windows, either.

I followed the kids up the stairs and into the house where they kicked off boots and parkas and threw them in the direction of the cobbler's bench lining one side of the entrance hall. There was a sweatshirt thrown over the banister of the open staircase and a basket full of clean laundry sitting on the bottom step.

The living room was to the left of the entrance hall, while the dining room was to the right. The big family-style kitchen was behind the dining room.

The kids, as usual, clattered through the dining room to the kitchen to raid the cookie jar. I followed to make sure none of them took more than two cookies—homemade oatmeal that Natalie cleverly laced with wheat germ and sunflower seeds—poured milk and got them seated at the table with their homework. Then I headed back to the living room.

Sure enough, Jeremy was still in his flannel pajama pants and an old football jersey, slumped on one of the two matching sofas, his bare feet up on the coffee table between them, his eyes glazed over from watching too much daytime television.

"Jeremy, we need to talk," I said.

"I've already applied every place I can think of, Abby," he said dully without taking his eyes off the television.

"I know that and that's not what I wanted to talk to you about anyway."

His eyes drifted toward mine.

"I just think that maybe it'd be better if you got dressed every day and did something around here. Even just one thing. That's all I ask, Jeremy. 'Cause I think you're slipping into a depression."

This brought his spine upright. "Oh, I can just guess who the topic of conversation was down at the diner this afternoon. I'll hang the damn Christmas lights, okay?"

"That would be a start—"

His jaw worked, but I'd known him since he was thirteen

and first started hanging around on my living room sofa. He was the boy who had cried when he'd lost a wrestling match in high school. The boy who had looked at Natalie with such love in his eyes as she'd walked down the aisle toward him when she was already three months pregnant with Matt. Jeremy could work his jaw all he wanted. It wasn't about to make me back off.

"—but that's not what I really wanted to talk to you about."

He looked wary but defiant and I saw my grandson Tyler in his face. How could I not love this man, even if I sometimes felt like sending the sofas out to be reupholstered just to see what he'd do?

"So, what do you want to talk to me about?" he asked.

"Ma—come on—what were you thinking?" Natalie demanded when she got home from work a few hours later.

"It's just that my business is going well, I could use the help and it would provide a little security for you and the kids. Since the two of you have been married, Jeremy has been laid off four times. Aren't you sick of worrying about layoffs and plant closings? Can't you see how each time it happens, Jeremy finds it harder to deal with?"

"Of course I can see that, Ma. That's one of the reasons I'm pissed that you talked to him without discussing it with me first. It's bad enough Jeremy has to depend on his mother-in-law for a roof over his head right now. How do you think he'd feel if you were his boss, too?"

I leaned against the kitchen sink and watched the kids out in the backyard tumbling around in the snow in the glow of the back porch light. A good four inches had already fallen. It didn't seem to be hurting Jeremy's manliness to not be out there shoveling snow. I wisely decided to keep that observation to myself.

"So, I'll sell him part of the business. For heaven's sake," I said in exasperation, "the point is, he'd be making money while in training and you wouldn't have to worry about layoffs and plant closings ever again."

My daughter Natalie, as usual, looked both sullen and beautiful. Her long sandy hair was tangled, her pale skin was bare of makeup so the sprinkling of freckles on her nose showed. She was as tall as me—five foot ten—but finer boned, leaner, less bosomy. She really took after her father more than me in looks. Of my two daughters, she had always been the more openly rebellious one. Her three kids had come so quickly that Nat still had some growing up to do. But she had a big heart and, in her own way, she was a terrific mother. But, as far as I was concerned, she was still too stubborn for her own good.

"Yeah, Ma, every out-of-work guy wants to be trained by his mother-in-law."

"Don't you think you're being a tad overprotective here?" I pointed out while I picked up a wooden spoon and went to stir the pot of chili on the stove. "He's got a family to help support."

"Ma—I do not want to talk about this now, okay?" Nat said through tightened lips. "Jeremy is upstairs taking a nap but he could be down any minute. I'd like to get through dinner without a scene for a change, if you don't mind."

I bit my tongue so hard to keep the words down that I was surprised I wasn't on my way to bleeding to death. I'd had enough scenes in the past months to last me a lifetime. I wasn't sure which was worse: listening to Jeremy and Natalie fight or listening to them have makeup sex. No wonder the man needed so many naps.

The three kids came tumbling in, cheeks rosy from the cold, trailing snow, spilling milk and getting more chili on the table than in their mouths.

I loved them. I did. But afterwards, as I stood in the middle of the ruins of dinner on the big, square oak table and looked at the puddles of melted snow on the parquet wood floor, I couldn't help but ask myself *isn't there someplace else I'm supposed to be?*

When had this new restlessness started? Was it after Nat and her brood moved in or had it been there all along? And if this wasn't where I was supposed to be, then where *did* I belong?

I got out the mop and told myself to get real. I was exactly where I was supposed to be. Where I'd *chosen* to be. Life wasn't so bad. So Nat and Jeremy had had to move in for a while. It was happening all over the country. The boomerang generation, they called it. It'd only been a little over three months. And surely having the grandchildren here would rekindle my Christmas spirit eventually, wouldn't it? Of course it would. Besides, things could always be worse. At least Gwen wasn't coming home for Christmas this year.

Not that I didn't love my oldest daughter, Gwen. I loved my daughters equally. Enjoyed being with them equally. I even fought with and was irritated by them pretty much equally. They were only a little over a year apart, but they were as different as peanut butter and steak: both of them delicious, but I'd prefer not to eat them at the same meal.

Nat and Gwen didn't share the sisterly bond that I imagined I would have shared with my sister if she hadn't been so much older than me. Basically, my daughters bonded by bickering. It was going to be a relief not to have that added to the cacophony that had become my auditory life. The bonus was, I didn't even have to feel guilty that Gwen wouldn't be here. Her husband, David, was taking her on a holiday cruise. Everyone was winning as far as I was concerned.

I'd always known that Gwen was the kind of girl who would grow up to marry the kind of man who could afford to take her on holiday cruises. Not to mention buy her just about anything she wanted. Gwen had lived her life toward that goal since she'd first discovered that she was not only smart but pretty, a phenomenon that had occurred to her around the age of twelve. Cheerleader. Prom Queen. Scholarships to good schools. A career in the city in banking that led to the kind of social life that got her invited to the right parties where she'd meet a man like David Hudson, an architect who was already making a name for himself at the age of thirty-five.

On paper, thirty-year-old Gwen read like the kind of young woman a mother never had to worry about. Yet I worried just as much about Gwen as I did about Nat. They were just different worries. For instance, I sometimes worried that Gwen loved her husband's money and family connections more than she loved her husband.

David came from a family of old banking money, although both he and his father were architects. I didn't know much about architecture, but even I had heard of Cole Hudson. I'd met him only once—at Gwen's wedding in Chicago last spring. Once was enough as far as I was concerned. He was one of those arrogant, larger-than-life types. Full of himself. Very different from David, who was kind and sweet and loving—and easily wrapped around Gwen's finger. I couldn't imagine Cole Hudson letting any woman wrap so much as a strand of his hair around her finger.

There was a sudden crash from the living room and Ashley squealed, "Give that back to me!" Then, "Mom!" I sighed. One thing I'd never have to worry about was Gwen moving back in. I was pretty sure she'd jump from its balcony before she'd give up the high-rise condo near Chicago's Loop—unless, of course, she'd be giving it up for a mansion on Lake Michigan.

I was finishing up the dishes while the kids were in the living room with Nat, who was checking over their homework before letting them watch TV, when I heard a plaintive voice behind me say, "Mother?"

I spun around. Gwen stood there with a look of such raw pain on her face that my heart immediately opened to her. "Honey," I said as I moved toward her, "what is it?"

"My marriage is over, Mother. I've left David and come home for good."

CHAPTER 2

Through the kind of sobbing that turns into hiccups, Gwen told me that she'd just found out that David never loved her.

"He doesn't want to be with me, Mom," she wailed as I took her into my arms.

"Baby, I'm sure David loves you. He's always loved you," I said.

She shook her head vigorously. "No. I just fit some kind of ideal that he wanted in a wife. It's not me he loves. It's his work. I was just—just arm candy!"

A tiny pinprick of guilt poked at me. I'd so recently wondered the same thing about Gwen's feelings toward David and now here she was, my brokenhearted daughter, feeling loved only for her facade.

"Oh, my God. What happened?" Natalie said from the doorway.

"David doesn't love me," Gwen blubbered.

Natalie shoved her hands deep into the pockets of her jeans as she came all the way into the room. "Oh, come on. We all know David is nuts about you."

Gwen sobbed more. "I don't think he's ever really loved me."

Compassion was one of Natalie's more endearing qualities, but she didn't usually waste it on her sister. Now it warmed my heart to see Nat take her hand out of her pocket to smooth

Gwen's long, expensively maintained, blond hair back from her face. "Come on. Tell us what happened."

"I just feel so betrayed," she said in a shaky voice.

Over her sister's head, Natalie mouthed the question *affair?*

I shrugged, but, given how crazy David had always been about Gwen, I thought it highly unlikely and I wasn't going to ask. Not now, anyway.

Natalie had no such compunction. "Did he cheat on you?" she asked.

The question brought Gwen's head up with a jerk. "What? Of course not. Why would he cheat on me?"

"Then what happened, for heaven's sake?" I asked, starting to lose patience.

Nat stepped closer to Gwen and put her arm around her shoulders. I hadn't seen them present anything like a united front since they'd both campaigned to skip school to go to a rock concert in Chicago when they'd been sixteen and seventeen.

Gwen, always the more delicate looking of the two, was only five six to Nat's five ten. She easily leaned her head on Nat's shoulder and gave a long, shaky sigh. "He—" she sniffed "—he canceled our cruise!" she finished with a wail.

Nat leaped away from her like she was going for the long jump in the Olympics.

"What?" she bellowed.

"He canceled our Christmas cruise because of some project that's in trouble. He's so selfish. That's all he thinks about is work. I spent months shopping for just the right clothes and then he—"

"Wait just a minute," Nat demanded, putting her fisted hands on her hips. "You're pulling this scene because your *cruise* was canceled?"

"You don't understand. We haven't been on a trip since our honeymoon in Hawaii last spring."

"Aw—that's real rough," Natalie said, her compassion morphing quickly into ridicule. "Boo-hoo."

"Nat," I warned.

"You don't know what it's been like," Gwen shrieked, totally undeterred by her sister's mocking. "He works all the time. We haven't even been out to dinner in over a week."

"Oh, really," Nat said as she cocked her hip out aggressively and crossed her arms over her chest. She'd been taking the same stance since she was just a toddler. Right after Charlie was killed, the smart-ass started to sprout out of her like someone had fed her liquid fertilizer. "My heart bleeds. Too bad Jeremy's unemployment ran out or we could take you to McDonald's for a Happy Meal."

Gwen abruptly stopped crying. "I simply will not take this kind of attitude from you," Gwen said with all the dignity of a royal. "Not when you're taking advantage of Mother the way you are."

Natalie shifted her weight to the other hip. "Excuse me?"

"She's practically ready for retirement and your whole family is living off of her," Gwen told her.

Ready for retirement? I was fifty-two. There was still time. I could still buy a pair of leather jeans and go out and get a life.

"Mom invited us to move in—and we pay our own way as much as possible," Nat said. "It's not Jeremy's fault he's out of work, you know."

I could see that Gwen was winding up for a retort that would wound. It was time for some mommy intervention.

"Okay, girls, enough!" I yelled. "Everybody has problems. And everyone's problems are important—if only to themselves. So let's show each other a little respect."

Natalie looked even more sullen, as she always did when she knew I'd hit the mark. Gwen sniffed and started crying silently. The phrase award-winning performance did come to mind. But still, she'd just left her husband. Being self-absorbed didn't mean you were protected from pain.

"Gwen, honey," I gently asked her, "are you sure this is what you want?"

"What she wants is for David to come running up here and beg her to come back to him," Nat said. "Oh, and maybe buy her another hunk of expensive jewelry."

"Natalie," I said sternly, even though I knew there might be more than a kernel of truth in that statement. "Please."

"You can be such a bitch," Gwen said before she blew her nose loudly into a big wad of tissues she'd pulled from her Dooney & Bourke handbag.

"Look, I'm stuck here living under Ma's roof again, trying to hold it together with three kids and an out-of-work husband. And you've got the nerve to come in here crying because David had to cancel your cruise? Give me a break."

Maybe Natalie was saying all the things to her sister that I wish I had the guts to say but I was too busy thinking about Nat's choice of the word stuck. Is that how she felt living with me? I knew it wasn't an ideal situation, but still the word stuck—well, it hurt, damn it.

"Mother, are you just going to stand there and let her talk to me that way?" Gwen demanded.

Right now I wasn't sure what was upsetting me the most. Gwen's self-absorption or Natalie's anger. I searched for the right words to say. "You know, Gwen, Nat's going through a hard time right now," I began.

Gwen dashed tears from her cheeks with an angry swipe of her hand. "Like I'm not? At least she knows where her husband is."

There was a burp from the doorway. We all looked up. Jeremy stood there, bleary-eyed, scratching his stomach with one hand and brushing his hair back with the other. "Did I miss dinner?" he croaked in a sleep-roughened voice.

"Oh, good," Gwen said, recovering rather quickly from her last outburst. "I'm glad you're here. I need help with my bags. If you'll follow me—"

"You bet, princess," Jeremy said as he rolled his eyes at us before following her.

"Look at that," Nat muttered. "She's taking over already."

"Nat, come on. Gwen is hurting."

"I'll tell you what Gwen is doing. She's finding a new way to make Christmas all about her. Like the time she had the chicken pox. Or the time she broke up with that guy she thought she was so in love with. She spent the entire holiday season crying her eyes out and refusing to eat. By the time Christmas break was over, she had a new boyfriend and claimed she'd never been so in love in her life. She does this kind of stuff on holidays, Ma. Haven't you noticed?"

Did she? I knew Gwen could be manipulative and maybe just a touch narcissistic. But chicken pox? "Nat, I don't think even Gwen could will herself to get the chicken pox."

"Don't be so sure," Nat said as she headed for the front hall. Seconds later she yelled, "Hey, Ma! You gotta come and see this!"

There turned out to be ten pieces of luggage. All matched. Pink crocodile. It made quite an impressive pile in the hallway. I was a little impressed to see Jeremy actually breaking a sweat for a change, too, as he hauled it all in.

"Last one," he said as he rolled in a suitcase big enough to hold a drum set.

"Mother, which room will be mine?" Gwen asked.

"Well, the only room free is the guest room off the kitchen."

"That'll never do," Gwen said with a dismissive wave of her hand. "It's barely big enough for my clothes."

"Well, you're not getting *our* room," Natalie said.

I totally agreed. It would really be starting off on the wrong foot to kick Nat and Jeremy out of the second largest bedroom in the house to give it to Gwen. And we certainly couldn't have any of the children sleeping downstairs by themselves. So that left—

Me.

"I'll take the guest room, Gwen. You can have my room."

Gwen took it like it was her due. "Jeremy?" she said, then picked up the smallest case and started up the stairs.

"If she offers me a tip," Jeremy muttered, "I'll kick her in her bony ass."

"Let's all help with the luggage," I hastened to suggest, grabbing a suitcase and starting up before anyone could argue with me.

Later that night, as I lay in the narrow single bed in what my mother had always referred to as the maid's room even though we'd never had a maid, I could hear Nat and Gwen bickering over the bathroom and, just like that, fifteen years peeled back. It was worse than déjà vu. I mean, I was actually going through it for the second time. But I had been younger the first time, I said to myself as I rolled over and pulled a pillow over my head.

I was feeling a little used and abused. And a whole lot sorry for myself. So Nat felt stuck. How did she think I felt? Did she think this was the life I'd planned to be living when I reached my present age? And Gwen was acting like a child throwing a tantrum. And even though I felt like kicking her in her bony ass myself, I had to be supportive, didn't I? Wasn't that part of the deal that came with motherhood?

Frankly, I wasn't feeling all that supportive of either of my daughters right now. I'd been a widow already by the time I was Gwen's age. At least she still had a husband who would eventually take her on a cruise. And Nat had Jeremy and the kids. I flopped onto my back again and tossed the pillow aside. The problem was, I wasn't supposed to be alone in this bed mulling over all this stuff by myself. Charlie was supposed to be here with me. To talk to. To hold me if I cried. To laugh with me over the absurdity of life. Was the restlessness I'd been feeling just a newly resurrected anger at the injustice of it all?

Charlie, always a careful driver, had been in the wrong place at the wrong time. He'd been on his way home to us from a conference in Green Bay when a semi had gone over the center line. It had happened too fast for Charlie to even react, the police had told me. I could hear the words like they were said just yesterday. "It's likely he never knew what hit him, ma'am," the cop had assured me.

Well, I knew what had hit me. Widowhood. Single motherhood. It was as if my life as me, Abby, had just stopped. By now, at the age of fifty-two, I'd thought I'd have Abby back again. But as I listened to the girls still squabbling overhead I knew that my time wasn't arriving anytime soon. In fact, I was pretty sure the train hadn't even left the station yet.

"Look," I said the next morning after listening to my daughters complain about the house having only one bathroom, "we're just going to have to start making a schedule for the bathroom in the morning and at night."

"We were here first," Natalie said tightly. "Let her go to a hotel. She can afford it."

"That's not fair! My marriage is crumbling and you want me to go to a hotel? Why shouldn't Mother be here for me, too?"

"Yeah, your marriage is crumbling because your husband put off a trip to the Bahamas to make another million. Excuse me while I don't cry."

"You are such a bitch!"

"Hey—little pitchers," Nat said sternly as she nodded toward her trio of minors. They were watching the sisters with their mouths dropped open nearly to the table.

Suddenly, Ashley jumped from her chair and ran up to me to clutch my leg. "Why are they yelling?" she whispered as she peered anxiously up at me. "Do Mommy and Auntie Gwen hate each other?"

I smoothed her hair back from her little concerned face. "Do you hate your brothers when you yell at them?"

Ashley solemnly shook her head. "Not really."

"Then I guess your mommy and your auntie are just acting like children."

"Would it kill anyone to try to see my side of things, here?" Gwen demanded before she flounced out of the room.

By now the kitchen table was a mess of cereal, spilled milk and whatever other chaos grade school children can cause in a kitchen on a Saturday morning. I went over to the sink and turned on the faucet, waiting for the water in the old pipes to get hot. The kids must have sensed more trouble brewing because they soon drifted off to wreak havoc in the living room.

I shot Nat a look. "You know, you're not helping matters any."

She had the grace to look shamefaced, something that always raised patches of bright red on her pale cheeks. "I'm sorry. I guess it's just that after losing your house it's a little hard to have sympathy for someone who has to postpone a cruise."

I put my arm around her shoulders. "Honey, I know. But this is still real to her. She feels let down by her husband. She feels—"

"Abandoned," Natalie finished for me. "I know. But she's not the only one who lost her father, you know."

I squeezed her shoulder. "We all deal with things differently, Nat." Was now the time to reminded her of her overprotectiveness of Jeremy? Probably not, I decided.

"Mother?"

Gwen had quietly come back into the kitchen. In her long rose-sprigged flannel nightgown with matching robe, her hair in a tangled mess and her eyes red from crying, she looked so much like the girl she'd once been. So when she asked in a small, plaintive voice, "Would you make me some pancakes?" I, naturally, said yes.

She smiled weakly. "I'll have them in my room."

"Oh, brother," said Natalie.

"So you're late for the Prisoners of Willow Creek Enrichment Society outing because you were serving your daughter pancakes in bed?" Iris asked. "Your thirty-year-old daughter, I might add."

I grimaced. "You might, but I wish you wouldn't."

Iris dipped the tip of her brush in pink paint. "Aren't we supposed to be escaping our bondage?"

"Yes, of course—"

"Well, I'm seeing you pretty tethered to the ground, honey," Iris said.

"Well, what am I supposed to do?"

"Kick them out on their asses and tell them to grow up?" Iris suggested tenderly.

"It's just not that easy," I whined.

"Oh, don't pay any attention to her," Jo said. "She's never had kids."

"Making me the smartest woman at this table," Iris stated.

We'd driven an hour in the snow to sit in the back room of an overheated ceramics shop and paint designs on large coffee cups. I was starting to think that none of the women at this table were very smart.

"This is a stupid way to spend a Saturday," I blurted out.

Some women at the advanced class's table who were working on painting little elves swung their heads our way, their faces registering disapproval.

"You trying to get us beat up or something?" Jo hissed.

"They do look a little hard-core," Iris said.

I started to giggle at the thought of hard-core ceramic junkies. More disapproving looks came our way. I wasn't sure if it was our conversation or the fact that none of us was wearing a sweatshirt with a barnyard animal, a snowman or sprigs of holly on it.

"Why do I get the feeling," Jo said out of the corner of her mouth, "that we're about to get kicked out of here?"

"Just as long as we don't have to serve detention," I said.

Iris threw down her paintbrush. "Let's get the hell out of here. I want a margarita."

There was a small gasp from a chubby woman at the next table, who was wearing a sweatshirt that featured a row of geese, each with a red ribbon tied in a bow at its throat.

"What's the matter, lady, would you rather have a rum and Coke?"

"Well, I never—" the woman said.

"Yeah, I'm betting you haven't," Iris quipped.

"I think now is the time to leave," Jo said.

I didn't argue.

Amid much giggling, we left our half-finished latte mugs where they were, went up front, paid what we owed and headed back to Willow Creek and the only Mexican restaurant in the area.

I ordered a regular margarita on the rocks, no salt, Jo ordered a blended strawberry one and Iris, skipping the niceties, ordered a double shot of tequila.

We were as different as our drink orders—Jo, Iris and I. Always had been.

Jo, the tomboy and the first of us to date, had been on the girls' hockey team in high school. She was the kind of girl who joined in a game of football with the guys at the park on Saturday afternoons, thus getting to know all the jocks and giving her the inside dating edge. Iris's high school claim to fame was getting caught smoking in the girls' room more often than any other girl of the graduating class of 1972. I was the studious, practical one. The one on the debating team. The one who usually followed all the rules.

The unlikely friendship had started when we'd all refused to dissect a frog in freshman biology. We'd all gotten detention as punishment for our stand on animal cruelty. Although I've secretly always felt that with Iris, it was more of a stand against the smell of formaldehyde. Jo and I, clearly out of our element, had glued ourselves to Iris, who was more than familiar with the drill and who was friends with nearly every scary boy in the detention room. Afterwards, we'd walked home in the dark together—it had been late fall and the smell of burning leaves had been in the air—griping about the unfairness of the world. We'd been best friends ever since.

"These chips are stale," Iris complained as she threw a half-eaten one back into the complimentary basket.

"The chips are always stale," Jo pointed out. "It's their way of getting you to order something."

"You guys want to split the fajitas?"

Jo and I agreed and we put in the order when our drinks were delivered.

Iris licked the back of her hand, sprinkled salt on it, licked again, threw back the double shot, then sucked a wedge of lime. This ritual never failed to fascinate Jo and me. We watched in admiration as we sat there sipping our gentile margaritas.

"You know," Iris said as she licked salt from her lips, "if the Prisoners Society doesn't start getting more exciting, we're going to need to form a society against the damned society."

Jo sighed. "Okay, so the ceramics didn't work out. So sue me."

"Maybe we should start planning another trip to Europe," Iris suggested, "while our passports are still good."

Jo shook her head. "I'm saving every dime I can get my hands on for the diner so when I get Mike to see things my way, I'll be ready."

"Fat chance I'm going anywhere soon, either," I put in. "I've got a full house. I bet they're all waiting at home right now wondering what's for dinner."

"Damn," Iris said, "how can you stand it? That's the main reason I've never wanted to get married, you know. The idea of being needed all the time like that—" She gave an exaggerated shiver of distaste.

I'd never really considered the concept of *not* being needed. What would that feel like? Right now I thought it would probably feel pretty damn good. But it might have just been the margarita.

"I'm starting to get depressed," Iris muttered. "I think it's time we did our ritualistic toast thingy again."

We'd started the toast—really a promise to each other—the year we'd had to cancel the trip to Europe. There was no clear anniversary date for the ritual. We generally hauled it out whenever any of us was having a bad time. It was a way of reminding ourselves that things were still possible.

Iris signaled our server for another round. When it came, we raised our various concoctions and clinked our mismatched glasses and repeated the promise. If one of us ever made it to Europe, we would toast the others out loud so at least our names would have been said there. If it was Rome, it would be wine. And if it was Paris, champagne, of course. Italy and France were the two countries we all agreed that we wanted to see.

"Hey, why don't you come up to Milwaukee with me next weekend?" Iris suggested after she'd finished her tequila ritual. "That guy I met last time finally called me. We're going dancing at a club downtown. I'm sure he's got a friend we could double with."

Jo groaned. "Milwaukee just doesn't sound as exotic as Rome."

Iris sniffed and straightened her shoulders. "Well, we don't all have a still semihunky husband to cuddle up to on Friday night."

"Sorry," Jo said.

Iris turned to me. "How about it?"

"No way," I said emphatically.

"Hey, you had fun that one time you came with me."

Fun wasn't what I'd call it. Okay, maybe at the time it had seemed like an adventure. But afterwards I just worried about whether I'd caught anything or if I was going to turn into a slut. That was over five years ago. I haven't had sex since. And I had no intention of having it again anytime soon.

"You're forgetting how paranoid I got afterwards," I said.

Iris made a face. "That's right. Forget it. I couldn't go through that again. Guess you'll have to find some other way to blow off steam."

Our fajitas came and we got busy divvying up the tortillas and sizzling platters of meat and vegetables. A guy in cowboy boots slid from his stool at the bar and ambled over to the jukebox.

"Oh, oh," Jo said, "I'm feeling some Patsy Cline comin' on."

But it wasn't Patsy Cline that came out after he'd stuck in his dollar.

"Hey, wasn't that our junior prom theme?" Iris asked as a song by the pop group Bread began to play.

But I was already there. I couldn't even see the face of the boy I went with or remember the color of the dress. But the same feeling I'd had then washed over me now. Excitement. Possibilities. A world at our feet.

I should have known after the evening's infamous punch incident that things weren't going to turn out as I'd planned.

I'd learned that the only thing you could really count on was getting old. Sure, fifty-two isn't old. But it's a lot older than forty-two, which is a lot older than thirty-two, which is a lot older than twenty-two. What if you didn't feel that old inside though? Lately I'd been wondering if my insides were keeping pace with my outsides. Like sometimes, inside, I'm still twenty-two. And then I pass a mirror or a plate-glass window and am shocked at the person looking back at me. Not that I look all that bad. My skin is still decent, although, like I said, those laugh lines are getting deeper. My hair is still more blond than silver. I weigh only a few pounds more than I did when I married Charlie. But I sure didn't look like the kind of woman who had something bubbling inside of me, still waiting to break free. And I sure didn't look like the kid I was feeling like right now, half buzzed from a couple of margaritas and the beat of a song that, until this moment, I'd forgotten all about.

When I got home that night, sure enough, the first question I got asked was what was for supper. It was nearly seven o'clock and it hadn't occurred to any of the other adults in the house to fix something.

"I've already eaten," I said.

They all looked shocked.

"But what about us?" Ashley asked.

I squatted down in front of her. "You know what, Ash? Your mom knows how to cook, too. Don't you remember?"

Ashley nodded enthusiastically. "She makes the best tuna casserole."

"Oh, yum," Gwen commented from where she was half reclined on one of the sofas. "Why don't we just open a can of SPAM?"

"Yes. Why don't you?" I suggested. "I've got some work to do."

I refused to look back to see what kind of impact my state-ment had on them. I just kept walking until I'd crossed the living room and opened the door to my office, careful to shut it quietly behind me.

My office was in a small second parlor off the back of the living room. It had a bow window that looked out onto the backyard and an old oak desk and chair I'd found at an estate sale and refinished. There were two small upholstered chairs for clients, a wall lined with file cabinets and an oval braided rug on the floor. I didn't want to be too cutesy—after all I did people's tax returns, kept their books, made out payrolls for some of the small businesses around town—so I'd replaced my mother's lace curtains with miniblinds and the needlepoint on the walls with pieces done by regional artists.

Numbers were one of the things that had saved my sanity after Charlie had been killed. I'd had to focus on something. And we'd needed money. Charlie's business had barely begun. He'd left me with more bills than anything. I knew that part of the reason that Gwen was so self-absorbed and Natalie was so defiant was because there had never seemed to be enough of me to go around when they'd needed me the most. I'd never claimed to be the perfect mother. But I'd given what I could. Done as much as I could. And I have ever since.

I sat down in my desk chair and leaned back. I felt drained. As if soon there wouldn't be anything left to give.

There was the sound of a skirmish outside my office door. Matt and Tyler, fighting again. I started to stand up but forced myself to sit. There were three adults out there. They could handle it. I looked nervously at the door. Couldn't they?

I turned on my computer and logged in to Ivan Mueller's account. Ivan insisted on keeping old-fashioned ledgers with handwritten entries. So once a month, I stopped by his jewelry store, picked up his ledgers and transferred everything into a spreadsheet on my computer. I hoped that the familiar comfort of the numbers would keep my butt in the chair.

I didn't leave my office that night until I was fairly certain, from the sound of things, that everyone had gone to bed for the night. Then I crept into the kitchen, grabbed a hunk of cheese from the refrigerator to stave off hunger pangs and went to bed in the maid's room.

Believe me, the irony of the name my mother had dubbed it all those years ago was not lost on me.

The next day, I had become Gwen's personal maid, spending a good portion of my time fielding phone messages between her and David.

"Did you tell her what I said?" he asked me anxiously during our latest chat.

"Yes, David. I told her exactly what you said. That you were sorry and were going to make it up to her."

"What was her reaction?"

Was I really supposed to tell him that she'd opened up the latest copy of *Vanity Fair* and hadn't said a word? "She's upset, David. Why don't you just let it go for today?"

It was his sixth call and I was, frankly, worn out. Gwen refused to take her husband's calls but as soon as I hung up the phone she'd call me from her bedroom upstairs, wanting to know what he'd said. I'd been up and down the stairs so many times I was getting jet lag.

"All right." The poor guy sounded both defeated and deflated. "If you're sure that's what she wants."

I assured him it was, told him to hang in there and hung up.

"Mother!"

It was uncanny how Gwen always knew the minute I hung up the phone. I ran up the stairs and arrived at her room, breathless.

"What did you tell him?"

"I told him to give up for the day."

She sat up straighter in bed. "*What?* You mean you told him to stop calling?"

I leaned against the door jam. "Basically, yeah. I mean, you don't want to speak to him anyway. So what's the point in his continuing to call?"

"But how can I make him suffer if he doesn't keep calling so I can refuse to speak to him?"

"Gwen, he's suffering enough already. And if that's what this is about—"

She shrank back into the covers and got a pouty look on her face. "No—of course not. I'm just not happy with him. Not like I thought I'd be."

"Life sucks sometimes, baby. What can I say?"

She slid her gaze in my direction, then immediately looked away. "You could say that I deserve to be happy."

I walked from the door frame to sit at the foot of the bed, patting her ankle over the covers. "Of course you deserve to be happy, Gwen. But maybe you need to adjust what your idea of happiness is."

"Oh, I should have known you'd take his side," she said, rolling so that her back was to me.

I raised my eyes to the ceiling and asked the floral wallpaper border to give me the strength to resist the urge to tell her she was acting like a baby. The room was still decorated with the blue-and-white striped wallpaper I'd hung when Charlie and I had taken over the room after my mother's death. The same white tieback curtains hung at the windows.

"I'm not taking sides," I said. "But I think taking David's calls would be the…ah…mature thing to do, don't you?"

Her back still to me, she shook her head. "Why should I be mature when he's not living up to his promises?"

"But he made promises to clients, too, Gwen. Maybe it'd be easier for you to understand if you went back to work."

She sat up straight in bed. "Has David said anything? Did he tell you that he thinks I quit my job too soon?"

"No, of course not. It's just that, if you don't have enough to do, maybe—"

"But I'd have enough to do if David had time for me!"

"Baby, it's hard to build up a business and a reputation. You've got to try to be understanding—to think of what it will mean for your future."

"Oh—so when I'm too old to look fabulous in a bikini that's when he'll have the time to take me on a cruise?"

Yes, Nat had been the rebellious one, but Gwen had been the demanding one. The one who wanted everything *right now*. She seemed only capable of seeing any situation for how it affected her. I shook my head. How could I have raised two such different daughters?

I sighed. "Are you coming down for dinner?"

"I'd rather just have a tray in my room if you don't mind."

I decided the extra trips up and down the stairs were worth not having her at the same table with Natalie. I wasn't sure there were enough antacids in the entire town to take care of the indigestion that might cause.

* * *

By Monday I couldn't wait to take Ivan Mueller's ledgers back to him. After which I planned to drive out to the discount store on the highway and get some Christmas shopping done. It was the last thing I felt like doing. My holiday spirit was still limping along like a wounded animal. But it would keep me out of the house long enough for Gwen to maybe answer one of David's calls herself. Maybe if they talked—really talked—David would get through to her. I certainly hadn't had any luck so far.

Ivan was his usual affable self.

"There's my beauty of a bookkeeper," he said when he looked up at the sound of the bell above the door. "And how was your weekend?"

"I've had better," I answered ruefully.

He put his palm to his chest. "No! You are unhappy about something during this happy time of year?"

Ivan had come to the United States in the late forties. He didn't really have an accent, but he had a courtly way of speaking that was very old world. He was short and still wore suits he'd probably had custom made in the early fifties—pinstripes and lapels a little too wide, but the fabric excellent. He wore rimless glasses and kept his thinning hair in place with something oily. Probably the same product he'd used when he bought the suits.

He had exquisite taste in jewelry, much of it he'd designed himself. Most Willow Creek couples had exchanged their vows over Ivan's rings. I couldn't really afford to be a customer but he regularly gave me earrings for Christmas. And I treasured every pair.

"My kids are going through a rough time, Ivan. Things ain't pretty at my house."

"I am sorry to hear this. I have just the thing that will cheer you up," he said. "Made for a special customer. Wait until you see."

I watched him toddle off to the back room then started to gaze at the cases of jewelry. Maybe I'd skip the discount store and just get each of the girls a pendant or something this year. Ivan had some beautiful ones. But Gwen already had better than anything I could afford and Natalie wasn't much into jewelry. Not the real thing, anyway. She'd find the cash more useful.

Ivan returned shuffling along, with a long, narrow black velvet case in his hand. He motioned me over to the counter and opened the case. I've never considered myself a diamond kind of gal. They didn't fit into my lifestyle, nor could I afford them. But when Ivan revealed the gorgeous diamond-and-gold bracelet reclining inside, I experienced the same feeling I had when I'd heard that song on the jukebox. Possibilities or maybe dreams that hadn't quite died—something that had only been a shadow of a notion up until now—still trying to break free inside of me.

"You like?" Ivan asked.

"It's—well, it's just the most beautiful bracelet I've ever seen."

"Here. You try it on," he said.

"No, I couldn't—well, maybe—"

He was already clipping it around my wrist.

"Those are perfectly matched brilliant-cut rounds. Oh—" he shook his head slowly, importantly "—very, very difficult to find stones that match so perfectly at this size. Set in eighteen karat gold. And you see how the clasp is made up of rubies and sapphires? The very best of everything."

The best of everything. What would that be like, I wondered. To have the best of everything?

There was a time when I thought I'd had it all. A husband I loved who adored me. Two beautiful, healthy little girls. A life as shiny as the diamonds twinkling on my wrist. This would have been our thirty-second Christmas together. I smiled softly—and a little sadly. By now, Charlie would have been able to afford to buy me something from Ivan for Christmas. Something I'd wear when we went out on New Year's Eve.

I held my arm out. The bracelet draped just right. But my nails—what a mess. It would be a travesty for a woman like me to own a bracelet like this. There was a time I'd taken better care of my hands—when Charlie had been here to hold them.

I took off the bracelet and handed it back to Ivan. "I'm sure your customer's wife will be very happy with it."

When I left the jewelry store I kept thinking about the shape my cuticles were in. How shameful they'd looked next to that bracelet. Iris's House of Beauty was across the street. It had been years since I'd had a manicure.

"Hey, kid," Iris said. "Did you come in here to sell raffle tickets or something?"

I laughed. "No—I actually thought about treating myself to a manicure."

Her eyes widened. "What's the occasion?"

"I was feeling nostalgic."

Iris looked puzzled. "Nostalgic for a manicure?"

"Something like that. Can you fit me in?"

"You better believe it. I've been trying to get my hands on your cuticles for years. Why don't you let me highlight your hair today, too? And maybe shape your brows."

"Don't push it. Just be happy I'm getting a manicure."

"Honey, I'd jump for joy if these boots weren't killing my feet."

The place was buzzing with gossip, as usual. Iris had three stylists and a manicurist working for her and they relished regaling the customers with details about their various love lives, diets and favorite soap operas. If anyone had gained weight in town, was on the verge of bankruptcy or divorce, this was the place you heard about it first.

It was, "Girl, did you see those hips in those boot-cut leggings?" or "They say the balance on her MasterCard has more digits than her phone number." I'd always felt a tiny bit uncomfortable with it all. Probably another reason I tended to avoid the place. Plus, I wasn't fond of having so many mirror images of myself to look at and be judged. I didn't need any reminders that my chin was getting slacker and my laugh lines were turning into crow's feet.

Sally, the manicurist, had graduated a year ahead of me so we knew each other only slightly. Still, I got every detail about her brilliant grandchildren.

"I told my son, you'd better start saving your money. The oldest is going to wind up in one of those expensive Ivy League schools out east—you mark my words."

I assured her I would.

She leaned closer. "Say, is it true what they say about Mary Stillman?"

I had no idea who Mary Stillman was, but Sally gave me the complete picture on what was being said about her, anyway.

An hour and a few dozen *confidential* tidbits later, I walked out with a set of fake nail tips elongating my fingers. I'd given in to Sally's choice of polish—a purplish red that looked even more garish out in the cold afternoon. And now I was really running late. I had two more clients to drop in on and I still wanted to start my Christmas shopping.

As did everyone else in the county, apparently. When I finally got there, the discount store was packed. I lost a fingernail nabbing the last of the most popular video game of the year off the shelf for Matt and I'd hovered near a woman who was deciding over a sweater that I knew would be perfect for Natalie. When she put it back down and looked away, I swooped in like a hawk on a field mouse. Before I got into line at the checkout counter, on impulse I turned down the music aisle and started to search. There it was—our prom theme—on a compilation disk of seventies soft rock. I dropped it into my cart.

The checkout lines were long. By the time I made it back to the car, I was exhausted, but I wrestled with the frustrating CD packaging anyway, losing another nail tip in the process. I wanted to hear that song again. Now.

I sat in the parking lot, puffs of my warm breath visible in the cold car, and listened to the song. Twice. I felt like I wanted to cry. Was it for the loss of the girl who'd danced with such hope in her heart? Was it for the woman who I was supposed to have become who'd never quite materialized?

God, this was insane, I thought. Sitting in a cold car—a rusty station wagon no less—listening to love songs from my high school years.

I popped the CD out of the player. It immediately switched to a radio station playing all Christmas music. I bit the bottom of my lip and shook my head. "Abby," I whispered into the icy air, "you picked a great time to have a midlife crisis."

I drove home, hauled the packages into the house, stowed them in the front hall closet and went into the living room.

"Well, it's about time," Gwen said from the sofa. "I'm starving."

Natalie looked up from her magazine. "I'm starving, too. And, Ma, the kids keep asking me when you're going to decorate for Christmas."

"Yeah, don't you usually have a tree by now, Mother? By the way," Gwen added, a secret little smile on her face, "David called seven times today. I think your answering machine is almost full."

The kids suddenly ran down the stairs, squealing, and Nat shushed them. "Daddy's napping."

You know that saying *I saw red?* Well, it's true. I saw red. And we're not talking festive lights here. I think it was the red of my blood boiling up to my eyeballs.

"What does *Daddy* have to nap for?" I asked testily. "He's not working. And he's certainly not doing anything around here."

Natalie got up and quickly glanced at the stairs. "Ma—shh, he'll hear you."

"Nat, I think Jeremy already knows he's not working. And he sure as hell knows he's not doing anything around here."

She cocked her hip. "What the hell has gotten into you?"

"That's another thing. Will you please watch your mouth? You gripe if anyone else uses bad language in front of the kids but you're the worst of all."

Gwen, wearing yet another expensive nightgown and robe ensemble, snickered from the sofa.

I swung around to face her. "And you. You're a grown woman. Isn't it time you got dressed and started doing something around here, too? Like maybe, for instance, making dinner?"

From the look on her face you'd think I'd asked her to sign up for boot camp.

Nat gave a short laugh. "Princess Gwen doesn't cook, Ma. She orders."

"Then what about you? You can't make a damn box of macaroni and cheese for your kids?"

As if they'd been cued from offstage, the kids came running through the living room again.

"Grandma! When can we get a Christmas tree?"

"Do you know where my skates are?"

"Can I have a sleepover this weekend?"

"Aren't you going to put stuff up outside this year, Grandma?"

"You know what," I said as I eyed the other adults in the room, "I think you'd better start asking your parents those questions— or Auntie Gwen—because as of right now, Grandma is on strike."

"What?" Both Nat and Gwen asked in unison.

"I am going on strike," I enunciated clearly. It wasn't something I'd planned to say. But while my blood boiled, the story Mike had told us on Friday at the diner bubbled up with it. If a man could go on strike against his wife for lack of affection, why couldn't a woman go on strike against her family for lack of cooperation? "As of this moment, all of you are on your own. For meals. For laundry. For Christmas."

There was a collective gasp.

"That's right," I reiterated. "No tree. No decorations. No cookies. I. Am. On. Strike."

I crossed the hall, passed through the dining room, went through to the kitchen, grabbed a bottle of water from the refrigerator, poured cereal into a bowl, added milk, grabbed a spoon and took it into the maid's room where I sat in my mother's old rocking chair and dined on Special K and silence.

Except the cereal lasted longer than the silence. Soon the kitchen just outside my door erupted into the noise of six hungry people who weren't even sure where the butter was kept. I listened to them as I crunched, willing myself not to go to their rescue. One question kept running over and over again in my brain. *When a woman finally decides that her time has come, where the hell is she supposed to spend it?*

CHAPTER 3

By the second day of my strike I knew I was in trouble. It was going to be impossible to keep from crossing the picket line if I stayed under the same roof as the rest of my family. For one thing, the maid's room was far from soundproof. I could hear the chaos going on around me as I rocked in my mother's old rocking chair, trying to talk myself into staying put.

Mealtimes were the worst. I tried to secrete myself in my office before anyone showed up looking for food. But I was forced to be an auditory witness to breakfast for two days in a row now because I'd overslept. It was like listening to a bad sitcom without the picture. I kept wondering why I didn't just go out there and make them all some damned eggs. Although maybe Natalie got some of her defiance from me because, ultimately, I refused to budge, unpleasant as it was.

My family needed to learn a lesson and I needed—what *did* I need? Space, certainly. Although the confines of the tiny room weren't exactly what I had in mind. I needed to not be taken for granted. And, above all, I needed to *not* be needed for a change. To just *be*. Peace and quiet. Ah, what a luxury that would be I thought just as the doorbell rang.

I was on strike so I didn't make a move to answer it.

It kept ringing.

I kept rocking.

Finally, whoever it was started to bang on the front door. Where was everybody? I looked at the alarm clock on the small table next to the bed. It was already after nine in the morning so the kids were probably in school. Nat was probably working an early shift or running to the store for a few more gallons of peanut butter. That still left Jeremy and Gwen. Gwen was undoubtedly up in her room waiting for me to come to my senses and show up with a tray of food and some sympathy. And if Jeremy wasn't slumped on the sofa, he had his head in the refrigerator. One of them would eventually act, wouldn't they?

The pounding went on.

"All right, all right," I yelled. "I'm coming!"

I didn't run into anyone while I made my way to the front hall. Someone *could* be upstairs yet I'd never know it because of the racket our visitor was making on the front porch.

I flung the front door open, but when I saw who was standing on the other side of it I wished I'd stayed in the maid's room where I belonged.

"Where the hell is my daughter-in-law?" Cole Hudson demanded as he swept past me without waiting to be asked in.

"Beats me," I said, as I waved at Ernie, the cab driver, waiting in the town's only cab idling at the curb. "Did you ask Ernie to wait?" I asked as I shut the door. "Because he's the only cab in town and—"

"Good God, how can anyone live somewhere that has only one taxi? And the closest damn airport is two towns away."

"For some reason, inexplicable as it may seem, Mr. Hudson, Willow Creek doesn't attract a lot of men who fly their own jets," I said, then turned to head back to my room.

He stepped in front of me before I made it halfway through the dining room.

"You don't know where your own daughter is?" he demanded.

I'd forgotten how hard his face could look. All etched lines and sharp angles. He had silver hair that fell to nearly his shoulders and light gray eyes beneath uncannily black eyebrows. He was taller than me, but not by much. He probably stood six feet or so. I could practically look right into those stormy eyes.

"She's a grown woman, Mr. Hudson. She comes and goes as she pleases. Besides, I'm on strike. I'm no longer responsible for knowing where anyone in this family is."

His frown grew even deeper. "On strike?" His voice rumbled with incredulity. "I thought you were self-employed."

"Oh, it's not my clients I'm striking against. It's my family."

His gray eyes shot to the ceiling. "Heaven help me, I'm dealing with another one of the Blake women." He looked me in the eye. "Tell me, are you *all* crazy?"

I felt my natural instinct to protect start to rev up but I eased off the pedal. I wasn't going to get in the middle of this. I was on strike.

"My daughter's room is upstairs. First door on the right. You might find her there." I shrugged. "You might not."

I stepped neatly around him and passed through the dining room and kitchen then went into the maid's room and shut the door. I heard his footsteps on the stairs and I peered up at the ceiling. I won't say I wasn't curious to know what was going on up there. I was. But I wasn't going to break my strike to find out.

As it turns out, I didn't have to. Moments later, the door to my room burst open.

"Mother," Gwen demanded, "how could you let that man come up to my room?"

"I'm on strike," I reminded her.

She stared at me. "Well, I'm not going back to Chicago and nobody is going to make me."

"I wouldn't dream of it," I said.

She stared at me some more. "I mean it."

"So do I. Now please shut the door on your way out."

I half expected her to stamp her foot like Scarlett O'Hara. She settled for slamming the door.

I could hear them talking, though the conversation was muffled. They must have gone into the living room. Then there were footsteps running upstairs—probably Gwen's—and the slamming of another door—probably Gwen's.

I couldn't help it. I smiled at the situation. Cole Hudson was an intimidating man but I was pretty sure he'd gotten nowhere with Gwen. This was the girl who had won the title of Miss Willow Creek two years in a row and graduated valedictorian of her class. Riding on floats in parades all over the county and giving a speech before practically the whole town hadn't even caused a flutter in her toned tummy. Nothing—or no one—ever intimidated Gwen.

The door to my bedroom opened again.

Cole Hudson glared down at me. "So you find this amusing, do you?"

"Ever heard of knocking, Mr. Hudson?"

"Would you have let me in?"

"No."

"Well, then," he said, his light gray eyes boring into me, "let's not play games. I need your help. For some inexplicable reason my son is in love with that woman up there—" he thrust his cleft chin at the ceiling "—and he wants her back."

"And you think I could help...how?"

"By intervening, of course. By convincing her that the right thing to do is to go back to Chicago."

"And how do I know that's the right thing for her to do? She told me she's unhappy with David."

His face hardened. "She was happy enough until he had to cancel that blasted cruise!" he bellowed. "She's acting like a spoiled brat."

That brought me to my feet. His assessment fit how Gwen was acting as well as the expensive clothes she wore. But no one was going to get away with calling my daughter a spoiled brat. Except for me, of course.

"Mr. Hudson, if my daughter says she's unhappy, then she's unhappy. And I am not about to do anything that would result in her making the choice to go back to a man that she's unhappy with."

He scowled and started to pace—unsatisfactorily, I'm sure, given the length of the room. As it was, the energy of his anger only seemed to make the room smaller. I was feeling slightly claustrophobic.

"Do you have any idea what David is dealing with in Chicago?" he demanded. "He's in the middle of the biggest project of his career so far and it's in crisis. There are dozens of men whose jobs depend on the decisions he makes right now. He doesn't have time for this foolishness."

"Then why is he calling here seven times a day?"

He stopped his pacing and glared at me again. "Because my

son is foolish in the ways of romance, like a lot of men of his generation."

"You're calling your son a fool?"

"When it comes to love, yes. Obviously he doesn't use his head."

"For love, Mr. Hudson, some of us use our hearts."

He made an angry sound of dismissal. "Spare me, please."

We were obviously getting nowhere. "Look," I told him, "even if I wanted to help you, I couldn't. Because I'm on—"

"Strike," he finished for me with a click of his large white teeth. "I see that the apple doesn't fall far from the tree."

I could feel the heat rise on my cheeks. Oh, I wanted to give him a piece of my mind, all right. Instead, I returned to the rocking chair and started, once again, to rock. I was pretty sure that Cole Hudson wasn't used to being ignored. And I was right.

"Damn it! You're even more infuriating to deal with than your daughter is," he proclaimed before stalking off and shutting the door behind him with a resounding thunk.

I heard his purposeful steps upstairs followed by the not-so-muffled voice of Gwen suggesting he go back to Chicago and tell David to come himself if he wanted her back so badly.

Back to Chicago. The phrase rang in my head with the echo of a bell.

Chicago.

Why not? Chicago, I told myself, would be a great place to carry out my strike. I didn't have a lot of money to spend on myself, but I had enough room left on my emergency credit card for a few nights in a reasonably priced hotel and transportation would be free, courtesy of Cole Hudson—even if he didn't know it yet.

I scurried out to the hall closet, trying to ignore what was going on upstairs. It sounded like Gwen was winning. I grabbed my suitcase and quietly hurried back to the maid's room. I threw the suitcase on the bed and started to fill it. My choice of clothing wasn't much since most of my wardrobe, what there was of it, was still upstairs. I threw in jeans, T-shirts, a couple of sweaters, some plaid flannel pajamas with matching robe. I'd be walking around Chicago by myself for a few days. What did it matter what I wore? Maybe I'd see a matinee performance of a play, have a massage, order some room service. A few days of solitude. A few days of not being needed. A few days to just be Abby again.

Okay, Abby in sneakers, but I wasn't going to risk going to my bedroom to get anything and giving Gwen a chance to talk me out of what I was going to do. I'd simply jump into Cole's taxi with him and off I'd go—traveling light and not very far, but traveling, nonetheless.

I had finished packing and was scribbling a note, telling my family I'd be spending the rest of my strike in Chicago, when I heard the front door slam. I grabbed my parka, purse and suitcase, but by the time I got out to the front porch all I could see of Cole Hudson was the tail end of Ernie's taxi.

I looked at the house. No. I couldn't go back in. *Now* was the time. And the opportunity was here, it had just gotten a little bit of a head start, that was all. I didn't see Jeremy's truck anywhere, meaning only Gwen was in the house. I'd have to make a run for the garage. I was afraid that all anyone would have to do was to try to talk me out of it. I was sure I'd cave like a soufflé after someone slammed the oven door.

Suitcase in hand, I hotfooted it from the house, thankful now that I hadn't much to pack. I winced when I pushed the button to open the old wooden garage door. It had always been loud.

Now it seemed as if it screamed. I tossed my suitcase into the station wagon, then eased the door shut. I knew Gwen would hear as soon as I started the car. Face it, the wagon's muffler had been damaged goods for a while now. But I figured that once I was down the short driveway, I was as good as gone.

I can't even explain what it felt like as I drove away from the house and headed in the same direction Cole's taxi had taken. I grinned. Yes, I could, I thought. *It feels like I've escaped.*

I tamped down the guilt at the same time I pressed harder on the gas pedal. There was no way Cole Hudson was taking off in his plane without me.

I averaged ten miles over the speed limit but even so, as I pulled into the small airport, Ernie was already pulling out. I rolled down my window and waved him to a stop.

"Which plane is Hudson's?" I asked.

"That one," he pointed. "Over there."

I followed his outstretched finger. The plane was sleek and white, accented with black-and-silver stripes. As elegant as its owner—and just as powerful looking.

"Thanks, Ernie," I yelled, not taking my eyes off of the plane.

Was I really going to do this?

Yes, I was, my heartbeat answered.

I parked, got out of the car, grabbed my suitcase and started to run. For the first time I appreciated the Louis Vuitton pilot's case that Gwen had given me years ago when Jo, Iris and I had started planning our trip to Europe. Its wheels had no problem at all keeping up with me. I was running into the wind and yesterday's snowfall was blowing around hard enough to sting my face. But I felt alive. Freedom was ringing! And, okay, it wasn't Rome or Paris. It was Chicago. The point was, it wasn't Willow

Creek. I was making a symbolic stand—and not just for myself. For all of us—Iris, Jo and me. I'd go to one of the best restaurants that would let me in wearing jeans and sneakers and toast the others just like we'd always promised we would if one of us ever left again.

Too bad I'd have to put up with Cole Hudson's company to do it. But Chicago was only about thirty minutes away by air. And a man like Cole Hudson was sure to have a driver waiting for him at the airport so I'd get a free ride into the city, too.

He hadn't started the engines yet when I reached the plane. He hadn't even taken up the stairs or shut the door. My luck was holding.

"Anyone home?" I yelled.

"Good God! What are you doing here?"

I spun around to find him coming toward me, his leather flight jacket plastered to his chest by the wind, his long silver hair streaming back from his rock hard face. I ran to meet him.

"I came to hitch a ride," I said with all the confidence and pluck I could muster. Surely, he wouldn't turn down pluck. And confidence he'd respect.

"Sorry, Ms. Blake. I don't take on hitchhikers."

I gave him my most winning smile. The pluck was fairly oozing out of me. "Come on. I need to get out of here. You're leaving. It's serendipity."

"Forget it," he grumbled as he kept walking.

I hurried to keep pace. "I'll sit in the back and be really, really quiet," I yelled over the wind.

"No!" he yelled back.

"Oh, stop being so argumentative. All I'm asking is to fly

along with you. You're going to Chicago anyway. You're using the fuel. You're depreciating the plane—or whatever it is planes do. You might as well have a passenger on board. In fact, it's practically your patriotic duty to have a passenger on board."

He stopped walking and turned to stare at me, those dark brows lowered over his gray eyes. I was pretty sure he was going to say no again, so I kept talking. "Just one way, that's all you have to take me. And then I'll be out of your hair and won't bother you again."

Finally, he spoke. "One way, you say?"

I nodded with the energy of one of those bobble-headed dogs in the back windows of cars. "I'll worry about how to get back once I get there. Just take me with you—please."

Was that a gleam I saw in his eye? Was he going to change his mind? I thought for a moment that he might even smile.

"All right," he said. "As long as the deal is for one way only."

"Well, you're not likely to be flying into Willow Creek again anytime soon, are you?"

"Heaven forbid," he grumbled.

"Then you'll take me with you?"

He stood back and held out his arm toward the stairs. "After you," he said.

The cockpit was to the right. It looked complicated and technical and interesting. I'd never known anyone who could fly a plane before. I started for the cockpit, fully intending to experience whatever I could.

"Turn left," Cole Hudson ordered from behind me.

I was flooded with disappointment. "There are two seats up there and—"

"Ms. Blake, I agreed to take you with me. I didn't agree to be your traveling companion. I prefer to fly solo and you *did* promise to sit in the back and be silent."

"Fine," I said shortly. "I'm sure it'll be more pleasant that way, anyway."

"Wise choice. Now sit down and strap yourself in. I'm behind schedule already."

There were four chairs covered in black leather and a black leather sofa with small round tables at their sides. All were bolted to the floor. It was practically a flying living room. I sat down on one of the chairs. Nothing like flying business class, let me tell you. I sank into glove-like leather and discovered that the seat swiveled a full three hundred and sixty degrees. While I twirled, I noticed what looked like a small wet bar between the cockpit and the cabin. I hopped out of my seat to investigate. By the time I got there, Cole was blocking my way. His jacket smelled like worn, expensive leather.

"I thought I told you to buckle in," he boomed.

"You haven't even turned this thing on yet," I pointed out. "I was just snooping. Looking for something to drink."

His frown deepened. "This isn't silence, Ms. Blake."

I put my hands on my hips. "Look, you spoke to me first. I was merely being polite. Frankly, I'm also thirsty."

He stepped aside. "Help yourself, by all means. Then kindly buckle in."

I opened my mouth to say something and he put his finger to his lips.

"Shh."

"Grouch," I muttered to his back as he returned to the cockpit.

I opened the little refrigerator and found, among other things, small bottles of champagne. I grinned. Might as well start toasting the other members of the Prisoners of Willow Creek Enrichment Society in flight. After all, I was pretty sure that I was the first of us to ever fly in a private jet.

"Would you mind taking your seat back there," Cole growled from the cockpit.

I quickly grabbed a bottle of champagne, located a crystal flute in a cabinet above the refrigerator then hightailed it back to my seat, strapping myself in for takeoff.

I could hear the crackle of the plane's radio and the rumble of Cole's voice, but not what he was saying. It was so unfair that I had to sit here, away from the action. It was akin to wasting the experience. Maybe after we were airborne and Cole was busy flying the plane I could sneak into the cockpit and grab the second seat before he noticed.

Finally, he started the engines. The louder they got, the harder my heart pumped. It was excitement, not fear. I had no way of knowing, but my guess was that Cole Hudson was an excellent pilot. He didn't get to be a famous architect by being the kind of man who settled for mediocre in anything.

I swiveled my seat around as we started to taxi down the runway. "Goodbye, Willow Creek," I whispered as we moved faster and faster. Then suddenly the plane gave a slight jerk and we were up and climbing.

And climbing.

It seemed to go on forever. I tried to relax and not white-knuckle the armrests. *Breathe*, I told myself. Every journey has to have a takeoff. When I felt calm enough to look out the window, it was as if we were traveling through cotton candy. Then the view cleared to a gorgeous blue and I was staring down on a floor of fluffy clouds.

Eventually, we leveled off. I popped the cork from the champagne bottle and filled the flute to the brim.

"To Jo and Iris," I whispered, as I raised my glass. Maybe I was escaping for only a short while, but I was doing it on a private jet while drinking the most expensive thing I'd ever tasted. I drained my glass and poured myself another.

I woke up with a jolt. It took a few seconds for me to get my bearings. Oh, right. Private plane flown by famous architect. I scanned the view. We were descending. I must have slept all the way to Chicago. I stretched and grinned as I swiveled my chair full circle. So far, no signs of the city.

In fact, there wasn't a sign of much of anything at all. And why was it so dark? We'd only been flying for thirty minutes, hadn't we?

I could see a control tower ahead but unless we were a lot higher than I thought we were, it didn't look very tall or imposing. And the runways, outlined by blue lights, didn't look very long. Still, the control tower seemed to be the tallest thing around. Everything, including the terminal, looked flat and low—and dark. We couldn't possibly be landing anywhere in Illinois. Where were the golden arches? The billboards? The neon of a gazillion franchises that lined every airport I'd ever seen?

With one final, gentle bounce, the plane landed. I unbuckled my seat belt and worked my way up to the front while the plane was still taxiing in.

I practically fell into the cockpit. "Where are we?"

Cole Hudson jerked his head around. "You should still be seated," he said curtly.

He gave me a look of annoyance when I bumped his knee as I struggled to land in the copilot's seat.

"That's not what I meant," he said before setting his mouth in a grim line.

"I know. But I'd like to see where I'm going, if you don't mind. This doesn't look like Chicago. Why is it so dark? How long have I been sleeping?"

"I'd say you've been sleeping for at least three hours."

"Three hours! Where are we?"

The grim line of his mouth morphed into a small smile. "Welcome to Goose Bay, Labrador, Ms. Blake."

I gasped. "Labrador? As in Canada?"

He glanced my way. "Someone did well in geography."

"What are we doing here?"

"Refueling."

Okay, refueling. That made sense. Sort of. "And then are you flying back to Chicago?" I asked hopefully.

"No, Ms. Blake. Then I'm flying to Iceland, where I will land and refuel once again."

"And then back to Chicago?"

He looked at me, one of his dark eyebrows raised. "You think we're out for a Sunday drive, Ms. Blake? I didn't just burn up thirty-six hundred pounds of fuel to turn around and fly right back."

The plane came to a stop and I heard the engines shutting down. Funny how I felt my stomach drop about the same time.

"After Iceland—then where are you going?"

"Paris," he said without looking at me.

I watched him flipping switches.

"But what about Chicago?" I asked.

He finally looked at me. "I never said I was going to Chicago, Ms. Blake," he said with exaggerated pleasantness.

I remembered the twinkle in his eye just before he gave in

to me. "Why you—you did this on purpose, didn't you?" I accused. "You knew I thought you were flying right back to Chicago!"

He didn't quite allow himself to smile. "I promised you one way, and one way you got."

"But what am I supposed to do in Goose Bay, Labrador?"

"You can get yourself a placard and an indelible marker, Ms. Blake, and picket, for all I care."

He had to lean close to me to get out of his seat. I was right behind him.

The wind hit me as soon as I reached the door. I struggled against it all the way down the stairs. The cold was biting. In Willow Creek, the cold just nipped. Goose Bay had gotten a head start on us in the snow department, too. There seemed to be several feet of it on the ground.

My face and ears were freezing by the time I caught up with him. I grabbed his arm.

"You don't think you're just going to leave me here, do you?"

"You'll be able to get a plane home," he said, then started walking again.

Openmouthed, I stared after him. I was going to have to use up my emergency credit card funds to fly back to Willow Creek from *Labrador?* No. Life couldn't be that cruel. But, apparently, Cole Hudson could.

"You can't do this," I yelled as I ran to catch up to him.

"Yes, I can," he affirmed as he kept to his stride. "You wanted to get away, well, Goose Bay is certainly away. Beautiful country up here. You'll love it. You could ski. Play a little ice hockey."

If I tried to argue with him much more out here, my nose was going to freeze and fall off. While he headed to what must be the service area, I headed for the terminal, hoping for something hot to drink.

Ah, civilization, I thought, as I spotted a small café. Inside, I ordered coffee. When it came I cradled the cup in my hands close enough to my face to melt some of the frost. I took a sip and it nearly scorched my throat, but the flood of warmth when the coffee hit my belly began to revive me. And the more I revived, the angrier I got.

Okay, so I hadn't wanted to spend my strike rocking in the maid's room. That didn't mean I wanted to spend it freezing my nose off. And what a letdown it was going to be to the Prisoner's of Willow Creek Enrichment Society to hear that I never made it to a place that had neon, never mind anything like the bright lights of Chicago. The thought of Cole Hudson tricking me into coming here, then abandoning me on his way to Paris was—

I sat up straight.

Paris.

I smiled. Paris was the perfect place to carry out my strike— not to mention one of the cities I'd always wanted to visit. I'd come this far, why not go all the way?

I looked up in time to see Cole enter the café with two other men in similar leather jackets. They sat down at a table, already engrossed in conversation. I didn't care. I had a message to deliver and I wasn't going to wait.

"When the new plant is built," one of the men was saying as I approached, "I might have to add to my fleet."

"It's going to get busier around here, that's for sure," said the other.

"I can help you find the planes," Cole offered. "I've got a connection with—"

"Excuse me," I said.

All three men looked up. Only one of them groaned.

"Guys, meet my human baggage, Ms. Blake."

The two men stood and introduced themselves as Dane and Oscar. Dane was gray haired, handsome and distinguished looking while Oscar looked rougher, more the outdoorsy type. They both offered their hands.

"Nice to see some gentlemen around here," I said as I shook them.

"If you don't mind," Cole said, "we're in the middle of a conversation."

"No, I don't mind. I did want to tell you that I'll be flying to Paris with you."

I started to turn to go, figuring a hasty exit might avoid the argument I was sure was coming. But he stood up and grabbed my arm.

"When pigs fly," he intoned—a Shakespearean actor spouting clichés.

"Why not? Don't you think you owe it to me after playing this lousy trick?"

"I've already made arrangements for Dane to fly you to Chicago tomorrow morning. I think that makes us even."

"But why won't you let me go along? What's the difference? I'll sit in the back and be quiet—"

"We already know you're incapable of that," he snapped. "Even when you went to sleep you snored!"

Swell, I thought. I guess it went with the parka and sneakers. At least I hadn't been in the cockpit where I might have drooled all over his thousand dollar jacket. Thus, I wasn't embarrassed enough to give up my idea.

"You're just being stubborn for no reason at all. You're going to Paris anyway, and—"

"Let me make this perfectly clear to you, Ms. Blake. As soon as they're done refueling my plane I'm flying out of here with the hope that I never have to lay eyes on any of the Blake women ever again. Understood?"

This time when he went back to talking to his pals, I didn't try to stop him. I had never in my life met a man so rude, so grumpy, so hard to bear. Why on earth I'd even considered flying on to Paris with him was beyond me. I bought a large coffee to go to help keep me from freezing outside. The wind catapulted me toward the plane where I planned to collect my suitcase. What a shame it was that I'd slept through most of the trip. It was such a beautiful airplane. Now I'd never get the chance to sit in the cockpit with Cole Hudson and watch him fly.

Imagine landing in Paris, I thought.

Yeah. Imagine.

I decided right then that I wasn't going to give up this easily.

On board I crawled into the copilot's seat to wait.

Cole showed up a half hour later. Good thing, too, because my coffee was almost cold and nearly gone.

"I thought I told you I fly solo," he said as he slid into the pilot's seat beside me.

"You're never too old to try something new," I said brightly enough to be Doris Day.

"As long as we're speaking in hackneyed phrases, Ms. Blake, perhaps you've also heard the one about how you can't teach an old dog new tricks."

"You're not that old. And since we're going to be together

all the way to Paris, I think you should start calling me Abby, Cole."

He stared at me. I grinned back.

Suddenly he erupted into a deep chuckle. "You're really incorrigible, you know that?"

"I've been called worse."

"I bet you have, Abby," he said. "I bet you have."

"Look." I leaned toward him earnestly. "Once we touch down in Paris you never have to see me again. I'll be completely on my own. And it'll still be one way. It's just that, well, I've always wanted to see Paris..." I let my voice trail off hopefully.

He scrutinized me for what felt like hours. I used the time to study his face. It was as interesting and unique as the buildings he designed. And his head was likely just as hard as the steel he used in his structures. His will was probably as unmovable as a block of marble, too, I thought. He was going to say no again. I could feel it.

"Even if I changed my mind it wouldn't work," he said with more gentleness than I'd expected. "You don't have a passport."

I threw my head back against the seat and squeezed my eyes shut to keep the tears from falling. So near and yet so far. Avoiding Cole's expression, I started to get out of the seat to collect my suitcase. And that's when I remembered.

"Wait—I'll be right back," I said.

I rushed to the cabin, grabbed my suitcase out of the luggage compartment and unzipped the outside pocket. I felt around. Nothing. And then my fingers touched it. I pulled it out. Yes! It was still there. Had been there all along.

I ran to the cockpit waving my passport.

"I've got a passport!" I announced breathlessly. "Been in the zipper compartment of my suitcase ever since I canceled a trip to Europe a few years ago."

He looked at the small blue book, dark brows lowered over light eyes, then looked at me.

I held my breath.

"I give up," he finally declared. "Buckle up, Abby. Next stop Iceland."

CHAPTER 4

I kept quiet while Cole communicated with ground control then started to taxi into position. I could see snow swirling in the lights along the runway. My heart was in my throat by the time departure control gave us the go-ahead to take off.

I couldn't take my eyes off Cole. His concentration was so complete, his energy so controlled as the plane moved down the runway and picked up speed. There was a bump as we let go of the earth and climbed straight into the darkness. I didn't speak until the plane stabilized and he'd finished talking into his headset.

"Wow—that was a rush," I said.

He looked at me with a raised brow. "I'm so glad you enjoyed it."

"I suppose to you it's no big deal, but I've never flown in a jet this size before. What kind of plane is it?" I asked.

"Cessna Citation Ultra. Nineteen ninety-seven," he answered, his eyes back on the instruments and the black sky in front of us.

"Have you had it long?"

"No."

I worried a tooth with my tongue, trying to think of something else to say. I mean, what do you say to a man who wishes he never had to lay eyes on you again?

"How long is the flight to Iceland?" I asked.

"Three and a half hours."

Oh, boy. Between my long nap and the caffeine in two large coffees I was wide awake. I stared out into the night sky. It was going to be a long, boring three and a half hours if every answer he gave me was going to be lacking a verb.

"You know, I really do hope that the kids get back together," I said impulsively. "I've always liked David."

He scowled my way and I swore I could feel the vibration of his anger floating around the cockpit in waves.

"Great timing, Ms. Blake. Why the hell didn't you show me any support back in Willow Creek?"

I sat up straighter in my seat and squared my shoulders. "Because it's got to be up to them to figure it out. We can't be rushing in to dictate their lives. If they're having differences, they need to work them out together."

"The only differences they're having is that your daughter is a spoiled brat and my son lives up to his responsibilities."

"My daughter," I told him firmly, "is no spoiled brat. It's not like she had everything handed to her. True, Gwen can be somewhat self-absorbed," I was willing to concede, "but she worked hard on her career and she's worked hard on this marriage, too."

"If you call walking out on it working hard at it," he muttered.

"Well, not that I expect it to raise your opinion of me, but I did tell Gwen that she needed to be more supportive of her husband's needs—but Gwen also has needs."

"Humph," he said.

I'd expected something a little more articulate. Probably not a wise choice of subject on my part, I decided. "So tell me why you're going to Paris."

"Business."

I raised my eyes heavenward. Surely, a man who was as successful and well known as he was had to be better at conversation than this. "Are you designing something there?"

"Yes."

"Is it some kind of state secret?"

"No, Ms. Blake, it is not."

I twisted in my seat so that I was facing him. "I know we're not exactly fans of one another, but if you're going to be so reticent, I might as well crawl in the back, pop open more champagne and sleep the rest of the way to Iceland."

I was about to unbuckle my seat belt when he said, "I'm going to Paris at the behest of some old friends. They want me to design a small art museum on the grounds of their estate to house their private collection."

I thought back to the structures he'd created. Okay, I admit it, I'd looked him up on the Internet when Gwen and David got engaged. Who wouldn't? Cole Hudson's career had gone way beyond something that small. He'd done skyscrapers and luxury condo developments. His last project had been a gorgeous black marble art-deco-style luxury hotel in Miami. I wasn't seeing him restrained to building a shrine to good taste in someone's backyard. "That doesn't seem like your kind of project."

"Ordinarily, it wouldn't be. But, as I said, Madeline and Andre Fontaine are special friends. They were my mentors when I was younger. And they're also philanthropists. They've recently moved into an apartment in Paris and plan to open both the Fontaine family estate and the art museum to the public with the proceeds to be used to set up a foundation that will award grants to promising young artists."

"They sound like wonderful people."

His face softened. "They are. I first met them when I was still a student. I was backpacking through Europe at the time. Living mainly off of bread and water, determined to see all the buildings in the world that had fascinated me since I'd been a boy. Art didn't interest me that much—but a certain Italian girl I'd met on the train did. She was an artist and knew Madeline and Andre slightly. She took me to a gallery opening where they happened to be and introduced us. We hit it off and they invited me and the Italian girl to spend the weekend at their estate.

"I'd never been around people like them. People who discussed ideas that had nothing to do with money or the economy or the stock market. I showed them some sketches I'd made of the kind of buildings I wanted to build." He shook his head, as if it still bewildered him. "They took me seriously. My ideas were more than a boy's dreams to them. I'd never had such encouragement. I owe them a lot."

The arrogant Cole Hudson was humbled by his feelings for the French couple. It was a side of him I never would have guessed existed.

"They must mean a lot to you."

"They're gracious, warm, wonderful people. They were the parents I wish I'd had."

We were silent for awhile. I had no idea what he was thinking, but I knew what I was thinking. I was wondering if my daughters ever felt that way—that someone else should have been their mother. That would be hard to take as a parent. Of course, if that's how they felt, they wouldn't keep boomeranging home, would they? I pondered that question as we flew through the darkness.

"Your turn now," Cole suddenly said.

I looked at him. "Excuse me?"

"Why are *you* going to Paris?"

I grinned. "Because you said yes."

"Oh, no," he growled. "You're not going to get off that easily. What makes the stalwart, loyal Widow Blake desert her family during the Christmas holidays?"

"Maybe I'm as selfish as my daughter, Gwen."

He glanced at me. "Not from what I've been told. I've heard the story of how you moved back to Willow Creek to care for a dying father, stayed to take care of an aging mother, then raised two children on your own when your husband was killed in a car accident."

My mouth dropped open. "How could you possibly know all that?"

"Your daughter is proud of you."

"Gwen?" I croaked.

"Gwen," he affirmed.

If my oldest daughter was proud of me, it came as a surprise. Of the two of my daughters, she'd always been the more critical one.

"You make me sound like some kind of saint."

"She made you sound like some kind of saint."

"Well, I'm not. Because if I were—"

I broke off. My mouth was running too fast. Must be the rarified air up here.

"Finish your statement, Abby," he coaxed in a voice that I figured got him a lot of things he wanted when it came to women.

It worked with me, too. "If I were a saint, I wouldn't be selfishly running away from my responsibilities. I'd be home, searching for Christmas decorations in the dusty attic."

"Selfish? Hogwash! You're on strike. And, from what I saw, with good reason. I'd hardly call that running away. I'd call it making a stand."

His words surprised me. "Why, Mr. Hudson, what happened to your assessment that all the Blake women are crazy and to be avoided?"

"I haven't stated any change to that assessment, Abby. But since we are each other's captive audience at forty-one thousand feet—"

"No kidding?" I looked out the window and down into the blackness below us. "Holy cow."

One corner of his mouth curved up. "I don't think I've ever met a woman who used the phrase 'holy cow' before."

"This is probably higher than I've ever been."

"And here I thought you were one of those people who got high on life."

I knew he was making a joke, but he'd just stuck a finger into one of my sore points. "People think I'm a Pollyanna because of how I look, I guess."

"How you look?"

"I have that certain Midwestern, corn-fed, content look. Lately, though, I haven't been all that content."

"Good God, do I feel a revelation coming on?"

I gave him a twisted smile. "You've designed important buildings for important people. Surely a small town widow's revelation wouldn't scare you off?"

"Do your worst," he challenged.

"I admit to a certain—ah—restlessness lately."

"Just lately? I would think life in Willow Creek would cause any thinking human being to be restless."

I considered what he said. "Actually, Willow Creek has its good points. It was a great place for the kids to grow up. I don't think this unsettled feeling started until the girls grew up and started lives of their own. For years I was able to contain it."

"And now it's breaking free."

I swung my head to stare at him. It astounded me that he'd used those words. Breaking free. It's what I'd been feeling—as if something inside of me was trying to break free. Somehow, high in that night sky, in our small bubble of dim, artificially lit suspended reality, Cole Hudson, of all people, seemed to know exactly what was going on with me. Which is why, I suppose, I kept on talking.

"I'm tired of being needed all the time. I know a woman isn't supposed to feel that way."

"Who says?"

I gave a short laugh. "Oh, it's on all the magazine covers, haven't you noticed?"

"Obviously, you're reading the wrong magazines," he said drily.

"Maybe. Let me know if you ever see a cover story with the headline 'It's Your Turn, Abby Blake' on it. Until then, despite my temporary strike, I'm pretty sure I'm destined to remain a dedicated middle-aged widowed grandmother, living out a life of semiboredom and obscurity."

Now why had I said that? And to this man? I suddenly felt far too naked—and not in a good way. Sort of like being observed in the middle of the impossible contortions one goes through trying to put panty hose on. I decided to keep my mouth shut for awhile.

That is, until I saw another airplane coming right at us. And it was a hell of a lot bigger than Cole's airplane.

"Ohmigod!" I screamed and gripped his arm. Didn't he see

it? How could he not see it? The thing was lit up like a Christmas tree. But he wasn't doing anything about it. "What's the matter with you? We're going to crash right into that plane!"

"Easy, Abby," he said calmly. "It's not as close as it looks."

"Are you crazy? It's right there. Coming right at us. Can't you dive or something?"

"Everything is under control," he insisted.

All right. He wasn't only arrogant. He was insane. I closed my eyes and prepared to die.

But nothing happened.

I opened my eyes again. The plane that had been heading straight for us was gone.

"What happened to it? Where did it go? You saw it, didn't you?"

"Will you take it easy? Of course I saw it. It was a 747. That's a big plane, Abby. I could hardly miss seeing it."

"I know it's a big plane! Why do you think I was screaming?"

He glanced at me. "You don't know a lot about air travel, do you?"

"Of course not! I'm a bookkeeper from Willow Creek, Wisconsin."

"Well, these days, airplanes are only required to keep one thousand feet between them. We were actually flying below that 747 by at least a thousand feet. I know it looked like it was coming right at us, but there was no chance for collision."

I leaned my head back, still breathing heavy, still trying to get my heartbeat under control. "You might have warned me."

"Like I said, Abby, I'm used to flying solo."

I took a couple of deep, calming breaths. "My husband Charlie used to say a miss is as good as a mile."

"Wise man."

"He was. Very kind. Very wise. Very sweet." I took several deep breaths. "What is David's mother like?"

He shook his head. "Not one of my favorite topics of conversation."

"How long were you married?"

He glanced at me, his dark brows lowered into another one of his scowls. "Are you always so tenacious?"

"I don't like to give up," I admitted. "Besides, moments ago, I thought I was going to die. I could use the comfort of a little conversation."

He sighed. "All right. We were married eight years."

"And then what happened?"

"We got divorced," he answered succinctly.

"Yes, but why?"

He lifted a shoulder. "I suppose we just grew apart. Grew bored."

"You wanted different things?"

"We wanted the same things—at least at first. She grew tired of waiting for them. She didn't realize that she'd married the black sheep of the family."

"Black sheep?" I asked, perplexed at the moniker being attached to a man like Cole Hudson. "But you're a famous architect. You own a jet. How could you possibly be the black sheep of the family?"

The silence between us lengthened until he said, "I suppose if I don't answer that question you'll just ask me again."

"Are you kidding? You can't put a statement like that out there and not elaborate on it."

He shook his head and sighed but I thought he was trying hard to hold back a small smile. "I come from an old, venerable banking family, Abby. I have three brothers who are all involved in high finance. I was supposed to get into line and carry on the family tradition."

"But you didn't."

"I didn't want to just move money around. I wanted to build something. Something lasting. To my father, it was foolish. A pipe dream."

"He must be proud of you now that you've proven him wrong."

"Proving him wrong only proved to alienate him further. In any case, he died before I did my best work."

"Do you think he would have eventually come around?"

"No. He prided himself on his consistency. I don't think he ever forgave me for turning my back on all the family name had to offer."

"Sounds like a pleasant fellow."

"David's mother, Monique, shared his opinion. She didn't want to be married to a struggling architect. I didn't know it when I married her, but she had plans to bring me back into the family fold so she could reap the benefits."

"But she obviously didn't succeed."

He shook his head, his silver hair shimmering. "I couldn't live the life she wanted. She couldn't live the life I wanted."

"That is just so sad. And it makes me wonder if—" I let the thought hang out there, not sure I should finish it. To finish it felt like it would be disloyal to Charlie.

"If what?" Cole Hudson demanded. "If we're trading secrets, it's only fair that I hear one of yours."

"Well, sometimes, like now, I wonder if Charlie hadn't died how we would feel about each other. That is, after years of marriage and gallons of water under the bridge."

"Surely, the stalwart Widow Blake would remain loyal for life."

I laughed. "I could tell you a secret that would shatter that image all to hell."

"I'm all ears."

"Once, when Charlie and I were making love, I pretended he was Neil Diamond."

He roared with laughter. It occurred to me that it was too bad you couldn't roll down the windows of a plane like you could a car. The wind could never snatch up that deep sound of pleasure and carry it out into space where it would become part of eternity.

"Do you laugh very often?" I asked.

He glanced at me. "I am not without a sense of humor," he said.

"Good."

"Why is that?" he asked gruffly.

"Because you have a really wonderful laugh."

"Disarming *and* incorrigible," he murmured. "Dangerous combination."

I decided not to ask him what he meant by that. I was much more interested in something else. "Why didn't you ever remarry?"

"Maybe I just never found the right woman."

"There's got to be more to it than that," I prodded.

"In the beginning, yes, there were other reasons. Almost everyone we knew was divorced, some of them multiple times. I saw what kids went through with stepparents upon stepparents. I saw the damage it could cause. Monique married a few times more, which meant the situation was already getting complicated for David." He shrugged. "It just never seemed worth it to me."

Silence, and then he said again, "Your turn now."

"You mean why didn't I ever remarry?"

He nodded.

"A small town like mine doesn't import many new men. I tried dating, but when I found myself sitting across from a man in a restaurant who I'd sat across from in second grade and who I personally knew had picked his nose every day of that long, long year, well, I kind of lost my appetite for dating."

"Yes, I can see how knowing those types of *tidbits*, shall we say, about one's past would be off-putting."

This time, I was the one who roared with laughter.

When Cole started flipping switches and talking into his headset, I realized that we'd talked and laughed our way through three hours.

Moments later, we started our descent. I looked out the window. Below us, I could see the faint outline of the coast of Iceland.

Iceland. It seemed almost impossible that I could have been in Willow Creek, Wisconsin, rocking in my rocking chair, just hours ago. Just like it seemed impossible that I could have enjoyed the company of Cole Hudson. But I had.

The terminal at Keflavik International Airport was a modern phenomenon. I might have wanted to explore it further, but Cole had a car waiting to take us to a hotel.

"It's another three and a half hours to Paris. I'd like to get a few hours of sleep and a shower before the last leg of the journey," he remarked.

I had no objection. It had been an incredible day.

The first thing that struck me was the temperature. "Why is it so much warmer here than in Goose Bay?"

"The name Iceland is something of a misnomer," Cole explained. "The temperature is affected by the Gulf Stream so the weather is often mild, yet highly changeable."

I leaned forward and asked the driver what time it was.

"One-thirty in the morning, ma'am," he answered.

"Iceland is six hours ahead of Chicago," Cole told me.

That made it dinnertime in Willow Creek. By now they would have found the note I'd scribbled, telling them I was going to Chicago for a few days. Like motion sickness, what I'd done suddenly hit me in the pit of my stomach. I'd abandoned my family! And during the holidays! I wondered how they were taking it. I didn't want anyone to worry. But why would they? They'd assume I was in Chicago. They'd never dream I was in Iceland. I could scarcely believe it myself.

I tucked away my guilt for the time being—as I'd tucked away other feelings throughout my life—and peered out the window of the car. I wished it wasn't so dark so I could see something of the country. As it turned out, we pulled up in front of the hotel in less than ten minutes.

The lobby was also modern, lots of pale wood and curves, with plush deep-blue sofas grouped together for conversation. The blond woman at the front desk obviously knew Cole and was used to him checking in in the middle of the night. He spoke to her at length then came back to me to announce that we were in luck and they had a room for me.

"We'll be leaving for the airport at nine in the morning," Cole told me in the elevator. "I've asked them to give you a wake-up call for eight."

"I guess you can tell I'm not high maintenance, huh?"

"Excuse me?"

"You're assuming I'll only need an hour to get ready in the morning."

"*Hoping* is the word I'd use."

"Don't worry, I'll be ready on time."

"I would greatly appreciate that. I have an important meeting tomorrow afternoon in Paris. I don't like to be late for meetings."

Our rooms were on different floors so I left him in the elevator on the second floor and found my room a few doors down.

The room was very Scandinavian—all muted earth tones and contemporary paintings on the walls. The nicest thing about it, aside from the wonderfully huge, soft bed, was the maple tray on the table that held a small bottle of wine, a basket of bread and a plate of cheese and fruit. There was a white card on the tray. I picked it up.

"Sweet dreams," it read. It was signed with a large C.

I smiled. Cole Hudson apparently had some pull at the hotel to get the kitchen to deliver my middle-of-the-night feast so quickly. I opened the wine and poured a glass.

I nibbled and sipped while I got undressed and pulled on my pajamas. I crawled into bed with a smile on my face. What a tale I would tell. I could just imagine the looks on Matt's and Tyler's faces when I told them about that 747 that looked as if it was coming straight at us.

My time in Iceland was going to be spent sleeping. Still, I figured I was doing the Prisoners of Willow Creek Enrichment Society proud.

And tomorrow, I'd be in Paris.

It seemed I'd barely fallen asleep before the phone rang. I lifted the receiver but no one was there. Was that my wake-up call? I got out of bed and went over to the window to pull back the drapes. It was still pitch dark. The call must have been a mistake. I gratefully crawled back under the covers and was oblivious again in seconds. The next thing that woke me was a pounding on the door to my room. What was going on? It was the middle of the night for crying out loud.

I dragged myself out of bed and went to the door.

"Who is it?" I asked.

"Who do you think?" came the answer.

The voice was unmistakable. I opened the door.

"Good God," he boomed.

"What's the matter?" I mumbled.

"Why aren't you ready to go? Didn't you get your wake-up call?"

I squinted at him. "I got *a* call. I thought it was a mistake."

"I told you we were leaving for the airport at nine, didn't I?" he asked as he scowled mightily at me. "And as I recall, you bragged about being a low maintenance woman and promised to be ready on time."

"But it's still the middle of the night."

"It's eight forty-five in the morning, Ms. Blake—"

Uh, oh. We were back to Ms. Blake.

"—the sun doesn't rise in Keflavik until after eleven in December."

"How nice it would have been if you had told me that, Mr. Hudson. You seem to like to keep a lot of important information to yourself."

"I don't intend to waste time arguing with you. Now kindly throw yourself together. You've got ten minutes to meet me in the lobby or I'm leaving without you."

He stalked off down the hall and I stared after him. Was that the same man who'd sent that note wishing me sweet dreams? The same man I'd shared secrets with at forty-one thousand feet?

Who had time to figure it out? I barely had enough time to brush my teeth.

"How was I to know that Iceland only got four hours of daylight this time of year?" I asked his stony profile.

We'd taken off from Keflavik Airport nearly an hour ago and he still hadn't spoken to me.

"I don't like being late for meetings, Ms. Blake."

"Don't give me that Ms. Blake business, just because I overslept," I said incredulously.

"I told you—"

"Yes, I know. You don't like to be late for meetings." I unbuckled my seat belt. "I'm sure you have no objection to my traveling as a passenger on the final leg of this journey."

"None at all," he assured me without so much as a glance in my direction.

I hated the fact that I had to brush against him as I got out of the copilot's seat—almost as much as I hated the fact that I'd told him some of the things I'd told him last night. If I'd known he was going to turn into the enemy again so soon, I would have kept my big mouth shut. Ohmigod. I'd told him I'd once fantasized that Charlie was Neil Diamond. Could this be any more embarrassing? How come there was never a parachute around when you needed one? I scrunched down in my seat and cringed the rest of the way to Paris.

There was another car waiting for us at Le Bourget Airport, which was outside of Paris and catered to corporate jets and helicopters.

"*Je voudrais aller à l'hôtel George V*," Cole told the driver before he settled back and pulled out his cell phone.

So now I was not only embarrassed but ignored. I glanced at Cole's stony profile again. Was that the problem? Was Cole Hudson just as embarrassed as I was about the things we'd told each other last night? Had I managed to penetrate a wall that he was now determined to erect anew between us?

Oh, who gave a damn. I was only a few miles from Paris. Once we reached the hotel, we'd part ways and I'd never have to see him again.

Cole spent most of his time during the ride speaking perfect French into his cell phone. A solemn rain fell as we drove into the city. I tried to keep my excitement in check, but the heavier the traffic got, the more quickly those tiny cars seemed to zip all over the place, the faster my heart beat. I was in Paris.

There was no mistaking it now as we turned onto a wide boulevard clogged with traffic and lined with old buildings. I had absolutely no idea what part of the city we were in—knew nothing, really, about Paris except for the Eiffel Tower, the Arc de Triomphe and the River Seine. But I refused to show my ignorance—or my enthusiasm—to Cole Hudson.

When we pulled up in front of the Hotel George V, I took one look at it and knew that my emergency credit card would be maxed out just by my walking through the door.

Uniformed doormen appeared like magic to assist Cole. When I didn't follow him out of the car, he ducked his head back in.

"Well, are you coming?"

"Um—could you ask the driver if he knows of a cheaper place?"

"Not necessary," he answered brusquely. "I've got a two-bedroom suite reserved. You're welcome to the second bedroom."

I hesitated. Did I want to share a suite with the unpredictable, arrogant Cole Hudson? I realized that he mistook my hesitation for worrying about propriety when he said, "Surely if you can tell me that you once pretended your husband was Neil Diamond while having sex, you can sleep in a bedroom separated from mine by a sitting room."

Damn it, I'd started to hope he hadn't really been paying attention up in that airplane. "I'd just like to be able to pay my own way, that's all," I said stubbornly.

He sighed and slid back into the car next to me. "Listen, it's the Christmas holidays. The likelihood of your finding a room anywhere in Paris is slim. And I'm not going to allow you to go wandering all over the city like a waif, looking for a bed for the night."

I turned to him. "I am not your responsibility. I'm the woman you'd hoped never to set eyes on again, remember?"

"I'm offering you a suite in one of the finest hotels in Paris. Don't be stupid as well as stubborn."

Inside I was seething, but what he said made sense. Besides, once I got my bearings and learned my way around, I could always shop for cheaper digs.

"Fine," I replied.

I followed him out of the car and into the hotel.

The lobby was a swirl of gold and marble and frightening tapestries that reached to the ceiling. It was exactly what I'd expected from a luxury hotel in Paris. There were gilt tables with immense vases full of huge but tasteful holiday floral arrangements. There were white marble statues on grand pedestals lit from behind and dainty armchairs upholstered in brocade. Holding command over it all was a huge crystal chandelier hanging from the center of the ceiling. I almost bumped into a half-naked man of marble staring up at it.

My sneakers squeaked as I followed Cole across the marble floor to the front desk. Our luggage had already been whisked away so I didn't even have the chic Vuitton suitcase to dilute the image of my polyester parka.

When we were shown to our suite, I tried not to gasp but it was truly magnificent. The sitting room was huge, scattered with pale green upholstered furniture and warm wood tables. Elaborate, heavy brocade drapes hung from the windows. The far end of the room was set up like a dining room with a table big enough to seat ten and beyond that were French doors that led to a balcony. It was almost too much to take in at once. A fireplace. More marble statues. Beautiful paintings on the walls. And a fat table-top Christmas tree decorated all in gold.

"You take that room," Cole said, nodding toward the door on the right side of the sitting room.

I walked over and peered in. I swear there was a crown over the bed—a huge swirl attached to the wall above the head of the bed that was draped with yards and yards of shimmering gold fabric, held back on either side by gold fleur-de-lis.

"Are you sure you want me to take this room?" I asked.

"Did you want the larger one?"

There was a larger one? "No, this one's just fine," I quickly assured him.

I think there were more lamps in my room than I had in my entire house in Willow Creek. The bed was covered in gold brocade that was echoed in the dressing table, the kind that little girls dreamed about.

Little girls like Ashley.

I sank onto the bed. I hadn't even stopped to think how my grandchildren were going to feel about my simply taking off without so much as a goodbye. Surely they'd believe I was coming back like I'd written in the note? What was the point in being here if I was going worry and stew? I figured I had two choices: get on the next available flight and go back home or convince myself that I deserved this and had nothing to feel guilty about.

I jumped to my feet. I was staying. I couldn't give up this chance. I couldn't go home until I'd experienced—*something*. Hell, anything. I was only going to be gone a few days. My family ought to be able to cope with temporary defection. It would probably be easier on them to have me out of the house in my present state of mind. Lord knows what sort of things I might have ended up getting off my chest once I started.

I was taking a break. That's all this was. A break.

It was likely time that I also took a shower.

I opened the door to what I assumed was the bathroom to find a huge tub encased in pink marble sitting smack dab in the middle of the room. There was an upholstered bench drawn up to it that held fluffy white towels and a large basket of toiletries; a huge window with a view of the courtyard was draped in more brocade. And above the tub, hanging from the ceiling, was a crystal chandelier that was almost as beautiful as the one in the lobby. A lot smaller, of course, but still luxurious. Across from the tub were two small armchairs. I suppose in case I wanted to dictate notes to my private secretary on which invitations to accept and what I might want for lunch that day and could she send my ball gown out to be pressed.

Oh, I definitely wasn't in Willow Creek anymore.

I looked up and saw myself in the gilt edged mirrors over the long vanity. Too bad I still *looked* like I was in Willow Creek, I thought with a frown. If I'd known I was going to Paris, I would have packed—

What? A newer pair of jeans? Perhaps that floral dress I'd been wearing to every party, shower or christening I'd attended for the past five years? Too bad I couldn't wheel my Louis Vuitton around with me everywhere I went to keep me from looking like a total yokel.

But what did it matter? I was in Paris. And there was a huge bathtub calling my name.

I went into the sitting room where Cole was just hanging up the phone.

"Is your room satisfactory?"

"More than. It's beautiful. Thank you for bringing me here. You have no idea what—"

I was saved from the certain humiliation of choking up by a knock on the door. Cole opened it and a waiter rolled in a cart draped in a snowy cloth and set with several covered dishes, a basket of assorted breads and a bottle of wine cooling in a silver ice bucket. There was a small vase of flowers next to two linen napkins rolled and held together with gilt napkin rings.

Cole spoke in French to the waiter, signed his name on the bill, then showed the young man out.

"I have to leave for my meeting. This—" he said, indicating the table "—should hold you over until I get back." He lifted the lids on the dishes. "Foie gras, Brie, fresh fruit, chocolates. If I'm not back by dinnertime, feel free to order whatever you'd like from room service."

"But I don't speak French."

"Ah, but they speak English," he said. "Always stay in the best hotels, Abby, when traveling abroad. You'll invariably find someone who speaks English."

Yeah, right, I thought after he left. I'll remember that bit of advice, Mr. Hudson, should I ever find myself traveling abroad again.

In my room, I unpacked my plaid flannel robe, which looked like it had been traveling for quite a few years already. Then I went into that incredible bathroom, planning on a shower. It would be a shame to waste that beautiful bathtub, though. Ignoring the glass-enclosed shower stall in the far corner, I started to draw a bath. I poured a liberal amount of the lavender-scented bubbling bath oil the hotel had provided into the running water and breathed in the soothing aroma. Once the tub was full, I shut off the water, went back to the sitting room and filled a small plate with goodies. Then I poured myself a glass of wine and took it all into the bathroom where I set it on the bench next to the tub. I slipped out of my robe and lowered myself into the warm, fragrant water.

When had I last taken a bath? I couldn't even remember. Baths were a luxury of time that I'd given up somewhere along the way. I picked up my wine glass and leaned against the slanted back of the tub, sinking to my chin in suds. I held the glass aloft.

"I made it!" I shouted up to the chandelier. "I'm in Paris!" I took a long, delicious sip. I had no idea what kind of wine it was. It was white and something I could never afford, that's all I could be sure of. I was totally out of my element. But wasn't that the point? I thought as I started to nibble the delicacies on my plate. Crusty pieces of bread topped with pate that was as foreign to me as France, perfectly ripened strawberries, a soft, creamy cheese served with slices of green apple.

This was the best. And I wasn't just talking about the wine in the crystal glass and the expensive silkiness of the water I was soaking in. It was also the time, the precious moments to myself when no one was looking for me, no one was asking anything of me, no one was waiting on the other side of the door to use the toilet. It was just me, Abby. I looked up at the sparkle of crystal above me and wondered what it cost, knowing that this precious time to myself was worth a lot more.

When I felt totally relaxed and the water began to cool, I climbed out, wrapped myself in one of the hotel's huge white towels and crawled under the gold coverlet. It was the first real nap I'd had in years.

It was nearly dark when I woke. It took me a moment to realize where I was. And even then, even when I remembered, I didn't believe it. I groped until I found the bedside lamp and turned it on. The small ornate clock on the table read five-fifteen. I crawled out of bed and found my robe before I opened the door to the sitting room.

The lights on the table-top Christmas tree were lit so I could clearly see the French doors that led to the balcony. I ran across the sitting room and threw them open. The stone balcony was cold on my bare feet and still damp from the rain. But the skies had cleared. I could see the outline of the Eiffel Tower, lit up like a Christmas tree, across the Seine. Lights were coming on all over the city. Traffic was so thick it was as if the streets were alive. It was so beautiful I could barely catch my breath. But breathe I did—and deeply—and that same feeling washed over me—like an old song on the radio, like a sweet memory yearning to be held once again. And wasn't that feeling just as responsible for bringing me to Paris as Cole's plane was?

I decided I couldn't just sit in the suite, beautiful as it was, like some wallflower in life. Paris was at my feet. And there was no way I was going to order room service.

CHAPTER 5

I decided that the lobby would not intimidate me. However, when I stepped out of the elevator, I realized that it wasn't only the lobby that could be intimidating. Everyone was so elegantly dressed. And what posture! Weren't the wealthy allowed to slouch? I felt like Cinderella whose godmother had forgotten her. Although, when I made it to the entrance, the uniformed doorman was as gracious to me as he was to everyone else. He opened the door for me and wished me a good evening in heavily accented English.

The sidewalk was so full of people, and the roads so busy with those little cars darting around that it was easy to forget to wonder if anyone was judging me by my parka. I walked the short distance to the Seine and crossed one of its many bridges, stopping in the middle to gaze at the river. The Seine was wider than I'd pictured and, on this night, at least, choppier. I could see the lights of traffic on the bridges in the distance and something of the skyline of the Right Bank. When I started to grow cold, I walked on, the Eiffel Tower, looming brightly ahead, my only guide.

The closer I got to it, the more I felt my heart opening. By the time I was standing under it, I was trying not to cry. I felt as if I'd made a pilgrimage I hadn't even known I'd been on. The fact that I was alone somehow seemed right. As much as I loved my family and friends, there was no one in my life that I'd really want to share this moment with. Even Jo's wisecracks and Iris's male ogling would have spoiled the moment.

This moment belongs to me, I thought as I stood under the tower and looked up. There was a message there for me, invisible to everyone else, among the lights and the steel girders.

Yes, it said, *things are still possible*.

I grinned and shoved my hands into my white fuzzy mittens. Then I started to follow the left bank of the River Seine. I turned onto Boulevard Saint-Germain just because it sounded familiar. The pace seemed slower on this side of the river, giving me time to stroll. I stopped to study aged buildings that revealed government ministries, universities and museums. Many of them were lit from below, showing off the magnificent architecture. No wonder Cole had been drawn to this city all those years ago.

I wandered off the Boulevard and discovered galleries, shops, cafés and bistros lining the curving, narrow streets. One shop window was full of cheeses of all kinds, colors and shapes. The word *Fromagerie* was over the door. Another shop had a sign that read *Boulangerie*. I could tell it was a bakery, and not just from the yeasty aroma of baking bread. There were pedestals in the window showing off cakes and pastries. I was hungry but the shop was closed for the night so I walked on.

Doors were swathed in greenery and fairy lights were everywhere. I absorbed the sounds, the smells, and considered how ancient the cobblestone beneath my feet was. The night was progressing and I was not only hungry, but getting chillier by the minute. And, let's face it, I was lost. I decided I was going to stop at the next open place I passed. Even if no one spoke English, I figured I could at least manage the name of the hotel so someone could point me in the right direction.

A few doors down, I came upon a narrow café with a dark red door adorned by a wreath made of an assortment of greens and branches. I went inside. Jazz was playing and people were talking loudly over the music. As I stood just inside the door, I realized that there wasn't a person over thirty in the place. And there sure as heck wasn't anyone wearing baby-blue polyester. I was trying to decide whether I should stay or go when a young man with dark, tousled hair and multiple piercings in one ear came up to me and said something in French.

I shook my head. "I don't speak French," I enunciated clearly.

The young man laughed. "Cool, 'cause I'm pretty sure I just mangled that sentence all to hell."

"You're from the States!" I exclaimed with relief.

He nodded. "You looked a little lost so I thought I'd come over and rescue you. We have a table over there. You're welcome to join us."

I looked over to the corner he'd indicated where two young women were sitting.

"Are you sure?" I asked.

"Of course. Come on," he said as he turned and headed back to his group.

I felt foolish standing there, so I followed.

He introduced me to his companions, Olivia and Rachel. "And I'm Todd."

I introduced myself and Todd asked what I'd like to drink.

"Coffee, I think. I've been walking for what feels like forever. I'm cold and completely lost."

Todd gave the waiter my order.

"Don't feel bad," said Olivia, whose short blond hair stuck out in interesting ways to frame her fresh cherubic face. "Getting lost happens to everyone on their first trip to Paris no matter how prepared you are. It's practically a rite of passage."

"Well, for me, coming to Paris was sort of an accident. I wasn't prepared at all. I don't even have a guide book with me."

Rachel flicked her long raven hair over her shoulders and put her elbows on the table. "An accident? How does someone end up in Paris by accident?"

So I told them my story—how I'd gone on strike against my family and had thought I was hitching a ride in a private jet to Chicago with a man I referred to as Mr. Big Shot Architect since I didn't know if Cole Hudson's name would be known to them. I didn't want to spread gossip about someone whose reputation they might be aware of. "But instead of Chicago, I wound up in Paris by way of Labrador and Iceland."

"That is so cool," said Rachel.

"Kids take off to 'find themselves'—" Olivia waggled her fingers into quotation marks "—all the time, but you never hear about somebody's mother taking off on an odyssey."

"Given my traveling companion, I think the word *oddity* would be closer to the truth."

Everyone laughed, then Rachel and Olivia raised their wine glasses.

"Here's to you, girlfriend!" Olivia said. "Your odyssey might be an oddity but at least you got to travel to Paris for free!"

"Power to the sisterhood!" Rachel shouted.

"So you don't think what I'm doing is selfish?" I asked.

"Fuck no," Olivia said. "Hell, I wish my mother would take

off once in a while. Might keep her happy enough to stay off my ass if she 'found herself.'"

The coffee was definitely warming me up and I slipped out of my parka. Todd called for another bottle of the *vin de maison* and an extra glass.

Olivia leaned closer to me. "Todd likes to show off his rather limited French. *Vin de maison* means house wine. Which means cheap."

"Is there any other kind?" I asked.

All three of my new companions laughed.

"Now tell me why you guys are in Paris."

Todd came from a wealthy family and was bumming around Europe on his Christmas break from Harvard. He was currently staying in an apartment owned by friends of his parents. Rachel and Olivia had come to live in Paris for a year. Rachel was working for an airline and Olivia, who was a sculptor, was studying part-time at the Sorbonne. The girls shared a tiny apartment in the Latin Quarter nearby.

"Is that where I am? The Latin Quarter?" I asked as the waiter set an open bottle of wine on our table.

"Or the Quartier Latin, as the French say," Todd told me as he filled my glass with red wine.

Olivia went on to explain that the Quarter had been the haunt of students and intellectuals for centuries. "Although it's gotten touristy over the years. But you still see a lot of students here. Aside from being close to the universities, there are plenty of cheap places to eat and drink."

"That's exactly what I need. A cheap place to eat."

"You hungry?" Todd asked. "Then let's finish this bottle and get out of here. You've just got to experience a real neighborhood bistro while in Paris. Not one that caters to tourists—but the real thing. Where the real Parisians eat."

"I'd like nothing better," I said.

Todd topped off all our glasses. When the glasses were empty, I put my parka back on and followed them out into the night.

We talked and laughed our way through the winding streets of the Latin Quarter. I asked about their families and Olivia told me she didn't get along with her mother and that she hadn't seen her father in years. Rachel came from a more traditional, conservative family who were against her taking off a year from college to work in France and refused to help her financially.

"That's the only reason we hang around with Todd, you know," Olivia joked. "He's always got eating money."

"And I thought you were using me for sex," quipped Todd.

"You wish!" both girls cried out at once.

We tumbled into a corner bistro and claimed one of its booths. I let the kids do the ordering for me and I wasn't disappointed. We were soon eating bowls of thick, delicious soup and breaking off chunks from a loaf of fresh crusty bread.

After we ate, the trio insisted I go to a cellar club with them, which they assured me was another essential Paris experience.

The atmosphere was smoky, the small tables were sticky, the music was loud and the wine was flowing. I refused to dance and finally convinced my new friends that I didn't mind sitting and people watching while they took to the floor. The place was full of beautiful people. And all so young and free, with their strange piercings and extensive tattoos and clothing the likes of which I'd never seen before. It was a joy to watch them and to soak up some of their attitude.

I have to admit, I was soaking up the *vin de maison,* as well.

After a while, Olivia came back to the table. "Whew. That's enough for me for awhile. It's so stuffy in here. Want to get some air?"

I nodded and we put on our jackets and went outside.

At the corner, there was a young couple embracing. I quickly looked away. "It's not as cold here as it is in Wisconsin."

"Cold enough for me, though," Olivia said, leaning against the building.

"I envy you, living in Paris for a year."

"Why couldn't you?"

"Why couldn't I what?"

"Live in Paris for a year, or for the rest of your life for that matter."

I laughed. "What would I do?"

"Get a job like everyone else. What do you do back home?"

"I own a bookkeeping service."

"Ah! What my mother would call a marketable skill."

"Not a good thing to have?" I asked.

"Oh, well, sure, of course it is. It's just that my mother always made growing up look like it took all the fun out of your life."

"I'm afraid that sometimes it does. That's why my two best friends and I formed the Prisoners of Willow Creek Enrichment Society."

Olivia looked at me. "Uh, what's the Prisoners of Willow Creek Enrichment Society?"

As we shifted from foot to foot, I told her about Jo and Iris and how we'd all ended up back in our hometown of Willow Creek—the last place we wanted to be—and how we'd vowed to struggle to keep from becoming stagnant.

"...and so we formed the society," I said.

"That is just so cool. I mean, how creative is that? For my mother, creative and fun is knitting in front of the TV while watching reruns of *The Love Boat*."

"Been there. Done that."

Olivia threw her arms toward the sky. "And now you're in Paris!"

Yes! I was in Paris. I threw my arms skyward, too. "I'm in Paris!" I shouted.

Olivia laughed. "See? My mother would never do something like that, either." She shook her head. "Your daughters are so lucky."

"Thanks, but I don't think they see it that way. Especially right at this moment."

"What makes you say that?"

"Because I've abandoned them a week before Christmas."

"Yeah, and I bet it's the first time you put your own needs ahead of theirs." She peered at me. "I'm right, aren't I? I'm also freezing. Our place is right around the corner. Why don't you come up and see my work. I could make some coffee—"

"That sounds wonderful. I'd love to see your work. But shouldn't we tell the others we're leaving?"

Olivia tossed her head. "They'll figure it out. Let's go."

We turned onto a cobblestone street and stopped at a narrow, ancient building that was leaning slightly to the left.

"This is it," Olivia said. "Sorry—there's no elevator."

I was breathless by the time I'd walked up the five stories.

"Terrible, I know." Olivia grimaced. "But it keeps Rachel and me thin. I mean, who needs a gym, right?"

I bent over, hands on knees, trying to catch my breath, while she unlocked the door. "Right," I managed to say between pants.

I'd probably just had the best cardiovascular workout I'd had in years. At that moment, I was sincerely thankful for my sneakers.

The apartment consisted of two rather dingy rooms with a galley kitchen between them and a bathroom down the hall that the girls had to share with two other apartments.

Olivia had converted the larger part of her room into a studio. Her sculptures were big, twisted-metal shapes. I recognized welding tools in the corner.

"You work in steel?" I asked, surprised. I had been expecting clay or stone. She was such a small, angelic-looking girl.

"Yeah. I love to torture metal into doing what I want it to."

I knew nothing about art, but I was impressed as I listened to Olivia describe the piece she was currently working on, which she referred to as a comment on privacy.

"Like, for some of us, we want to keep a part of us in a cage, away from prying eyes."

That explained why the piece looked sort of like a distorted cage.

"But you can still see through the cage," I said.

"Exactly! See? You get it! We can't hide ourselves no matter what we do. And some of us do a lot of self-destructive things trying to hide parts of ourselves—something that just can't be done. Not without a lot of pain, anyway."

That would explain the barbed wire, I thought.

When she went to the kitchen to fix the coffee, I studied the room. There was a narrow mattress in one corner draped with black velvet and a sorry-looking stuffed chair with a mismatched ottoman. Clearly, her work was more important to her than creature comforts.

Olivia came out with a tray that held two steaming cups of

coffee. She set the tray on the ottoman then sat on the floor. I gratefully took the chair. My knees were already protesting the five flights of stairs; sitting on the floor would just incite my joints into further mutiny.

"You know," she said, "given what I'm working on now, don't you think it's sort of weird that we met at this particular point in our lives? I mean, with you escaping and all that."

"I think it's weird that we met up at all, if you want to know the truth. I'm a middle-aged grandmother and you're—what? Twenty-one?"

"Almost twenty-two," she said, as if a couple of months would make a huge difference.

"So do you have other fifty-two-year-olds you hang out with?"

"Hmm—I see what you mean. But this is Paris. Things are different in Europe. I don't think age differences matter as much as they do in the States." She shrugged. "Or maybe I just feel more free from convention here because I'm so out of my element."

"That would probably explain why I'm sitting here, too." I grinned. "You might not believe this, but I don't usually go clubbing with twentysomethings."

Olivia grinned back. "I think it's more than that, though. Do you believe in destiny?"

I took a sip of coffee while I thought about it. "Before this trip, I might have said no. Now, I don't know."

"If you'd come to Paris any later, we might have just missed each other. My year is almost up," she added sadly.

"It sounds like you want to stay."

"I'd stay in a heartbeat if I could afford to. But the only way I could afford it is to get a full-time job and then I'd have no time for studies or sculpting, so what would be the point in staying? Back home I do have friends I can move in with for next to nothing."

I told her how Nat and her family had had to move back in with me.

"Honestly, I'd rather live in a car than move back in with my mother. If I *had* a car," she said with a joyful laugh.

Oh, to be young enough to laugh at life's problems. Had I ever been that young? I'd certainly never managed to make the kind of escape Olivia had. I hadn't been that brave. Not brave enough to go far enough—not brave enough to stay away. Yes, my father had gotten sick, but I had two other siblings who could have moved back home with no more upheaval than I'd had. Why had it been me who went running home? My mother had asked me to, that's why. I was the youngest child—the last to leave home. I lived closer to Willow Creek than my brother or sister. I'd agreed with my mother at the time that it made sense for me to be the one to come home.

Or had I just not had enough courage to build a life elsewhere? And after my mother died, there had really been no good reason to stay in Willow Creek. Except I hadn't wanted to uproot the girls. Had that just been another excuse to stay put, to live the life I was used to instead of the life I really wanted?

There was the sound of footsteps on the stairs.

"That'll be Todd and Rachel," Olivia said.

"We thought we'd find you here," Todd said after they'd come in.

Rachel got cups of coffee for her and Todd and they joined Olivia on the floor where we entered into a lively discussion about ambition versus talent.

When I finally looked at my watch it was after midnight.

"Oh, my God, I've got to get back to my hotel!"

"Will Mr. Big Shot Architect be waiting up for you?" Olivia asked.

"I doubt it. The less he sees of me the better. But I think I better start to find my way back. It could be daybreak before I make it."

"Where are you staying?" Rachel asked.

"The George V."

"Whoa, guess he really is a big shot," Olivia commented. "That place is about as luxurious as it gets, even in Paris."

I nodded. "It's almost worth putting up with the ogre. The tub alone is about the size of my bathroom back home."

"There's a metro station near there," Todd said. "Why don't we take you home on the metro?"

"That's like the subway, isn't it? Is it safe this time of night?"

"Safer than New York," Rachel assured me.

"Just watch your purse and pockets," Olivia said. "Pickpockets are likely to be the worst thing you'll face in Paris."

The metro proved to be clean and fast. The kids knew just which station to get off at. They insisted on walking me to the hotel, which proved to be only a short distance down Avenue George V.

As we stood in front of the hotel saying good-night, Olivia peered over my shoulder.

"Is Mr. Big Shot Architect a middle-aged hottie with long gray hair?" she asked.

"A hottie? I guess so. Why?"

"It looks like he waited up for you, after all."

I turned around. Incredibly, there he was, hands stuffed into his black suit pants, suit jacket flying out behind him as he paced the lobby with a scowl on his face.

"He doesn't look happy," Rachel said.

"He rarely does," I told her.

"Need an escort into the lion's den?" Todd offered.

I could see he was relieved when I told him it wouldn't be necessary.

The doorman was already holding the door for me so we said our last goodbyes while Olivia quickly scribbled her phone number on a ragged-looking receipt she'd fished out of her jacket pocket and pressed it into my hand.

We did the whole European thing of kissing each other on both cheeks and I promised Olivia I'd call before I went back to the States. I passed over the threshold and there Cole was, standing on the other side of the door, fists on hips, looking angrier than I'd ever seen him, and I'd seen him look pretty damn angry.

"Well, it's about time," he said, his jaw tight.

"What's your problem?" I asked.

He took my elbow and steered me toward the elevators. "We'll discuss it when we get back up to our suite."

"You're acting like an angry father," I said as the elevator doors closed.

"Perhaps that's because you're acting like an irresponsible child."

"Don't tell me you're going to give me one of those lectures that begins as long as you're living under my roof!"

By now we'd reached the seventh floor. Cole walked ahead of me and unlocked the suite. Once I'd followed him inside he bellowed, "Where in the hell have you been?"

"I've been sightseeing."

"Until the wee hours of the morning?"

"Well, I got kind of lost—"

"And I suppose that trio of reprobates found you and got you drunk."

"I am not drunk."

"I'd say from the looks of you, you've been drinking in cheap cafés all evening."

I looked at myself in a tall, narrow mirror hanging over an ornate console table. My cheeks were red from the wind. My lips red from the wine. My eyes shining from—well, because it was Paris and I'd had a good time.

"You know, for a guy who never wanted to lay eyes on me again, you're putting up a lot of fuss over my being gone for a few hours."

"A few hours wandering the streets in a foreign city on your own! Anything could have happened."

"Something *did* happen."

"I knew it!" he exclaimed triumphantly. "What?"

"I spent a few hours in the company of some young people who didn't expect me to make their beds, do their laundry, run their errands or cook them a meal. And I enjoyed every minute of it."

He grunted. "I suppose you'll be heading out to a discotheque next."

I frowned. "Do they even have discos anymore?"

"How the hell should I know? I was out acting my age all evening."

"Look, I appreciate the roof over my head. But I'm on strike and I refuse to punch a time clock. I didn't come all this way to follow somebody else's rules. So, if you'd like me to leave, then say the word."

He scowled at me for several seconds and I started to hope

there was a Holiday Inn nearby. He dragged a hand through his hair. "I'm not about to kick my son's mother-in-law out on the streets of a foreign city in the middle of the night."

I let out a breath. "Good. 'Cause I'm tired and I'm going to bed. Sweet dreams, Mr. Hudson," I said, then blew him a quick kiss before I shut the door to my room.

I was so tired and full of wine and exhilaration that I let my clothes fall where I took them off and crawled beneath the coverlet. Naked. Another first. But there were no grandchildren to come rushing in in the morning demanding pancakes or asking where their homework was. And there were no adult children to burst in and ask where the jumper cables were and could they borrow money for a new car battery?

There was just me, Abby, curling up on sheets that felt like heaven against my bare skin.

"Good night, Paris," I whispered just before falling into deep, luscious sleep.

Around ten the next morning I crawled out of bed and opened the drapes at the nearest window. Just the sight of Paris started to ease the slight hangover I had.

Ah, Paris.

And a whole day to do nothing but whatever I wanted. I went into my sumptuous bathroom to wash my face, brush my teeth and push the hair out of my eyes. Then I headed for the sitting room, figuring I'd order a nice big breakfast, courtesy of Mr. Big Shot Architect. But when I opened the door, Cole was seated at the dining table at the far end of the room, having breakfast while reading some papers.

I hesitated, wondering if it was too late to retreat. Come on,

Abby, might as well enter the lion's den and get it over with. Besides, the lion had food in his den and I was hungry.

"Good morning!" I announced brightly.

He grunted without looking up. There was a place set for another person across from him so I sat down, poured myself some coffee and reached for a silver basket. I chose a croissant from beneath a snowy white napkin and smeared it liberally with jam from a silver pot. Even the simplest food tasted better in Paris. Apparently, I was making appreciative noises as I ate and drank because Cole looked up at me and said, "Didn't those hoodlums feed you last night?"

"My *friends*," I said, emphasizing the word, "took me to a restaurant where I had the most fantastic soup and bread. I can't remember what the place was called but they said it was an authentic neighborhood bistro. Then we went to a cellar club to dance."

"Cellar club? Where on earth were you last night?"

"The Quartier Latin," I said, proud for having pronounced it right.

"Good lord! How on earth did you end up there?"

"Well, I found my way to the Eiffel Tower, then I walked along the Seine for a while and before I knew it I was lost among these really old narrow streets."

"You're lucky you didn't have your purse stolen. Too bad, however, that no one stole that jacket you wear."

I laughed. "Tell me about it. I stood out like a sore thumb in the first place I went to. I was lucky that Todd rescued me."

"Todd, is it? And the girls?"

I told him about Rachel and Olivia.

"Rachel works for an airline and plans on going home soon.

Olivia is an artist studying over here. She does these fantastic sculptures in steel. You know, I was thinking—"

He looked up from his papers again. "This doesn't sound good."

"Well, Olivia might have to go home soon, too, because her money is running out. Maybe your friends would be interested in seeing her work."

"Abby," he said with the exaggerated patience people often use with children, "Andre and Madeline aren't interested in seeing work from a wannabe artist who is doing the obligatory year in Paris thing before she goes home and marries her engineer boyfriend."

"Oh, but Olivia's not like that. She's serious. I don't know anything about art but I think she might have talent."

"I can almost guarantee you that she doesn't," he said, his mind back on his papers again.

I glared at him while I ate my croissant. "Do people let you get away with being that condescending?"

He put his papers aside and looked up. "I don't mean to be condescending. It's just that you yourself say you know nothing about art. And then on your first night in Paris you miraculously *discover* a sculptor you think might be worthy of a grant from a foundation that hasn't even been announced to the public yet."

"All right. All right," I said. "Point taken. Still, I think she's got talent."

"Please, spare me further demonstrations of your tenacity. Instead, let's discuss another of your eccentricities."

"Such as?"

"I know you're on strike, but do you think it'd be breaking the rules to accept a dinner engagement tonight with people more your own age?"

I gave him a twisted grin. "I've got a pep rally scheduled but if it's important I could cancel."

He arched a brow. "How generous of you. I'm having dinner with Madeline and Andre. I thought you might like to meet them."

"Are you kidding? I'd love to!" I said enthusiastically. But I sobered quickly enough when I thought of my wardrobe. "I'd better go shopping for something to wear, though."

"I couldn't agree more. And I've cleared the rest of my morning so I can take you."

"Excuse me. You what?"

"I said—"

"I heard what you said. I assure you that I'm capable of shopping by myself. I've been picking out my own clothes since I turned fourteen."

"And doing a brilliant job," he said sarcastically.

"So you're afraid I'll embarrass you, is that it?"

"Frankly, no, that's not what I'm afraid of. I've got an important meeting later this afternoon and I don't intend to leave for it worrying about where you've gone off to or whose garret you're being held prisoner in."

"That's ridiculous. I got home all right last night, didn't I?"

"Well, you got home. I'm not sure you were all right."

I stood up and spread my arms wide at my sides. "See? One piece."

"And your head?" he asked me with a slightly sardonic look. "It's not pounding from all that cheap red wine?"

"Not even the ghost of a hangover," I declared, which wasn't exactly true. I was feeling somewhat queasy but it was nothing a few croissants and some fresh air couldn't cure. "I assure you,

Mr. Hudson, that I look both ways before I cross the street. I don't need an escort."

"Ah, but you're forgetting something."

I frowned. "What?"

"You're on strike. That means you'll need someone to carry your shopping bags and to buy you lunch."

I laughed. "Good point. Just let me eat another croissant and I'll go get ready."

This time I settled for a shower. It was almost as luxurious as the bath. The stall was huge, lined with pink-and-white marble, and had several jets at varying heights pulsing out water at varying strengths. It pounded the rest of my hangover right out of me.

I'd managed to throw a pair of black matte jersey pants in the Vuitton so I put those on with a black turtleneck sweater. Unfortunately, I couldn't do anything about my somewhat grubby sneakers. I put on a little makeup and gelled and blow-dried my hair. I was ready to go in under thirty minutes.

"I've never known a woman to get ready that quickly," Cole said when he saw me.

"It's not like I had a lot to work with."

"You look fine—except for the shoes, of course, and that jacket. I think our first mission should be to find you a coat."

I'd been promising myself a new winter coat for years. So I agreed.

There was a soft rain falling when we left the hotel. But it scarcely mattered. It only made the city look more romantic. As we passed shops and restaurants I noticed our reflections. What an odd couple we made. Me, in my dirty sneakers and cheap jacket, him in a black cashmere coat and a pair of shoes that would never squeak on any floor. He was wearing a heather-gray turtleneck and I have to say, with his hair neatly tied back in a ponytail, he looked almost as magnificent as the scenery. I couldn't wait to get that new coat and a pair of real shoes.

Just before we reached the river, we turned onto Avenue Montaigne. That's when I started to get nervous. I'd seen ads for these designer clothes in the glossy magazines at Iris's House of Beauty. Courtesy of Jil Sander, Chanel, Dior.

I grabbed the sleeve of Cole's coat.

"What's wrong?" he asked, clearly perplexed and a little put out at the interruption in our progress.

"Um, Cole, I can't possibly afford to buy a coat—or anything else for that matter—in these kinds of places. Isn't there a reasonably priced department store somewhere we could go to? I'm a small-town bookkeeper, remember?"

"Which is why I'm prepared to pay for the clothes," he stated. It seemed to be a nonissue for him and he began to walk away.

I hurried to catch up and grabbed his arm again. "Um—but I'm not prepared to let you pay for them."

He scowled at me. "Don't be stubborn."

I raised a brow. "Don't be tyrannical."

For a moment, I thought he was going to really blow, right there with throngs of shoppers having to skirt around us. Instead he took my hand and firmly drew me closer to the front of a boutique where there was a pocket of space.

"Can't you just consider the clothes as payment for being my companion on this trip? It's not always easy to be the only man who's alone at the table, you know."

"Don't you know any French women?" I asked.

"Yes, of course I know French women. However, my last

relationship here ended badly. I'm not in any hurry to repeat the mistake."

I thought about it. "So I'd be doing you a favor?"

Finally, he smiled. A small smile, but still—

"Yes, Abby," he said. "You'd be doing me a favor. And since you'd be going home with several thousand dollars' worth of clothing, I don't think anyone could accuse you of breaking your strike."

I gulped. Several thousand dollars' worth? Surely, going out to dinner wearing expensive clothing would be a good thing, right? Cole sighed and looked at his watch.

"Must you always be so stubborn?"

"Hey, I don't know what sort of women you usually hang around with but I'm the sort who likes to pay her own way."

"Fine," he bit out. "I'll find some way for you to pay me back."

"Like what?" I asked suspiciously.

He moved his head impatiently. "I don't know. I'm sure something will come to me."

"Just as long as you don't forget that I'm on strike."

"How could I possibly forget?" he muttered.

He put both hands on my arms and scrutinized me—head to foot—the scowl on his face going deeper.

I sighed. "Do you find anything at all you approve of?"

He looked into my eyes. "Of course. Surely you know you're an attractive woman. I'm just trying to decide what designer might be right for you."

I was barely listening as he rattled off some possibilities. My mind was too stuck on the fact that he'd said I was an attractive woman.

"So, I take it your silence means Lauren is fine with you?"

I blinked. "Lauren? Ralph Lauren?"

But he was already leading me through the crowds on the sidewalk. We passed some of the most beautiful shops I'd ever seen, all of them swagged to the hilt. We turned onto the Champs-Elysées and I promised myself to come back after dark to see the decorations all lit up.

Cole's cell rang and he answered, speaking in French, but still holding my hand as we twisted and turned our way until we reached it. Ralph Lauren.

I started to tremble.

"Abby," Cole said softly after he'd disconnected his call.

I looked up at him, my mouth dry.

"You're with me. I have money. Therefore, you deserve to be here. Now hold your head up, stop shaking like a schoolgirl and let's get you a Paris wardrobe."

I licked my lips. My mouth was no longer dry as we held each other's gaze for several heartbeats. Then I laughed at the incredulity of it all. "How did I get here?" I blurted.

"By sheer force of will, Abby. Now let's use some of that will of steel to buy you a coat, shall we?"

He offered his arm. I put my hand through it and we walked through the doors.

It wasn't nearly as scary as I thought it'd be, possibly because of the man at my side. In any case, the staff were all friendly and much too gracious to stare at my shoes. Cole spoke to an assistant in French and soon I was being shown outfit after outfit. There was a suit in winter white with a spreading portrait collar and large black buttons. There was a black swirling cocktail skirt paired with a frothy ruffled white fitted jacket with a wide black belt. There was a tailored pants suit in taupe that I could barely keep my hands off, the wool was so soft.

Cole sank into an ornate chair next to a fitting room, as if he was preparing for a private fashion show.

"You're kidding, right?" I asked. "You expect me to come out here and parade in front of you like a pig at the fair?"

The sales assistant looked a little aghast. I had a feeling that she understood more English than she was letting on. Or maybe a pig was a pig in any language.

"I like to see what I'm buying," Cole said matter-of-factly. "Besides, design is my field. Don't be too stubborn to take advantage of my expertise."

I'll just bet he had expertise, I thought, as I was led into a fitting room bigger than the bedroom I'd planned to spend my strike in back home. I wondered how many other women Cole Hudson had taken on this little shopping spree. He certainly didn't seem to be a novice. I pulled on the taupe trousers. No doubt he'd treated many women to such luxuries. Of course, in my case, he was doing it to make sure I wasn't going to embarrass him at dinner that night. That was probably a first for him. I put on the taupe jacket. I was sure he wasn't used to escorting the kind of women they grew in Willow Creek, Wisconsin.

I turned around and looked in the mirror.

"Holy cow." Amazing what great tailoring could do for a woman.

"Are you coming out?" I heard Cole's voice booming. "Or am I coming in?"

I dutifully marched out of the fitting room.

"Perfect," he said. He turned to the sales assistant and spoke in French. She beamed.

"What did you say to her?"

"I told her we'd take it."

"But there are others to try on—"

"Yes. So get moving. I've got a meeting, remember?"

I stared at him for a moment, feeling the hair on the nape of my neck start to rise, but then I thought about that beautiful winter-white suit waiting for me in the fitting room. If Cole wanted me to spend some of his money, then spend some of his money I would. It seemed that my fairy godmother was a man— and he hadn't forgotten me!

The winter white suit's pencil-thin skirt looked surprisingly good on me, thanks to the Prisoners of Willow Creek Enrichment Society's recent forays into yoga and Pilates. I was what the sales assistant referred to as statuesque, which was the only word I understood when she saw me in the outfit. From the look on her face I gathered that it was spectacular. The jacket was short enough for the wide belt from the skirt to show and cut low enough to show a hint of cleavage. The standout portrait collar made my neck look longer and more delicate.

When I stepped from of the dressing room the look on Cole's face made me feel—well, it made me feel like a woman. Not a mother. Not a wife. Not a grandmother. Or a girlfriend. Just a woman. A woman who was still capable of putting that kind of look on a man's face.

He smiled at me. "*Oui*," he said to the sales assistant.

She totally agreed.

By the time we were finished, I owned the winter-white suit, the black cocktail skirt with the white ruffled jacket, a pair of beautifully tailored black trousers, a cream-colored organza shirt and a couple of cashmere sweaters. I was wearing the taupe pantsuit under my new black cashmere coat.

Cole picked up my baby-blue polyester parka by two fingers and held it out to the assistant. "Could you dispose of this for us, *s'il vous plaît?*"

She had no trouble understanding what he wanted. "*Oui,* monsieur," she replied.

"I was afraid we might have to pay them to take that monstrosity," Cole said when we were back out on the sidewalk.

"Don't knock the parka. It saw me through four winters."

"Then it deserves to be retired."

I had to admit, he was right. The clothes were transforming. I was amazed anew every time I caught my reflection in a window. Now I looked like I belonged walking next to a man like Cole Hudson.

We were both loaded down with shopping bags as we retraced our steps to the hotel. We left our purchases with the doorman then walked a few blocks to a lovely little restaurant tucked away on a side street.

"It was nice to see you finally relax and enjoy yourself this morning," Cole said after we were seated.

"I guess I'm not used to people doing things for me. It's usually the other way around."

"Then I'm glad I could give you that experience," he said.

"Have you given many women that experience?" I asked.

His mouth twitched as he tried to hold back a smile but his sparkling gray eyes were a dead giveaway. "One or two. But none of them quite matched this morning, Abby. It gave me a lot of satisfaction to see you once you relaxed. You're so—"

While he groped for a word, I worried. So gauche? So naive? So small town?

"*Unguarded,*" he finally said. "*Genuine.* When you tried on that white suit, the pleasure in your eyes was so obvious. So real."

"Today was like a dream, Cole. A fantasy. I mean, I'm used to shopping at Wal-Mart."

"Now, see? That's what I mean. The women I'm accustomed to would simply smile coquettishly and bat their lashes a few times."

"While I let my naiveté just pour out unabated?"

"No," he said, his gray eyes on mine. "While you say what you think. What you feel. You're a rare bird, Abby Blake."

I smiled. "A rare bird still wearing dingy sneakers. We forgot about shoes."

Cole laughed. "I don't suppose those sneakers would do anything for that cocktail suit tonight, would they?"

When the waiter came, Cole asked if he could order for me. Relieved, I assured him he could. I'd gotten through my first designer boutique; I wasn't going to push my luck by trying to figure out the menu, which was all in French.

"Just don't get me anything icky—like snails or squid."

"Fair enough," he said, his eyes glittering with amusement. "Nothing icky."

Lunch was a delicious cassoulet of chicken in a wine-flavored sauce with mushrooms and tiny green beans. I was wiping up the last of the sauce with a hunk of crusty bread when I looked up to find Cole watching me.

"I suppose most of the women you know don't eat like I do, either."

"Certainly not in public. It's a joy to watch a woman really enjoy a meal for a change."

"Does that mean it's okay with you if I order dessert?" I asked.

And there was that wonderful laugh again. If I didn't watch out, I was going to become addicted to it. In fact, if I didn't watch out I was going to become addicted to it all. To Paris, to beautiful clothes, to handsome men escorting me around.

I had to keep reminding myself that this was for a few days only. That none of it was real. I may have found my prince but he was on loan and eventually there would be a price to pay.

"Have you decided on what services I'll have to provide to pay you back for all these clothes?"

"I'm working on it," he said.

I watched him watching me and wondered if the payment would have anything to do with taking off the beautiful clothes he'd just bought me. Fat chance, I thought. Olivia had been right. Cole Hudson was a middle-aged hottie. While I—well, I was just middle-aged. The idea gave me a thrill anyway. Just a tingle of electricity that reminded me that there were other aspects of being a woman that I'd also done without for a long, long time.

After lunch, Cole gave me a wad of euros and sent me off in the direction of the Givenchy outlet store across from their flagship store on Avenue George V.

"You'll find shoes and accessories there. Get whatever you think you need."

I pretended shock. "You mean you're going to trust me to buy a pair of shoes all by myself?"

"I think you can manage it," he said. "In fact I'm beginning to think you can manage just about anything."

CHAPTER 6

I'd had no problem at all finding a pair of shoes at the Givenchy outlet. Several pairs, in fact. And a pair of leather boots. Plus an organza evening bag, a large taupe leather bag and several pieces of costume jewelry.

I'd gotten some real deals and when Cole came back from his meeting, I couldn't wait to show him everything and to tell him the amount of money I'd saved him.

"Those faux pearl earrings and bracelet were a steal," I said, all flushed with the triumph of a bargain hunter. "And you wouldn't believe what I paid for this organza evening bag—"

He started to shake his head and laugh.

"What?"

"I've just never met another woman like you, Abby."

"You keep saying that."

"Well, it's true. You take as much pleasure from finding a bargain on fake pearls as you did when you tried on that white suit at Ralph Lauren."

I felt my enthusiasm start to sag. I should have realized a man like Cole Hudson wouldn't be interested in my bargain finds. He was obviously used to women with a lot more sophistication. At this moment he was probably coming to the conclusion that no matter how many designer duds he draped me in it wasn't going to do any good. I was still missing the sophistication gene. "I guess I'm hopeless, aren't I?"

"Hopeless?" he echoed, his dark brows forming a scowl. "Unique is the word I would have used."

I stood there for a moment, rooted in surprise. *Unique*. Not a bad adjective at all. Much better than hopeless. He started to unknot his tie and I watched his graceful fingers work at the silk. That tingle of electricity went through me again and I finally looked away.

"I'd better go get ready," I said. "I know how you hate to be late."

I wore the black-and-white cocktail suit that night, with the faux pearls at my throat and on my wrist. My shoes had three-inch heels, which was about two inches higher than I was used to. But they were beautiful black suede with tiny flowers off to the side made of seed pearls.

I did what I could with my limited supply of makeup. I put plenty of gel in my hair then blow-dried it until it was in deep waves pushed back from my face.

Cole was waiting for me in the sitting room when I came out of my bedroom. He stood as I approached.

"You've done Ralph Lauren proud this evening, Abby," he said.

"It works, then?" I asked as I brazenly twirled around.

"Oh, it definitely works. You look beautiful."

That was certainly more than I'd hoped for. Beautiful. How many years had it been since anyone had said that to me?

Had Charlie ever called me beautiful? Pretty, I think he would say. Or cute. But never beautiful.

I immediately felt disloyal at the thought. Which was a little absurd considering how long Charlie had been gone. And it wasn't as if I was interested in Cole in that way—or he, in me. Although, my reaction to Cole's compliments made me consider how long I'd actually been without male companionship, or the appreciation in a man's eyes like I was seeing in Cole's at that moment.

He held out my gorgeous new coat for me and I slipped into it, smiling my thanks. Cole grabbed his coat and we left the suite.

Walking through the lobby on Cole's arm, dressed as I was, was a whole new experience. If anyone was watching us, I was pretty sure they saw a woman who looked as if she might really belong here.

Cole had a car waiting to take us to the restaurant where we were meeting the Fontaines.

"I wonder if I'd ever get used to the way Parisians drive," I said as our driver swerved to miss another car that had zipped in front of us.

"It can be pretty wild, which is why I generally hire a car and driver. The added convenience of that is that I can also work or make phone calls enroute."

"I noticed you didn't bring your work with you tonight. I thought this was a business dinner."

"I haven't seen Madeline and Andre for a few months, although we've been in touch by phone, of course. So, it will be mostly pleasure, not business. Especially now that I'm bringing you with me. Madeline would never let us neglect you to talk business."

"But I thought that might be one of the services I could supply in payment for the clothes," I suggested with a grin. "I listen avidly to everything you say, applaud every idea you come up with and occasionally gaze at you like I'm captivated by your genius."

Cole gave me a look. "Somehow I can't see you applauding anything you didn't believe in, even if your escort has paid for the Ralph Lauren."

I laughed. "You're probably right about that. I could try to fake it."

"I doubt that you'd succeed."

"Aren't you the man who called me tenacious? I could learn."

"Learn to be a yes man?" He frowned. "Yes woman? Yes *person*? Confound it all, this age of political correctness can be damn irritating."

I was finding his irritation a touch amusing at the moment but I was trying not to laugh.

He sighed loudly and the irritation seemed to disappear when he exhaled. "What I'm trying to say is that you've stood your ground all the way from Willow Creek to Paris, Abby. You've managed to get what you wanted out of me without resorting to feminine wiles or erecting a facade." He reached out and touched the earring at my ear, his fingers brushing my neck. "The only thing fake about you, Abby," he said softly, his silver eyes looking into mine, "are your pearls. The rest of you is as real as it gets."

I shivered as the tips of his fingers slid across my skin to cup my chin.

"I did tell you how beautiful you look tonight, didn't I?" he asked.

Luckily, I didn't have to answer him. His cell phone rang. I was pretty sure my voice would have come out in a pathetic croak. Abby, I told myself, you're fifty-two years old. Get a grip. Who wouldn't look beautiful in Ralph Lauren?

"David!" Cole exclaimed into his phone as he shot me a look. "How are things going, son?"

I watched his face eagerly as he listened.

"Good. I'm glad the project is back on track. How is everything else?"

He put his hand over the receiver and whispered, "Do you want him to know you're here?"

I quickly shook my head. I wasn't ready to end my strike yet. If the girls knew where I was, the frantic phone calls would start and I'd lose my nerve and be back in Willow Creek basting a turkey and wrapping everyone's last minute gifts for them in less time than it took for Cinderella's coach to pop back into a pumpkin.

"Yes, David," Cole was saying. "I think that might be the wise thing to do. Force the issue. Get stubborn about it. Don't take no for an answer until she's agreed to hear you out."

When he disconnected the call I was ready to pounce.

"What's going on? Has he spoken to Gwen? Did he say anything about how Gwen or Nat are doing? Did he—"

"If I might get a word in," Cole said, slipping back into irritation as easily as I'd slipped into my coat.

"A word—or even two—would be greatly appreciated," I said, feeling a little irritated myself.

"David knows nothing about what is happening in Willow Creek. Your daughter refuses to take his calls. I don't think he even knows about your strike. Somewhat against my better judgment I agreed with him when he said he was going there in person."

"Against your better judgment? I thought the reason you showed up on my doorstep was to get Gwen to go back to David?"

"I did. Yet if this is your daughter's usual way of handling adversity in a marriage, David is in for a rough time of it. Frankly, he has too much to offer to settle for a miserable marriage."

I felt my temperature go up a notch or two. "Settle? My daughter might be difficult at times but I assure you that she is not a consolation prize."

"Now is not the time for this conversation, Abby," Cole said as the car pulled up to the curb in front of the restaurant.

Damn it, I thought. I'd been so looking forward to tonight and to meeting the couple who had seen talent in Cole so many years ago when his family refused to be supportive. Now here we were, at odds over our children again. Cole opened the door for me. His arm, when I took it, was as stiff as if he were one of the statues I'd passed on my way to the Latin Quarter last night.

The restaurant looked beautiful. Its entrance featured huge gold wreaths and was flanked by elaborate evergreen topiary lit with fairy lights. Inside, we checked our coats. While Cole spoke to the maître d' in French, I tried to take in the elaborately decorated room without rubbernecking like a tourist. I wanted to be able to give Iris and Jo a colorful description. With Cole in this mood I was pretty sure this would be the only time I'd see the likes of a restaurant like this for the rest of my strike.

We were shown to a table in an alcove where an older couple was already seated. Cole made the introductions and Andre rose to his feet and kissed me on both cheeks. He was fairly short but wonderfully handsome, with closely clipped white hair and a trim white mustache.

"We are happy to see our friend not be alone during the holidays," he said in the kind of accent that could make a woman's toes curl.

Neither man sat down until I was comfortably seated.

"My dear," Madeline said, taking my hand, "I have been absolutely dying to meet you."

"Me?" I asked in astonishment. "But, why?"

Her laugh was light and musical. "Because, my dear, I have never met a woman who has gone on strike against her family before—although I am certain that most of us have wanted to at times."

I chuckled. "So my reputation precedes me."

"Yes, Cole has told us all about you," Madeline said. "I hope you don't mind."

"Not at all. Especially if you don't think the whole thing is silly."

"Silly? What we women put up with sometimes is what is silly."

While Andre and Cole discussed the wine list Madeline and I traded information about our children—she and Andre had two sons and a daughter. When she learned that I had two daughters she said, "Oh—daughters are the worst, are they not? I mean, yes, they can bring great happiness into your life, but they are so much more demanding and critical of their mothers. My sons—I just have to cook them their favorite meal and I am like a queen to them. While my daughter, she is never satisfied. Even with my choice of shoes!"

I couldn't imagine Madeline choosing the wrong shoes, or anything else wrong. She was a tiny woman. Her silver hair was drawn back from her beautiful, nearly unlined face into an elaborate twist. She was expertly made-up and chicly dressed in basic black jersey that clung to her petite body.

The sommelier brought the men's wine selection to the table and they went through the ritual of sniffing, swirling and tasting—something that, up to now, I'd only seen done on the cable food channel. After the men gave their approval, the sommelier poured for Madeline and me.

"Let's toast to new friends," Andre suggested.

"Yes," Madeline agreed. "To new friends."

For a moment, I was afraid Cole was going to refuse to toast. A few seconds passed before he raised his glass and clinked it with mine. "To new friends," he said softly as he held my gaze for several heartbeats. Long enough to make me wonder if he was willing to forget our argument in the car.

Andre offered to order for me and I was happy to accept. Although this meal was very different from having soup in a corner bistro, I wasn't disappointed. Course after course was presented, one more beautifully arranged than the other. The restaurant specialized in nouvelle cuisine, which meant the portions were small works of art. Delightful and much less rich than the French cooking I'd experienced up until now.

"I suppose our architect friend has told you that he's generously volunteered his services to design our modest art museum," Andre said.

"Well, yes, I knew he was designing it—" I gave Cole a speculative look but he avoided eye contact. It surprised me to hear that he was donating his services. It was a side of him I hadn't suspected existed, even though he had told me how much the Fontaines meant to him. And it also made me realize how little I really knew him.

"Mentoring and occasionally helping to support young artists has always given us pleasure in life," Madeline confided. "The foundation we plan to set up will allow us to do so much more than we could on our own."

"It will also allow Madeline a chance to use her special talent of raising money for good works for the rest of her life," Andre said with a warm smile for his wife and an affectionate squeeze of her hand.

"Andre knows I like to talk people who have more money than they know what to do with into parting with some of it. The Silver Ball is the first big event to help raise funds for the foundation. I am happy to announce that every ticket, although frightfully expensive, has been sold."

"That doesn't surprise me at all, Madeline," Cole said. "I know your powers of persuasion."

Madeline laughed, then addressed me. "I hope Cole has not forgotten to tell you that all the women are being encouraged to wear silver gowns."

"Oh, but Cole hasn't—"

Madeline gave Cole a disapproving look. "You haven't told her yet? You naughty boy. A woman cannot be expected to come up with a silver evening gown overnight, you know, even if this is Paris."

I hurried to correct her. "No, what I meant was that Cole isn't—"

Cole put his hand on mine and I was so stunned I stopped speaking.

"You're right, Madeline. I did forget to tell her. But Abby is a very enterprising woman. I'm sure she'll find the perfect gown to wear."

Obviously, Cole was trying to rescue both Madeline and me from an awkward moment. I wasn't sure if I should rescue him right back and explain to Madeline that Cole hadn't asked me to the ball. Could I give Cole the out he was surely looking for?

I laughed lightly. "I'm afraid I'm not exactly safe to have around when people are dressed in formal wear. Several girls I knew in high school still aren't speaking to me because I tripped right after my date handed me a full cup of fruit punch." I grimaced and rolled my eyes. "I had to work two summer jobs to pay all the dry cleaning bills."

Everyone at the table laughed, including Cole.

"No fruit punch, my dear," Madeline assured me. "We will be serving champagne."

"Well, that would certainly make it perfect," I said.

"Why is that?" Madeline asked.

I told her about Jo and Iris and the Prisoners of Willow Creek Enrichment Society and of our aborted trip to Europe and our pledge to toast each other if any of us ever made it.

"If one of us made it to Paris, we were supposed to toast each other with champagne."

Madeline laughed. "That is such a charming story. I would love to meet your fellow prisoners one day."

"And by all means, we will most certainly toast your friends at the ball," Andre added.

"They'd love it, I'm sure."

I caught Cole staring at me with amusement in his eyes. I hadn't a clue whether that was good or bad. I hoped he wasn't laughing at himself for wasting the money on the ensemble I was wearing and wishing he'd come to dinner alone. After the tiff we'd had in the car, I figured our relationship, such as it was, had been rewound back to where it had started. A very rocky one indeed. One I wasn't sure I wanted to try to repair again.

When the dinner was over, the men left us at the table to go smoke cigars over cognac in the bar. Madeline and I sipped delicate cups of strong coffee.

"My dear," Madeline said, "Cole seems very taken with you.

When we spoke on the phone last it was Abby this and Abby that."

I liked this woman too much to lie to her. "Actually, the truth is, we really don't like each other very much."

She gave a small, gentle smile. "Really? I could have sworn I felt some sort of electricity…"

"Fireworks," I corrected. "And not in a good way."

"Can there be bad fireworks?" Madeline asked. "They are colorful, beautiful, passionate—"

"Loud," I said before I could stop myself.

Madeline laughed. "Yes. Cole can be loud—and impatient. It's all part of his passion. It comes with the package, you see."

"Well, even if I liked Cole's *package*, I don't think he's too crazy about mine. In any case, I won't be staying in Paris for long."

"No? You do not like Paris?"

"No. I *love* Paris. My family is back in Wisconsin and so is my business."

"What sort of business are you in?" Madeline asked.

"I own a bookkeeping and tax preparation service in Willow Creek."

"And you are good at this?"

"Very. Numbers are my thing. I like the order of it. The sense it all makes. When Charlie—he was my husband—died, numbers helped me stay focused so I could do all the things I had to do."

"How long have you been a widow?"

"Twenty years."

"Yet you still wear your wedding rings," Madeline said as she nodded toward my hand.

The diamond solitaire sparkled up at me. "Out of loyalty, I

suppose. Charlie was such a fine man. And we had such fun together during the few years we had. I have yet to meet a man worth taking my rings off for."

Madeline smiled. "Perhaps the glow of the stone has blinded you."

"It's not that big a stone," I said with a laugh, but I suppose in a way she was right. If I'd really been in the market for a man, I would have taken the rings off long ago.

"This business you own—tell me how you started it."

We talked for several minutes about my work and then she said, "It's a pity you're not staying in Paris. The foundation could use someone like you. And I think we could work well together, you and I."

"That's very flattering and I'd like nothing better than to stay in Paris. If I did stay, I'd have to get a job."

"But that's what I'm offering you!"

"You mean, a job with pay? I thought you were talking about volunteering."

"No, no! Our fund raising department will need a financial—oh—what's the word? A financial secretary of sorts. You understand?"

I nodded. "I think so."

"You would keep basic records. Act as liaison between me and the financial officer—who, I must admit," she added with a laugh, "I do not always understand. Abby, you are a woman of business. A woman who understands numbers. There could be any number of positions in the foundation you might be suitable for." Her eyes twinkled as she added, "If you found a reason you would wish to stay in Paris, that is."

I knew what she was referring to. And she knew that I knew.

And it was making me slightly uncomfortable, so I decided to change the subject.

"How would the foundation go about awarding these grants? Will you and Andre be in charge of that?"

"We would be heavily involved, of course. We will have a panel of experts. It will be a process one will have to go through, you see?"

I nodded.

"Do you have some special reason for asking?"

Oh, boy. Cole was not going to like this one bit, I thought. But now that I'd been handed such a beautiful opening, I had to take it.

"Yes, as a matter of fact, I do."

"Then tell me, Abby, please."

"Well, the other night I got lost in the Latin Quarter, and I met this wonderful girl named Olivia who is a sculptor and—"

I'd hoped to make it quick, before the men returned to our table. However, Madeline seemed genuinely interested and asked a lot of questions. So, when the men came back I was just finishing relating to Madeline how Olivia had described the piece she was working on.

"And that's what the barbed wire signifies," I was saying as Cole pulled out his chair and sat down.

Madeline nodded slowly. "Most interesting."

"Barbed wire?" Andre asked as he sat down. "We leave for a cigar and come back to find our two beautiful women discussing such things?"

Madeline laughed. "Silly man. Abby has been telling me about the work of an artist friend of hers. A sculptor who works with metals."

I gave Cole a quick look. He was glaring at me under those dark brows so I didn't look for long. The way I figured it, the damage was already done. Cole was already angry so why not try to do Olivia some good?

"I think she's got a really interesting take on universal themes," I said.

Andre put his elbows on the table. "In what manner?"

"There's anger in her work, I think, but redemption, too. I mean, I realize I don't know a lot about art, but I think her work might be worth examining—when you've reached that stage, that is."

"Certainly," said Andre.

Suddenly, I felt Cole's hand on mine again and not in a way that caused any sexual electricity, either.

"I explained to Abby that it's way too early in terms of the project to bother you about this. Now, I'd like very much to take a drive out to the estate tomorrow and have a look around so I can start making preliminary sketches if neither of you have any objection…"

When we finally said good-night in front of the restaurant, Madeline and I embraced warmly. "Please call me tomorrow if you have difficulty finding a silver gown. I know so many people, I may be able to help."

I thought it best at this point to just thank her and let it go at that.

Andre kissed me on both cheeks again and we said a heart-felt good-night.

"I expressly asked you not to bring up that girl with the Fontaines, didn't I?" Cole asked as soon as we were in the car.

"Yes, but—"

"I owe these people a lot, Abby. Most of all, I owe them respect. This foundation is very dear to their hearts. I assure you their intention is not to coddle mediocrity."

"Now if that isn't classic Cole Hudson," I scoffed. "How do you know it's mediocre when you haven't even seen it?"

"The law of averages is against it being anything but."

"Wait a minute. *You*, the creative type, are talking to *me*, the woman of numbers, about the law of averages? So out of five women, how many will become worthwhile artists, Mr. Hudson?"

"The point is, these are people you just met and you know nothing about art and yet you have the—the—"

"Spunk?"

He gave me a look. "I was going to say *temerity*. You have the temerity to propose a candidate for a Fontaine Foundation grant."

"I did no such thing. This was merely a casual suggestion. If you had a chance to help a friend, wouldn't you?" I shrugged. "If I'm wrong and Olivia's sculptures suck, then what's the harm? The Fontaines will simply know for sure that what I told them is true. I know nothing about art. They'll have a funny story to tell at parties and fund-raisers and all that'll be wasted is an hour's time."

He was silent for awhile. Then, "Still, you shouldn't have gone against my wishes without discussing it with me first. And you shouldn't have traded on my friendship with Andre and Madeline to try to curry favor for this girl you barely know."

"You know, sometimes it amazes me that you didn't stick with family tradition."

"What does that mean?"

"It means that sometimes you sound and act stuffy enough to be a banker."

He threw back his head and laughed. I smiled at the victory.

"Look, Cole, I know it was a little awkward tonight when Madeline assumed you were taking me to the ball and that you only went along with it to avoid embarrassing me. So, please, don't feel obligated in any way."

"I have absolutely no intention of letting you out of this particular commitment, Abby. You're going to that ball with me."

I was shocked at how my heart soared at his words. I wasn't the ball type. For the past few decades any occasion that required me to squeeze into a pair of panty hose could put me in a bad mood, but the idea of Cole wanting to take me excited me a lot more than I'd guessed it would. Had my recent foray into fashion merely whetted my appetite for more glamour? Or was it Cole himself and the memory of that shiver I'd felt when his fingers had brushed my skin during the ride to the restaurant that was exciting me?

"You can consider it part of your duties," he said, interrupting my reverie. "You still owe me for that white suit."

Well, that settled that. We were back to business, I thought as I stared out of the car window. It was better this way, anyway. The last thing I needed was the complication of a crush on a moody, unpredictable man added to my midlife crisis.

Such foolishness, my mother would have concluded.

And she would have been right.

The next morning, dressed in my new black trousers and a pale-blue cashmere sweater, I was standing on the balcony of the suite. I sipped a cup of café au lait and luxuriated in the sights of a morning in Paris.

Memories of the times I'd had coffee on the front porch in

Willow Creek surfaced. On beautiful summer mornings Charlie and I would eat breakfast at an old ice-cream parlor table and chairs I'd rescued before the Willow Creek Creamery had been demolished. The girls, both barely toddlers, would be content in their playpen under the shade of a maple tree in the front yard. Special times. Happy times. Too often forgotten in the toll and toil of everyday life.

A chilly wind brought me back to Paris in December and the realization that it was time I called home.

I knew Nat and Gwen thought I was in Chicago and I'd only been gone a few days, but I still felt some guilt about walking out on them. It didn't help that they had no idea where I really was. I had been hoping that when Cole talked to David last night, there might be some news of my daughters. Were they doing okay without me? I hoped for the sake of my grandchildren that they'd managed to pull together and start some sort of preparations for Christmas. And I hoped that Gwen was seriously considering whether or not she wanted to end her marriage to David. David was much more even-tempered than his father and I'd liked him from the moment I'd met him. With me out of the picture, Gwen would have plenty of time to do some soul searching and maybe some growing up, as well. Although, if I'd suggested she needed any maturing, she would have had a fit. Gwen was so sure she was the mature, responsible one of the sisters. But, in truth, when the chips were down it was Natalie who stood by her husband, not Gwen.

I went inside and found the phone. The answering machine picked up after three rings. Was this the kind of thing I wanted to tell my family via an answering machine? I hung up without leaving a message but hovered over the phone, my fingers tapping on the receiver, wondering if I should call back and leave a message.

"Good morning."

I spun around to find Cole emerging from his room.

"I didn't know you were still here."

"Sorry. I didn't mean to startle you. I'm headed out to Versailles to take a look at the site for the museum on the Fontaine estate. I thought you might like to come along."

I cocked my head. "Hmm—I don't know. Would accompanying you to Versailles pay for this sweater?"

Cole laughed. The sound of it filled the room with rich warmth.

"One of the things I like about you," he said, "is that I never know what is going to come out of your mouth."

I grinned. "I never know what's going to come out of yours, either, so that makes us even."

His eyes held on to his laughter. "Then how about coming along for the ride and we'll see if we can continue to surprise each other?"

How could a girl resist an intriguing invitation like that? I went to get my coat.

To my surprise, Cole had rented a small car and was doing the driving himself. I had all I could do to keep from laughing when his anger got the best of him as he tried to conquer the outrageous Paris traffic. He honked his horn liberally and rolled down the window to shout out French words that I was pretty sure weren't included in the average guidebook.

Once we were out of the city, Cole visibly relaxed.

It was a sunny, cold day and the countryside was beautiful. We passed farms where cows grazed languidly. We passed fields, brown for the winter. We passed cottages and manor houses and even an amazing castle.

"That's the Château de Versailles," Cole said, "brought to you by King Louis XIV. Believe it or not, it started out as a hunting lodge. He just kept adding and adding to it until it was large enough to seat his entire government."

"Old Louis sounds like the kind of client that could drive an architect nuts."

"I've never heard him explained quite that way, but you're probably right. If the weather holds, we can stop there after I'm finished at the Fontaine estate if you'd like. The fountains alone are spectacular."

But when we reached the Fontaine estate, I couldn't imagine anything that could be more spectacular.

"Imagine growing up in a place like this," I said as we turned into the long, straight, tree-lined drive that led up to the stone mansion.

"I think that's one of the reasons Andre is such a philanthropist. For him it's not just noblesse oblige. It's partly guilt at having had everything handed to him."

"But they were both so passionate about this project."

"Don't get me wrong, they are very passionate about art and the idea of helping young artists develop. That's one of the things that Madeline brought to Andre's life—her love of art. But when he was younger, Andre suffered the same thing a lot of wealthy students suffer."

"And what is that?"

He shrugged. "There's a certain feeling of unworthiness."

"Unworthiness?" I asked, truly puzzled about what he meant.

"You watch other students—some of them more passionate

than you are, smarter than you are—struggle to get an education. Struggle for their place in the sun, while you were born with it already shining on you. And sometimes, despite knowing how lucky you are, you wish to hell the sun would go shine somewhere else for a change."

It was obvious Cole was no longer only talking about Andre.

"But it's the luck of the draw, isn't it?" I asked. "I mean, it's not your fault if your parents are rich any more than it's Gwen's and Nat's fault that their parents weren't. Gwen had to work to get through school. She was smart enough to get scholarships, but still she had to work summers and holidays. And she worked damned hard to keep her grades up so the scholarships and grants would keep coming. I would have loved to have handed it all to her, but I couldn't."

He gave me a rueful look. "No wonder you were so upset when I called Gwen a spoiled brat."

"Absolutely. Aside from my hackles rising as a mother, I know what kind of woman my daughter is. She might need a lot of male attention due to losing her father when she was so young, but she isn't spoiled. Although, I will concede she can be a brat at times. Gwen's always been demanding of people, but never more demanding than she is of herself. She's a perfectionist and I've often suspected that she's confused her perfectionism with maturity."

He looked at me, the surprise evident in his eyes.

"I'm not oblivious to my children's faults," I assured him. "I've watched enough daytime TV to figure out that both of my daughters have been affected by losing their father when they were so young."

"Yet, they both picked very different ways of dealing with it."

"You noticed that, huh?" I asked with a wry smile.

"I have to hand it to you, Abby. Dealing with one child who is very different than I am is about all I can handle. I don't know how you deal with two."

"Do you ever look at David and wonder how you ended up with a kid like him?"

"Constantly. And what a relief to know I'm not alone in that. Makes me feel like much less of a failure."

"You think you failed with David? No way. David is a great guy."

He glanced over at me. "You really think so?"

So Mr. Big Shot Architect wasn't so arrogant and sure of himself about everything in his life. He seemed to be actually waiting for an answer to his question.

"Yes. I really think so," I said sincerely. "I've always liked David. And I really do hope that Gwen comes to her senses and tries to work out their differences."

We'd reached the house and Cole had driven around back and parked the car in an elaborately carved stone carport. He turned the engine off before he spoke.

"I'm glad you feel that way, Abby. I'm not one of Gwen's biggest fans at the moment, but I hope they work it out, as well."

I laughed. "Yeah, well, I'm not one of her biggest fans right now, either."

"Show me where that museum is going to be built," I said as I got out of the car.

For the next hour or so we tramped around the site while Cole fed notes into a tiny digital tape recorder, took measurements and snapped pictures with a digital camera.

He pointed out trees he wanted to be able to keep and spoke

of aspects of the land that he wished to incorporate into the design. When we were through thoroughly inspecting the site, I went to sit on a low stone wall that bordered the winter ruins of a garden and watched him think as he retraced his steps.

That marvelous silvery hair of his was blowing in the wind and his long, dark coat, which he never seemed to button, was billowing around him. He stood with his legs braced far apart as he stared off into the distance and I thought he looked like a conqueror. I laughed at myself. Or maybe one of those incredibly virile models in the men's cologne ads in one of Iris's glossy magazines.

Finally, he came over to sit next to me.

"You've been very patient," he said.

"I enjoyed watching you work. Do you have any idea what kind of building you plan to design?"

"I was thinking of something long and low that would blend in with the surrounding grounds rather than try to mimic the design or the materials of the house."

I listened to him talk. Some of what he said I didn't really understand, but I wanted to learn because what he said excited me. Or was it the man himself who excited me? I'd never met a man so passionate, so talented, so creative, so handsome, so sexy—

Well, a woman would have to be as cold as the stone wall I was sitting on not to notice, wouldn't she? That's all it was.

That's what I told myself when we stopped at a country inn to eat some of the most wonderful roast chicken I'd ever tasted. And again while we explored the palace of Louis XIV. And again on the ride back to Paris.

By the time we got back to the suite, Cole had retreated emotionally again. Now, I felt nothing but relief. I told him I was tired and was going to bed.

As I lay there in the darkness, I told myself again that I was not falling for Cole Hudson.

This was supposed to be "my time." And, so far, it had turned out better than any daydream I'd ever had. I would do well to remember, though, that this wasn't my real life. I belonged in Willow Creek with my kids and my grandkids—not on the arm of a handsome, famous, interesting and provocative architect.

I grinned. Of course, that didn't mean I wasn't going to enjoy the journey while it lasted. I hadn't come all this way to worry about the future. Whatever I was feeling for Cole was part of the journey. In a few days, my strike would be over and the widow of Willow Creek would be back where she belonged, her heart intact and her feet once again on the ground.

CHAPTER 7

The next day I decided that I really, really had to call home. I wasn't ready to end my strike, but I was starting to feel the need to know that my family was all right. And, face it, I needed to get my feet back on the ground after my romantic schoolgirl thoughts last night. A few offhand compliments and there I was, lying in bed with the kind of fantasies I'm pretty sure a fifty-two-year-old woman was no longer supposed to have. I hadn't thought of myself as a sexual being in a long time. Believe me, the added frustration in my life didn't appeal. I had enough frustrations without adding sexual frustration to the mix.

So, I called home. But no one answered. When the answering machine finally engaged I got one of those digital voices telling me that the machine was full. I tried again, thinking I must have dialed the wrong number, but got the same results.

Okay, was I supposed to start worrying now? Wasn't I on a strike from worry, too? Still, where was everyone and why were there so many messages on the machine? Like fast-forwarding through the previews on a DVD, scenario after scenario rushed through my mind. Most of them involving emergency rooms or at least EMTs. What if Jeremy, humiliated by my outburst, had started to hang the outside lights and electrocuted himself? What if one of the grandkids slipped on the icy sidewalk because I wasn't there to sprinkle it with salt?

Apparently mothers never got a vacation from worry.

I sank onto the plush sofa and willed myself to stop all the gory film clips playing in my mind and try to come up with something more fitting for a romantic comedy.

Of course, I thought, practically smacking myself on the forehead. David. He'd probably been calling several times a day and Gwen was refusing to pick up. The messages had piled up and everyone had been too busy to erase them.

That made sense, I thought as I headed for the bathroom to brush my teeth. Gwen and Natalie were both grown women. Jeremy was there, as well. Three adults could certainly handle three kids. Had I come to think I was indispensable to my family in order to raise my self-worth quotient? Or was I just looking for a reason to slip back into my usual element where I would be safe and sound, and nothing like going to a ball would be expected of me?

"Oh, my God," I gasped at my reflection in the mirror. 'I'm going to a ball in two days! In Paris!"

Okay, no panicking. I'd raised two children by myself and owned my own business. I could do this. Couldn't I? Of course I could. Just as long as I remembered not to eat or drink anything that might stain someone's Versace or Valentino.

I peered more closely at my reflection in the mirror. Cole liked that I didn't hide behind a facade, but maybe it was time for a veneer of sophistication, at least. I picked up the phone and asked to be connected to the salon and day spa at the hotel. Luckily, they could fit me in.

* * *

An hour later, I was standing in a too short black silk wrap-around robe while three women, one more gorgeous than the next, circled me, shaking their heads and consulting with each other in French. I didn't understand a word but I gathered they weren't too impressed.

Finally, one of them spoke—in English, thank God.

"We think madam should have new coiffure, manicure and pedicure, of course. Herbal body scrub, mud wrap, aromatherapy facial, seaweed chest treatment and bikini wax. No?"

"Um—no."

They all looked very sad.

"I mean, just no to the bikini wax—um, and the seaweed chest treatment."

"But, madam, the seaweed chest treatment is known around Paris as the wonder bust treatment for its immediate lifting effects, you understand?"

"Yes, I understand. But being wrapped in mud is about all I can handle today, *s'il vous plaît.*"

I did let them talk me into the thirty-minute Daylight Touch George V makeup session, though.

I spent over three hours being shampooed, conditioned, cut, highlighted, moisturized, massaged, exfoliated and wrapped in mud. It was both relaxing and invigorating. When they were through with me, I felt like my body and hair would glow in the dark. And I ended up liking the results of the makeup session so much that I made an appointment to have the Cocktail Makeup session the night of the ball.

Several hundred euros later, I walked into the lobby and felt almost like one of the sophisticated women who lounged on the antique furniture. I even caught a few men giving me a second glance on my way to the elevator. I won't say I didn't enjoy it, either, because I did.

Moments later, I stared at myself in the mirror in my bedroom and whispered, "Abby, is that you?" It definitely wasn't the same Abby who'd snuck out of her own house a few days ago to escape Willow Creek. I knew I'd be going back soon to face whatever mess I'd made by leaving, but no one could ever take away the experiences I'd had. Or was yet to have.

I picked up the flowered hand mirror from the vanity and checked out my new look from every angle. After Charlie died, bit by bit I'd discarded many of the things that used to mean something to me as a woman. It hadn't been a conscious decision. There'd been more important things than makeup and hairdos to deal with. What difference did it make if I wore perfume or lipstick? I was the widowed mother of two kids plus caretaker to an aging mother and an aging house.

I put the hand mirror down. Those excuses didn't hold anymore. They hadn't for a long time. Why had it taken Paris for me to put on some lipstick, for heaven's sake? Iris had forever been trying to talk me into highlights. I could have driven to Milwaukee or Chicago for the same makeup that was now on my face.

With a sigh, I left the bathroom and lay down on my crowned bed. For the first time since I'd arrived in Paris, I was missing my girlfriends. How I would have loved to discuss all this with Iris and Jo over coffee or margaritas. Especially Iris. She'd consciously avoided marriage and, as a result, had dealt with—and test driven—men of all makes and models. If she were here, she would have dissected every second look from the men in the lobby and, based on clothing, haircut and firmness of butt, would have chosen her quarry and been sitting at the hotel bar with him at this very moment. Yes, I could have used my girl-friends right now. To talk to—and certainly to shop with. I had to find a silver evening gown. That seemed as if it would be a more painful experience than the bikini wax would have been. For one thing, I fully intended to make this purchase on my own, with my own money. It would be just too embarrassing to ask for money from the man I'd been fantasizing about half the night. Obviously, I had to find someplace a lot cheaper to shop than the designer boutiques in the area. But I had no idea where to go. I also wasn't enthusiastic about asking Madeline for help, even though she'd offered. For one thing, she must have a million things to do since she was in charge of planning the Silver Ball, for another thing, I wasn't sure she'd know where to shop for an inexpensive gown. She didn't exactly look like the kind of woman who ever had to pinch pennies.

I was debating the wisdom of asking the hotel concierge to point me in the direction of a cheap evening gown, when I thought of Olivia. Who better than an art student to show me where to buy inexpensive but fashionable clothing?

I found the crumpled receipt with her number. I was just about to hang up when Olivia answered on the sixth ring. Her hello sounded breathless.

"Did I catch you at a bad time?" I asked.

"Who is this?" she demanded, sounding none too friendly.

Swell, I thought. Maybe Olivia was one of those people who regularly handed out her number figuring no one was ever really going to call her.

"Um—Olivia, this is Abby."

"Abby!" she immediately exclaimed with enough glee to

make me sure of my welcome. "No, it's not a bad time. I was just working, but I could use a break."

"And I could use a favor," I said.

"Okay—shoot. I'm listening."

"I've got this ball I have to go to—"

"With the Mr. Big Shot Hottie Architect?"

I grinned. "Right."

"Awesome! So, how can I help?"

"I need a dress. And it's got to be silver. And it's got to be something I can afford but it also has to be something that won't scream *discount diva* when I walk into the room. Any suggestions?"

Olivia laughed. "Girlfriend, you definitely called the right number. I know just the place. I'll take you there myself."

"Oh, that's not necessary. I don't want to interrupt your work."

I could hear the smile in her voice. "Shopping is my favorite interruption. Do you know the Place de la Concorde?"

I frowned. "I don't think so."

"It's that huge square at the base of the Champs-Elysées—the one with the obelisk. If you get lost, just ask anyone where the giant obelisk is. I'll meet you there in an hour."

I decided that as long as I was made-up, coiffed and buffed to a glow that I'd wear the winter white suit. The day wasn't too cold so I threw my cashmere coat over my shoulders and left the suite.

The hotel was near the Champs-Elysées and I easily found the Place de la Concorde and the giant obelisk. The square was crowded with tour busses and local traffic, but Olivia had no problem spotting me.

"You look fabulous!" she cried as she gave me a hug.

"So do you," I said. And I meant it. She was wearing jeans

that had what we used to call bell bottoms with high heeled boots, a short rough tweed jacket and a colorful scarf wrapped around her neck several times.

"It's wild here this time of day, but I knew you'd be able to find it easily enough."

As we crossed the square Olivia pointed out the United States Embassy. "Just in case Mr. Big Shot Architect kicks you out on your butt some night."

I laughed. "That's not as far-fetched as you might think. He's the most changeable man I've ever met."

"Moody is the word," Olivia said. "We creative types are always moody."

"Hmm—moody. Maybe you're right."

"Ask Rachel. I drive her nuts when a piece isn't turning out like I want it to. If I've got something in my head that I can't translate with my hands, I can get very moody and isolated. It's like the idea takes over my body until it can work its way out. Like giving birth to an alien."

I told her about visiting Versailles and viewing the Fontaine's museum site with Cole the day before and about how quiet he got when he was thinking and how he'd isolated himself as soon as we'd returned to the hotel.

Olivia nodded. "I can relate. Unfortunately, my mother never could. That was always one of the problems between the two of us. She couldn't understand that sometimes I just couldn't let it go. Sometimes solitude and silence were necessary. She was forever worried that I was depressed or sick or something. She was always trying to cheer me up and turn me into her idea of a normal teenager."

"The Prisoners Society once had a discussion about this. We

debated whether allowances should be made for creative or talented people. Was it fair to expect them to bend to convention, to follow the same rules as everyone else?"

"Now, see, I couldn't even begin to have that conversation with my mother. She doesn't even want to try to understand. The whole concept would be as foreign to her as that Indian street musician over there." She nodded toward a man playing a pipe of some kind.

I was amazed at Olivia's mother's attitude. If she were my daughter, I'd be so proud of her for what she was doing—for the chances she was taking. Hell, I was proud of whatever my kids accomplished. I was proud of Gwen for working hard for a college education. I'd been proud of her when she'd moved to Chicago. I knew first-hand that leaving a small town for the city took courage and ambition. I'd been equally proud of Natalie for being a good mother, for coping so well every time Jeremy got laid off and for getting a job at the Mega-mart to try to hold her family together when Jeremy couldn't find work during this latest, longest, layoff. My walking slowed a little. Did my daughters know how I felt? Did they realize what great young women I thought they were? Did I need to tell them so more often?

And what did my daughters think of me? Did they ever discuss me with the kind of disdain Olivia showed when she talked about her mother? Cole had told me that Gwen was proud of me, but had she said it in the heat of the moment—perhaps during an argument with her father-in-law? Were they proud that I'd gone on strike? Did they understand why I'd had to? Why would they when I'd seldom asked for what I'd needed or wanted? Maybe Cole had been wrong when he'd said that I didn't hide behind a facade. Maybe my strident independence and willingness to sacrifice was as much of a facade as this veneer of sophistication I now wore.

"Here we are," Olivia said. "Now, this place is sort of like a consignment shop."

"You mean used clothing?" I asked dubiously, wondering if I wanted to show up at the ball in someone's cast-offs.

"Gently used," Olivia emphasized. "Stuff from the kind of women who wouldn't be caught dead in the same gown twice. And sometimes some leftover stuff from a designer's last year's collection. You never know what you'll find. Versace. Dior. Stella McCartney."

"Any relation to Paul, the Beatle?"

Olivia laughed. "You're kidding, right? She's his daughter. Come on, let's get in there and look for your gown."

The place was nothing like a consignment shop in Willow Creek. It was all very glamorous. Beautifully dressed women looking for their next ensemble. I could swear a few of them were coveting my suit and it gave me the guts to head right for a rack of Versace.

But it was a Dior I fell in love with. Vintage Dior. An ivory gossamer fabric shot with silver threads. A full, swishy skirt. An off the shoulder neckline that stood out slightly from the body. When I tried it on, I knew Olivia saw it, too.

"It's like it was made for you, Abby. Just waiting for you to come and claim it."

So claim it I did. And at a very good price. Yes, more than I'd ever paid for a dress in my life, but nothing close to what Cole had spent on the cocktail suit I'd worn to dinner the other night.

We found silver shoes and a bag at another discount designer place. We both agreed that earrings were the only jewelry I should wear and found a pair of vintage ones at a street vendor that were silver swirls crusted with clear crystals.

"I hope you'll let me take you out for a late lunch for all your help," I said.

"I never turn down free food," Olivia confessed with a laugh.

This time she suggested we grab a sandwich at one of the many places that specialized in panini. We came upon one that still had a few tables outdoors, despite the chill December air.

"Want to sit outside?" she asked.

"Love to. It will probably be my only chance to experience a Parisian outdoor café."

"And it'll probably be my last chance to do it."

"You'll be leaving Paris soon?" I asked her.

She sighed. "I have enough left in my bank account for a ticket home."

"That's pretty much what I have left on my emergency credit card, too."

I debated telling her about the Fontaine Foundation but the process probably wouldn't happen fast enough to keep her in Paris. And if Cole had his way about it, Madeline and Andre would never see Olivia's work, anyway.

Our server came out with our food. Hot coffee and steaming panini sandwiches, oozing melted cheese. We were the only customers braving the December weather. It was sunny and pleasant and the coffee helped keep us warm while we watched the human parade go by.

"I hate the thought of leaving it all," Olivia said. "Last night I was even considering just getting a job and staying. Give up the whole art thing."

"No!" I insisted, surprised at the alarm in my voice. "You can't give up that dream, Olivia. Have you thought of applying for any grants?"

"I've applied to every one that I'd be even remotely suitable for. I did get a small one a few months ago. Materials ate up most of it. You know, I wonder sometimes if life is easier if you don't have a dream."

"No—it's just longer. Or seems that way."

Olivia laughed.

"Besides, you already have a dream. It's not like you could say *time's up, dream be gone*. You'd be fighting against the instinct for the rest of your life. Making compromises right and left. You'd always have that dream in you, wanting to burst out."

"You sound like you know what you're talking about, Abby," Olivia said as she watched me. "What kind of dreams did you have when you were my age?"

"Nothing as lofty as yours," I answered. "Mainly, I wanted to live in the city. As far as I was concerned, Willow Creek didn't have much to offer. I always pictured Charlie and me going to plays, meeting other young professionals for cocktails, discovering art and culture at the same time as our children did. I guess you could sum it up by saying that I wanted something different than what I'd always known."

"You sound as if you think it's too late for that."

"Isn't it?"

"Abby, you're fifty-two. In today's world, that's not old at all. From where I'm sitting, I'd say you still have time for another kind of life. Have you thought any more about getting a job and staying?"

I wasn't sure I should tell her. I hadn't yet mentioned it to Cole. I'd barely allowed myself to think about the possibility of taking the job that Madeline had offered. Olivia might be the perfect person to try out the idea on.

"I actually got offered a job," I said. "Right out of the blue."

Olivia leaned forward, her fresh, young face brimming with enthusiasm. "What kind of job?"

"It'd be working with numbers." I wasn't sure if I wanted to tell her about the Fontaine Foundation yet. Given Cole's attitude and the fact that the project was barely off the ground, I didn't see any point in getting Olivia's hopes up. "I'd be working for a non-profit group," I simply said.

"Then you can stay!"

I shook my head. "It's not that easy. I have a life back home. Responsibilities. My strike is only temporary."

"Unless you decided to up and quit the union."

"I don't think there's anywhere you can go to quit being a mother."

"Well, if you ever find such a place, let me know. I'd love to send my mother there."

"Olivia, maybe you should try to be a little more understanding of your mother. It's not an easy job, you know. Especially once your kids become young adults. It's hard to let go. Hard to let them make their own mistakes. Have you ever considered that your mother's lack of enthusiasm for your art might be driven by love?"

Olivia wrinkled her nose. "Love? If you love someone, don't you want them to have what they want?"

"Not if you think it might hurt them. The maternal force to protect is pretty strong, Olivia. I think a lot of mistakes we mothers make are linked to that force. None of us want to see our kids struggle. Your mother no doubt knows that the artist's life isn't an easy one."

Olivia frowned and leaned back in her chair. "Now I'm feeling guilty for not being more understanding of my mother's point of view."

I grabbed her hand. "Oh, no! Not guilt! I've felt enough of that for the both of us. Especially lately. I certainly had no intention of burdening you with the emotion. I'd rather you tried to understand your mother's side of things."

We ate in silence for a few minutes, then Olivia said, "You know, it's kind of cool having a friend your age. I've never really considered my mother's motives before. I just figured she was being a bitch about my ambition. Like she knew I'd never make it as an artist so why waste my time."

I sipped my coffee and wondered how often my own daughters had misunderstood my intentions.

"If you could ask for only one thing from your mother, what would it be?" I asked Olivia.

She put her elbow on the table and rested her chin in the cup of her hand. She was obviously taking my question seriously, so I kept quiet and gave her a chance to think.

"I think it would be to just have her listen."

"Just that? Listen?"

Olivia nodded. "Yes. To listen and not judge. To listen and really hear. To listen and ask questions instead of give opinions."

That sounded simple enough, I thought. But was it? Did Gwen and Natalie think I really listened to them? And even more importantly, *did* I really listen to them? I liked to think I did. From now on, I would make sure of it. I'd listen with my heart and not just my head.

Gwen and Natalie. My love for them suddenly filled me up. I pushed my plate away.

"Do you think you could help me find something really special for my daughters for Christmas?" I asked Olivia.

She thought for a few moments, then her face brightened. "There's a wonderful perfumery nearby. You can just tell them the kind of scents you like—like citrus or floral—and they find the exact thing for you. Or you can explain someone's personality and they'll come up with the perfect scent."

I liked the idea, so we went there. Among the thousands of small glass bottles with stoppers, the shop assistant listened to me describe my daughters then suggested two divine choices—both perfectly in tune with how I saw Gwen and Natalie. I bought each in the smallest sizes available and had them gift wrapped.

"I know this guy who makes these great marionettes," Olivia suggested when I mentioned that I still needed gifts for my grandchildren.

His shop was in a tiny street. The window display was filled with all sorts of puppets, marionettes and masks.

While Olivia chatted with the puppet maker, I chose a marionette for each of my grandchildren. It'd be a good thing, I told myself, for them to play with something that they didn't have to plug in and didn't require batteries. For Ashley, I chose a princess. For Tyler, I chose a clown and for Matt I chose a pirate.

After we left the puppet shop, we spent some time examining the wares of a street vendor who was selling scarves and berets. I decided they'd be the perfect gift from Paris for both Jeremy and David—who I hoped would still be part of the family when I got home.

Noticing the time, I gasped. "Holy cow, I'd better get going."

"Will Mr. Big Shot Architect be scowling and pacing the lobby again?"

"I certainly hope not," I said, then thanked her for the wonderful afternoon. "I never would have found that dress if it hadn't been for you. Or the marionettes, or the—"

She laughed and gave me an exuberant hug. "I'm the one who should be thanking you. I had fun. Come on, I'll walk you to the metro station."

Flushed with the success of taking the metro alone back to the hotel, I burst into the suite, hoping to stow my purchases away before Cole returned, but he was already there.

The dining table at the far end of the room was strewn with sheets of paper and he was pacing out on the balcony. He was running a hand through his hair over and over again. I moved as quietly as possible to my bedroom where I threw my coat on the bed, hung the Dior in the closet and put the rest of my packages on the closet floor.

In the sitting room, I carefully approached the table and picked up a few of the papers. He'd been sketching—and obviously wasn't happy with the results. Remembering what Olivia had told me about the creative process, I wasn't sure if Cole would want the interruption or not. I decided to go out there and at least let him know that I was here.

I opened the French doors and stepped onto the balcony. Cars honked from below and the pleasant late December afternoon had turned cold enough to see your breath.

"Are you warm enough? Would you like your coat?" I asked.

His head jerked up in surprise. "I didn't hear you return," he said.

"I knew you were thinking about work so I didn't want to interrupt. It's a little cold out here so I thought you might like your coat—or something. I could ring down for coffee—or drinks."

"There's a bottle of brandy in the cabinet across from the sofa. I could use a shot of that, if you wouldn't mind."

I found snifters in the cabinet alongside the bottle. I poured a shot of brandy in two of them and carried them out to the balcony. Cole took his and threw back his head to take a generous swallow.

"I can't get it right," he said as he started to pace again. "It's just not coming."

His struggle was painful to watch.

I'd glimpsed some insecurity in Cole on this trip, but it never occurred to me that he would ever be insecure about his work. I walked up to him and put a hand on his arm. His black V-neck sweater was soft, the muscle beneath it hard and tense. I wanted to help him in some way, but I didn't know what to do.

Maybe Cole, like Olivia, just wanted someone to listen.

"Is this the way it always is at the beginning of a project?"

"No—not always. Only the ones that mean the most to me. The ones that I want to be masterpieces." He gave a bitter bark of laughter. "It's folly to try to set out to create a masterpiece, you know. Far better to be working with a clear eye as to what is best for the site and the use of the building."

"But because it's Madeline and Andre, it means too much."

He took another gulp of brandy. "Yes. I can't fail them."

He looked bleak as he walked over to the balustrade and leaned on it, staring out at the Paris night for several minutes. I was shivering, though the brandy was helping. I was ready to listen. The question was, how was I going to get him to talk?

"Why don't we get out of here for a little while?" I suggested.

"But—my work."

"A walk might clear your head—give you a fresh start."

His gaze raked over me. I fully expected him to turn me down. "You may be right. Besides, you look far too beautiful tonight to spend the evening sitting in the suite."

There was that word again. *Beautiful.* Maybe it was a word that Cole Hudson tossed around on a regular basis. The women he knew probably took it as their due. There was no way he'd know what a word like that could mean to a woman like me.

He helped me on with my coat and I straightened the collar of his after he'd put it on. When we left the hotel, we walked along Avenue George V until we reached the Champs-Elysées. The trees lining the avenue were lit and twinkling. The shops, stores and cinemas were showing off their neon. And up ahead, at the end of the avenue, the Arc de Triomphe was glowing like an oasis in the night. And the traffic. Always the traffic. This time several lanes of it.

We walked all the way to the Arc, Cole keeping up a brisk pace. As we stood and gazed up at the Arc, he explained to me how it had first been commissioned by Napoleon as a memorial for the French Army.

"But you can see now it's a central hub with twelve avenues emanating from it like spokes on a wheel. The stone facade was done by three sculptors," he said.

I gazed up at the massive work and felt its power. It gave me some understanding of what it must be like for Cole to want to build something that lasted beyond a lifetime.

We retraced our steps along the Champs-Elysées, walking more slowly this time. I could feel in the movement of his body next to mine how much more relaxed he was than he had been when we'd left the hotel.

As we walked, Cole started to talk about the problems he was having with the Fontaine project. As I listened, I began to feel connected to him in a way I hadn't before. I felt like less of an inconvenience and more of an equal.

I'd been trying to learn some French by listening and watching so when we stopped at a restaurant, for the first time since I'd reached Paris, I decided to try to order off the menu myself.

"*Artichauts à la vinaigrette et des médaillons de veau, s'il vous plaît.*"

Cole ordered then leaned back in his chair to smile at me. "I'm impressed," he said.

"You might want to hold your praise until we see if I actually get what I thought I was asking for."

"If you meant to order artichokes vinaigrette and medallions of veal then my praise stands."

"I did. And I will accept the praise, thank you very much."

We'd already ordered drinks, white wine for me and another brandy for Cole. The wine was fruity and just a touch dry. Delicious.

"So, tell me what you did today."

"First, I tried calling home."

"Ready to come out of hiding, are you?"

I cocked my head as I considered his question. "No, it's more like I'm starting to wonder how everyone's doing. You know, without me."

"So, how did the call go?"

"I didn't get through. The answering machine was full and no one picked up."

"Hmm—does that happen often?"

"Never."

"And you're worried?"

"I'm trying not to be, but I will admit that several horrible scenarios spun through my mind earlier today. Guilt can do funny things."

"Guilt is a wasted emotion," Cole stated brusquely. "What good has it ever done anyone?"

"It did my mother a lot of good. She got me to stay in Willow Creek."

As soon as the words were out of my mouth, I quickly looked up and met Cole's gaze. I'd tossed off the comment without thinking. And now it was sitting out there, like the salt and pepper shakers on the table between us.

"Go on," Cole prodded.

"Our stay was supposed to be temporary—just until my father passed away."

"But it didn't turn out that way."

I shook my head. "My mother was afraid to be alone in that big house."

"After she passed on, what made you stay?"

I stared at him for several seconds. "Me," I finally said. "I made me stay."

It was the truth. I was the one who'd made the choice to stay in Willow Creek. I hadn't been a prisoner, but a willing captive. There had been other solutions, other choices I could have made.

I grabbed my wine glass and gulped the rest of the contents down. "Holy cow, that was a sobering revelation."

Cole tilted his head. "Why sobering?"

"Because it means that I haven't been very brave in my life. It means I've used other people as excuses for things I haven't done."

He reached across the table and took my hand. "Abby, it means that you're human."

I liked the feel of my hand enclosed in his. I liked the new softness in his eyes as his gaze held mine. I liked that he seemed to understand something that I'd only just realized. It had been so long since I'd had a man to comfort me or to share confidences with.

"Abby," Cole said while his thumb started to rhythmically stroke the back of my hand, "you're far too hard on yourself."

"I thought I was supposed to be comforting you tonight."

"No reason why we can't comfort each other."

He was doing more than comforting me. The warmth his thumb generated was spreading throughout my body. I suddenly felt more relaxed—and more alive—than I had in years.

"What else did you do today?" Cole asked.

"Hmm? Oh—Olivia took me to do some Christmas shopping."

He let go of my hand. "Olivia, again," he muttered.

"She's a friend, Cole," I said after I'd recovered from the jarring change in the atmosphere. "Why shouldn't I go shopping with her?"

"Just as long as that's all it is—friendship. I won't have you trying to push this girl's work on Andre and Madeline."

Our server came with our food so I kept silent until he'd left our table again.

"Did I say anything about her work, Cole?"

"No—but I'm sure it was coming."

"Well, it wasn't." I grinned at him. "But since you've brought it up—"

Cole groaned as he sliced into his steak.

"Well, really, Cole, what if no one had believed in you when you were starting out?" I asked as I cut into my veal. "What if the Fontaines had seen you as just another rich student with artistic pretensions when they'd met you?"

His mouth twitched slightly. "The tenacious Ms. Blake rises again. All right, I concede that you have a point. However, at the moment I'm wondering if my mentors made a big mistake in judgment."

"Why?"

He took another bite of steak.

"Come on," I urged. "Talk to me about it."

He shook his head. "Why bore you?"

"Right. Listening to a world-renowned architect talk about his latest project would put me straight to sleep."

"I've had dates yawning, believe me." He studied me for a few seconds. "But you wouldn't be one of them, would you?"

"Absolutely not. I find what you do exciting." I find *you* exciting, I wanted to add, but didn't. After all, it might only be the magic of Paris that was making me feel that way. A few days ago, I could barely stand the sight of the man. And he still easily infuriated me. Yet, Olivia's words about artistic temperament came back to me. What I'd learned from and about her made me want to know more about what drove Cole's moods.

"Tell me what kind of problems you're having," I coaxed.

He started to talk and we sat there for hours, drinking, talking, sharing dessert.

"I thought round at first—like the circle of life—with a courtyard in the center. But the problem with that would be—"

Every once in a while I'd find my mind drifting from what he was saying to just watching his face—so animated, so changeable. I don't think I'd ever met anyone who was as full of life, in all its many facets, as Cole Hudson.

It wasn't until the restaurant started to close that we stood and he helped me put on my coat. He held my hand as we strolled along the Champs-Elysées, nearly deserted now by the late hour. His hand felt warm, strong. Our steps seemed to match perfectly. I wished we could go on walking forever. We reached the hotel far too soon.

But even the palatial suite couldn't seem to contain me that night. I went out on the balcony, not wanting the evening to be over, not wanting to be inside when Paris was still out there. I tried to examine what I was feeling, tried to make sense of it. How could I be having these feelings about a man who was so unlike my Charlie? Because there was no denying it now. I definitely had feelings for Cole Hudson. I just wasn't sure what the feelings were.

Lust? He'd certainly awakened something in me. My skin was on fire. My body was humming.

Or was it just the wine and the city?

Behind me I heard the French doors open but I didn't turn around. I was afraid of what might show on my face. I heard his footsteps on the stone. Felt the heat of his body as he came up behind me.

"You'll catch cold out here."

I shook my head. "I'm too full of wine to get cold. In fact, I feel like I'll never be cold again."

"I think you're drunk on Paris," he said and I could hear the smile in his voice. I already knew exactly what his face would look like when his voice sounded that way.

I leaned back until I could feel his chest against my back. He sighed heavily, almost angrily, and then I felt his hands at my waist and the heat of them as they slid forward to join in front of me, pressing against my midriff just under the short jacket of my suit. It was then that I let my head drift to his shoulder.

It was magic. It was like the answer to everything I'd ever felt when that certain wind from the past caressed my face or that old song played on the radio.

I turned my head, thrust my hand into his hair, and brought his mouth to mine.

His lips were as clever as his mind. When I broke the kiss, he pressed his mouth against the side of my neck and my gaze moved languidly to the Eiffel Tower, the lights blurring, my body blooming. I'd forgotten what it felt like to be a woman ready for sex.

"You know," he murmured, "I think I've finally come up with a way for you to pay me back for everything."

Thank God. We were finally getting to the good part. Damn it. Why hadn't I gotten that wonder bust treatment? "How?" I asked, my voice barely above a whisper.

"I'd like you to find me a place to live while I'll be working in Paris."

"What?" I croaked and spun around.

"I'll need an apartment. I'd like you to find one for me," he stated.

Hell, and I'd been hoping for ravishment.

"Of course," I said, moving around him, going into the suite.

He followed me. "You'll work with an agency, of course. Madeline gave me the name of a good one."

"Great," I said, heading for my bedroom.

"Abby."

I turned.

"We've both had a lot to drink—"

"You don't have to explain," I said as fast as I could. And then I went to bed. Though not to sleep.

I laid there trying to remember if I'd ever made a pass at a man before. Nope. I was pretty sure I'd remember the humiliation I was feeling at this moment.

Oh—right. I'd kissed Bobby Saunders in the first grade during recess. At least Cole hadn't run around spitting afterwards.

So what had Cole been thinking coming up behind me like that and putting his arms around me? Had he just been trying to keep me warm? And hadn't that been him nibbling my neck and ear? Were we headed anywhere? Had I read all the signals wrong? And why couldn't life have a rewind button, so that I could examine the entire scene again and figure out if I'd really made as big a fool of myself as I thought I had. What a time for my dormant sexuality to surface.

CHAPTER 8

The rental agent and I weren't seeing eye-to-eye.

"Monsieur expressly wished for us to examine apartments in the area of the Place du Trocadéro, Madame."

"I know, but everything we've looked at has been so—cold."

"Madame, our apartments all have central heating."

I shook my head. "No, that's not what I mean. They're too modern. Not Parisian enough."

The agent, a pretty young woman dressed in a little gray suit, was looking at me like I was a crazy tourist. Which, I suppose, I was.

"Have you got anything in the Quartier Latin?"

"Madame, I don't think that section of Paris would be appropriate for this client," she said as she perused her file on Cole Hudson again. "It is not even on his list of possibilities."

The apartments we'd looked at so far were all glass and chrome and granite countertops. There wasn't a French door or a balcony among them. No crown moldings. No fleur-de-lis. No wrought iron. Not even a fireplace. Nothing romantic at all about them. And shouldn't an apartment in Paris be, above all, romantic?

"Have you got anything in the Quartier Latin?" I asked again.

The agent sighed. "One or two that would fit in Monsieur Hudson's criteria and price range. But, Madame, I assure you—"

"I'd like to see what you have in the Quartier, *s'il vous plaît.*"

I could see that she wasn't happy with me, but Cole had hired a car and driver for use in finding him a place to live, so I really didn't see why the agent should have any objection to moving on.

Moving on. Something I absolutely had to do after last night. Talk about embarrassing. The scene on the balcony at the hotel last night was definitely cringe-worthy. I'd lost some sleep over it, but I wasn't going to let it ruin my day. I watched out the window of the car as we made our way across the Seine to the Left Bank.

If I'd misread Cole's signals, then I'd better go back to grade school because it had definitely been him nibbling me and getting me all hot and bothered last night. For whatever reason, he had stopped what he'd started, which was probably the wise thing to do. However, it didn't mean I had any intention of thanking him for condemning me to a night of frustration. I was beginning to enjoy sleeping in the nude, but last night the feel of the expensive bed linens against my skin just made me want to touch myself. And that was something I hadn't done since I was a teenager. I finally flung back the covers, got out of bed and put my flannel pajamas on.

Our driver stopped the car in front of an old ornate building. Wrought iron balconies abounded. The front door was huge and made of heavy, ancient-looking wood. The door knocker in the center was tarnished and obviously original to the building.

"This is more like it," I said.

"Madame, there is no *l'ascenseur*."

"Excuse me?"

The agent sighed. "No—um—*lift*, madame."

"Lift? Oh—you mean no elevator."

"*Oui*, madame. Monsieur expressly wished for an elevator."

"What floor is the apartment on?"

"Floor four, madame."

Four floors? I thought of Cole's body—with just the tiniest influx of heat to my veins. Yeah, he should be able to manage four floors. I'd done five floors at Olivia's and lived to tell the tale. In a year's time he'd be thanking me for his improved cardiovascular health.

"Since we're here anyway, we might as well take a look at it," I told the agent.

We climbed the four flights. I was barely breathing heavily. Okay, maybe panting a little, but when the agent unlocked the door I pretty much lost my breath anyway.

The walls were painted deep pink. The ceilings were high and surrounded by fancy plaster moldings in contrasting white. There was a pink-and-black marble fireplace and tall French doors opened onto the black wrought iron balcony. I unlocked the doors and stepped out.

The view was charming. The tree-lined street had apartments, shops, bistros and cafés. The yeasty smell of newly baked bread drifted up from the *boulangerie* across from the apartment and I could see that the *fromagerie*, or cheese shop, next door to the bakery was doing a brisk business.

I went back inside where the agent waited to show me the bedroom.

"More French doors to the balcony!" I exclaimed. How wonderful. And there was another fireplace, less detailed than the one in the living room, but imagine cuddling up in bed on cold winter nights with a fireplace crackling just a few feet away.

The kitchen was rather large, but old-fashioned, with a stone floor and an old wooden drain board. Windows over the sink opened inward and there was room enough for a small kitchen table and a few chairs in one of the corners.

"Monsieur wanted a formal dining room, as well."

"I know, but the living room is so big. I'm sure a dining table—maybe a round one—could fit on the far end."

I wandered from room to room again, picturing what would go where. Checking the view of the rooftops nearby.

"I think this is it," I said.

The agent looked dubious but relieved. I gave her the check Cole had given me as a deposit, which got me the key. Then I used the driver's cell phone to call Cole.

"You've found something already?" he asked in surprise.

"Cole, it's perfect. Can you meet me to take a look at it?"

"I'm meeting with the finance people," he said. "It's going to be easily another two hours before I'm free."

"All right. Tell me where you are and I'll have the driver pick you up in two hours."

I told the driver to take the agent back to her office and then gave him the address Cole had given me and told him to meet Cole there in two hours.

I knew the Luxembourg Gardens were nearby—Jardins du Luxembourg—so I decided to explore a little. There were fountains, but the water was turned off for the season. There were elderly men in black berets bowling on the lawn. There were young people bundled up and hunched over chessboards. There were other groups of young people likely students, talking passionately in French. The flowers had mostly given way to winter, but I imagined how the place would look in the spring and summer. It was a short walk from the apartment. One could stop at the *boulangerie* and the *fromagerie* along the way for a simple yet elegant picnic.

I wandered the park for awhile, aware of something missing. I thought back to that first night when I'd gone to the Eiffel Tower and how being alone seemed fitting and not at all lonely. It was different now. Now I knew what had been making me restless. Not just lack of stimulating surroundings, but lack of stimulating male companionship. Cole's companionship. As I thought of him in this moment, that same feeling washed over me. The feeling that had been bedeviling me for months now. Longing. That's what it was. Longing.

I remembered the feel of my hand enfolded in his when he'd reached out to me at the restaurant last night after I'd blurted that revelation about my mother. He'd shown me his tender side and it had caused me to entrust him with a piece of me that I'd hidden from everyone, including myself. Unlike Olivia's sculpture, my jail didn't have barbed wire and the key had been in my hand all along.

But with the freedom had come complications. Not just the lingering guilt I felt about taking this time for myself, but also my growing feelings for Cole.

Okay, so he didn't want me that way. So he didn't have those kinds of feelings for me. I still intended to enjoy every moment of the rest of my strike in Paris. Besides, maybe Cole was right when he said I was drunk on Paris, not on love. The fact that I was still capable of emotion like that for any man was cause for celebration, wasn't it? And if it was Paris I was really in love with, I could always take Madeline up on her offer of a job. Like Olivia had said, there was no reason I couldn't live in Paris for a year if I chose to.

I looked at my watch. There was more than an hour before I had to meet Cole at the apartment building. I wondered how far I was from Olivia's place. Judging by my surroundings, it seemed pretty close. I passed a red telephone kiosk and decided to call her.

But when I placed the call, I was told that the number was no longer in service. I hung up the phone, perplexed and puzzled. Wouldn't Olivia have called me if she'd suddenly decided to go back to the States? I felt that, despite our knowing each other only for a brief time, we'd bonded enough that she would certainly call me if she was leaving Paris. Instead, it was much more likely that she was so low on money that she hadn't paid the phone bill. My experiences with Natalie had taught me that the phone was always one of the first casualties of interrupted cash flow.

What if Olivia had already gone home? I didn't even know for sure where *home* was. We'd talked about so many things, I didn't remember her ever saying where she was from. It seemed important to me not to lose her altogether. She was a symbol of the newly liberated Abby.

No, it was more than that. Despite our differences in ages and the fact that we didn't have much in common, I considered Olivia a friend. It was pretty cool to know a young woman who liked me just because of the person I was. One who would never plaintively ask me to make her pancakes while I was on my way out the door or whose kids would never clog my bathroom sink with jelly beans just to see how long it would take them to melt.

Because she was my friend, I wanted a happy ending for Olivia as much as I'd always wanted one for Jo and Iris. I still believed that if Andre and Madeline ever saw Olivia's work, they'd be willing to help her stay in Paris.

I decided to call Madeline. Luckily, she'd given me her number the night we'd met at dinner, just in case I wanted to discuss the possibility of a job. I found it in my purse and called her.

"I'm in the middle of a manicure," she told me. "How important is this?"

"Remember that artist, the sculptor, I told you about?"

"*Oui*. Olivia."

"Right. Well, I'm afraid that Olivia might have to go back to the States anytime now. Her phone's been disconnected and that can only mean the money situation has become dire."

"Yes—I see."

"I promised Cole that I wouldn't bother you with this again, but I just feel that maybe if you saw Olivia's work, that—"

"You say Cole told you not to bother me with this?"

"He's got some idea that it's a waste of time and not worth your notice."

"Ohhh, men. They can drive you crazy, can they not? I love Cole like he's my son, but he has no right to decide these things for me. I am more than capable of making these decisions for myself."

"Does that mean you'll come?"

"Give me her address. I shall catch a taxi as soon as I can and meet you there."

Finding Olivia's apartment was a near disaster. The streets were such warrens here. It was easy to make a wrong turn and find yourself at the spot where you started. Eventually, I located the narrow building that leaned to the left.

I managed to make it up the five flights with only two stops to take a breath. When I knocked, there was no answer.

Damn it. I had stuck my neck out with Madeline. And when Cole found out, he wasn't going to be happy. And now Olivia might not even be home.

I pressed my ear to the door and heard the unmistakable hiss of a welder. So I pounded harder.

Suddenly, the door burst open.

"What?" an angry-looking Olivia demanded. Her hair stuck out like a scarecrow's and she was wearing an old pair of coveralls that were pockmarked with little burn holes.

"Can I come in?" I asked.

"Suit yourself," she said.

She left the door open, so I followed her in.

"Is this a bad time?"

"I'm working," she answered curtly.

"Well, I did try to call first, but—"

"Yeah, I was behind on the phone bill. I'm behind on the electricity, too, so don't be surprised if you find yourself suddenly sitting in the dark."

Her cherubic face looked about as angry as I figured cherubic could look. Olivia was clearly having one of those moody days she'd spoken of.

"Work not going well?"

She gave me a look, then just slammed a welding helmet on and started working again. Well, that answered that. Olivia had been telling the truth when she'd said she possessed an artistic temperament much like Cole's.

Too bad I hadn't found out she was having a bad day until after I'd called Madeline.

So here was my dilemma—should I interrupt Olivia's work to tell her she was about to be visited by a woman who could have a lot of power over her circumstances? Or do I just let her keep working and hope for the best?

I decided I'd let her keep torturing the metal until Madeline arrived. We would probably all be safer that way.

I went back downstairs—five flights down was so much easier than five flights up—to wait for Madeline.

When she got out of the taxi, I went to warn her that she might want to tell the driver to wait.

"Why? Is your friend not home?"

"Oh—ah—she's home, all right. But she's sort of in a foul mood. I've never quite seen her this way—although she did warn me she could be temperamental."

Madeline laughed. "I've been working with artists for years. I've known Cole since he was nineteen. You think I am capable of being shocked or wounded by an attack of artistic temperament?"

I laughed. "No, I guess it would take more than that."

"Exactly. So—how many floors must I walk up to meet this sculptor friend of yours?"

As it turned out, Madeline was a lot less winded when we reached the fifth floor than I was.

"You're in amazing shape for your age—or any age, for that matter."

"We live in a walk-up, my dear. The best exercise in the world."

I didn't bother knocking on Olivia's door this time. Madeline and I went right in. Olivia didn't even acknowledge us; she continued welding. I didn't know whether to get all motherly about manners or what. And then it occurred to me that I wasn't Olivia's mother. Her behavior didn't reflect on me whatsoever. I was simply someone who was interested in her work. All I had to do was hope that Madeline saw something in it. Olivia could be as disagreeable as she wanted to be.

Madeline seemed content to sit on the lumpy ottoman and watch.

Finally, Olivia lifted the glass on her helmet.

"Who the hell are you?" she asked.

Instead of cringing, I headed into the kitchen to make some coffee. It turned out to be a good idea. Soon I could hear what sounded like civil conversation coming from the other room.

By the time I came in with the tray of filled mugs, Olivia and Madeline were deep in discussion about her work and about what it would take for her to stay in Paris to study. I mostly kept out of the way and let the two of them talk.

Olivia gave me a big hug when we left, so I gathered that the visit, although it had started rocky, had turned out to be all right.

"What do you think?" I asked Madeline when we were on the sidewalk.

"She's very raw—but there is something there. I think I might be able to find a way to finance part of another year here. She has agreed to consider working for the foundation in some capacity in repayment."

"That's wonderful."

"You had good instincts about her, Abby. Have you given any thought about staying in Paris and accepting a job at the foundation?"

I shook my head. "I have to see my kids again before I can decide something like that. I have to know they'd be okay."

"I understand," Madeline said. "But your children are not such children anymore, no?"

"No. They just act like it sometimes."

Madeline laughed. "You know, walking these streets brings back so many memories. It was all so different when I first came here in the early fifties. There were many artists and writers starving in garrets back then. In fact, it was not so far past Hemingway's time here. You have no doubt heard the stories of how he often dined on pigeons he captured in Jardins du Luxembourg to keep from starving." Madeline shook her head. "Oh, how I wanted to be an artist in those days. But I had no talent whatsoever. I was impossible. I ended up selling small paintings to tourists at a kiosk along the Seine. And I knew that was as far as my art career was going to go. Tourists who knew no better," she said disdainfully. "So I finally gave myself permission to quit trying to be an artist and to start studying art history, instead. I was working part-time as a docent at the Louvre when I met Andre. He knew nothing of art. I knew nothing of business. We argued our way through our first few dates."

"You and Andre? Arguing?"

"Oh, my dear, we had so much to learn about each other. I think that always produces conflict, especially in two passionate people. Oh, there's a taxi. Let's try to flag it down."

Cole was waiting when we arrived at the apartment building. And not very patiently by the looks of it.

"Madeline!" he exclaimed in surprise when she slid gracefully out of the taxi.

"My darling, I have to run. But I just had to give you a hug and kiss and tell you what a wonderful time I've had with your Abby today. I'll let her tell you all about it. I am very late as usual."

"Where on earth did you run into Madeline?" Cole asked as soon as her taxi had pulled away.

"I didn't exactly run into her. I called her. I thought that now might be a good time for her to take a look at Olivia's work. Since Olivia lives in the area, I mean."

Cole gave me one of his mightiest scowls. "I thought I made it clear that you weren't supposed to bother Madeline about this girl?"

I made a show of studying him while I tapped my finger on my chin. "You know, you're too tall for a Napoleon complex. You can't tell me what to do. Besides, it was now or never. Olivia's money has run out. Another day or two and she might have been on her way back to the States."

"If it was a matter of now or never, then I think it should have been never," Cole said harshly.

"And I think you should discuss that with Madeline. Madeline actually liked Olivia's work—despite the fact that Olivia is in the same kind of snit that you're in right now. Artistic temperament is flowing all over the place in the Quartier Latin today. Luckily, Madeline has known you long enough to know how to deal with it."

"Very funny. Now tell me what I'm doing in the Latin Quarter, anyway."

"You're here to see the apartment I found for you."

"Is this some kind of joke?" he demanded.

"A joke? Of course not. Why would you say that?"

"Well, for one thing, this is not the Trocadèro."

"Well, no. It's the Latin Quarter, but the apartment is just so much better than any of the other places the agent showed me."

"You do realize that this means I'd have to drive through the city every time I had to go out to Versailles?"

"Well, yes, but I think the quality of life in this area would make up for that small inconvenience."

He frowned. "That's the first time I've heard Paris traffic referred to as a 'small inconvenience'. But, now that I'm here, let's have a look at it."

"Isn't that door knocker the coolest?" I asked as I unlocked the main door.

"Abby," he said wearily, "I could really care less about the door knocker."

"Oh, well—"

"Where's the elevator?"

"There isn't one."

"No elevator?" he boomed in a voice loud enough that I heard a door on the second floor open and saw an older woman peer down the stairs at us.

"It's only on the fourth floor, Cole. The stairs will do you good. Better than time at any gym. In fact, did you know that's one of the ways that the Fontaines stay in such spectacular shape? They live in a walk-up."

"I'm well aware of where they live," Cole said as he started to climb.

"See?" I said when we'd reached the fourth floor. "You're barely winded."

"Abby, I'm fifty-six years old. I deserve an elevator."

"You'll get used to it in no time. Believe me, your cardiologist will thank me."

"And I'll be cursing you every time I have to carry home groceries."

"That's another thing. There are cafés and bistros everywhere and a *boulangerie* and *fromagerie* right across the street. You just have to get one of those cute string bags and bring home fresh whatever you want to eat that night. Very healthy," I added when he seemed unmoved by my little speech.

He sighed and I started to feel some real apprehension. "Just unlock the door, Abby."

I unlocked the door and stepped back.

"Good lord, it's pink!"

I grimaced. "Well—not really."

"No? What color do they call that in Willow Creek?"

"Um—I don't think we have that color in Willow Creek."

"I'm guessing that'd be a safe bet."

Okay, this wasn't going as I'd planned. I started to rush around, pointing out the fireplaces, the balcony, the huge kitchen.

He leaned in the doorway, clearly unconvinced.

"You're wasting my time. I've got work to do."

My heart sank. It suddenly became clear to me that I'd picked out this apartment for *me*. It had been me I'd pictured at the sink in the kitchen and on the balcony. Fine, fine it had been me and Cole. How foolish could a woman my age get?

"Are you coming!" he said as he scowled from the doorway.

I quietly walked past him and down to the car.

"I'm sorry," I said on the way back to the hotel.

He grunted.

"I guess I got carried away."

He grunted again.

At the hotel he gave me the silent treatment all the way up to the seventh floor. I gave up. Once inside the suite he mumbled something about having work to do and shut himself up in his bedroom.

Not even bothering to turn any lights on in the sitting room, I retreated into my room, as well. I remembered what Olivia and

Rachel had said to me that first night. There was no reason I couldn't take a year to live in Paris just as they had. Of course, if I did, there would be no way I could afford that apartment on my own, anyway, even if I took Madeline up on her job offer. But there were cheaper apartments to be had. There were possibilities open to me. Other choices I could make. My family would always need me, but being needed like that wasn't enough anymore. I wanted to be needed the way a man needed a woman.

Damn it. I was feeling miserable. I should have stayed in Willow Creek where I belonged. I'd been right all those years ago when I'd gone back. When I returned this time, everything would probably go back to being exactly the way it had always been. My time in Paris would grow dimmer with each passing year and I'd eventually wonder if it had been nothing but a bittersweet dream.

I undressed and put on my flannel pajamas. When I went to hang my beautiful white suit in the closet, I saw the Dior gown hanging there. I ran my hand over it. How I'd wanted to wear it to the Silver Ball tomorrow night. No chance of that now, I thought. Mr. Big Shot Architect was surely way too angry to take me anywhere.

And the Widow Blake from Willow Creek had wanted to, just once, play Cinderella.

And guess what? She was going to! This Cinderella wasn't going back home until she'd danced with the prince!

I flung open my bedroom door and marched to Cole's room where I rapped hard on the door.

"What?" he demanded.

"Get out here! I want to talk to you."

The door opened and he stood there, wearing flannel pajamas that weren't all that different than my own.

"You're wearing flannel pajamas," I said.

"Is that what you pounded on my door to tell me?"

"Uh—no. I just figured you for black silk or something."

"Sorry to disappoint," he said grimly.

I grinned. "Actually, it's not a disappointment at all."

He raked a hand through his hair impatiently. "Abby, what do you want?"

"I want to go to that ball tomorrow night. So if you're sitting in there brooding, thinking that because I screwed up your life again you're going to get out of taking me, well, you're wrong."

"I have every intention of taking you to that ball tomorrow night." He started walking toward me. "Just like I have every intention of kissing you right now."

"You—um—do?"

He grabbed me and pulled me up against him. "You think it was easy going to bed by myself last night?"

"Then why did you?"

"Because we'd both had a lot to drink. I wanted to make sure it was me that was making you tremble out on that balcony last night and not the wine."

I gave him a little grin. "I guess there's only one way to find out."

"Yes, there is," he said gruffly.

And then he kissed me. Long, hard, expertly. When he finally took his mouth from mine, he murmured, "You're trembling, Abby."

"I know," I whispered. "And I haven't had a drop of wine all day."

This time when I thrust my hand into his hair and pulled his mouth down to mine he moaned and I felt something inside of me break free. Break free? Hell, it exploded.

Before I knew it we were at each other's buttons and flannel was flying all over the gilt furniture. His hands on my breasts made me gasp with pleasure. I didn't even have time to think about the wonder bust treatment before he had his mouth on me, teasing one nipple until it was hard and throbbing and then moving on to the other one. I ran my hands over his chest, feeling the coarse hair that curled there. I ran my hands up his arms, the muscles, the tension, measuring the broadness of his shoulders with my palms. I ran my hands down his back then grabbed a handful of his long, glittering hair to bring his head up so I could kiss him again, so I could bring him closer and feel his chest against my bare breasts. I cried out into his mouth at the feel of it—my taut nipples against the coarse, curly hair on his chest.

"Abby," he said hoarsely. "I want you to come to my bed."

I wasn't going to argue. I needed him inside of me with the kind of ache I thought I'd never feel again.

We kissed all the way into his room, our tongues seeking, our hands unable to get enough. There was no hesitation as he brought me down to the bed with a gracefulness that belied the passion that was pulsing between us.

"Don't make me wait," he said.

"No—now. I want it now."

He thrust into me, sinking into the slickness of my body. So ready. I felt like I'd been ready for him for years. When he started to move inside of me my body met his every thrust, trying to hold him there with my pulsing muscles so that it was almost a battle between us, both of us demanding, both of us hanging on to a tiny thread of control, unwilling to let it go and have it end too soon until finally our bodies took over and left us with no choice at all.

In the end we both won—his heat pouring into me just as I lost all control.

When our bodies stilled, I heard his soft laughter. I rested my head back on the pillow and looked at him.

"You continue to surprise me, Abby," he said.

"Does that mean I've earned the clothes even though you didn't like the apartment?"

He laughed again. "After that, I could almost say yes to pink walls."

"Let me work on that," I said as I started to kiss my way down his body.

His laughter turned into a gasp then a moan.

As I took him into my mouth, I felt powerful, alive and totally in love.

"If you keep smiling all day like that, people will know we've become lovers," I said the next morning over breakfast.

He raised one of his dark eyebrows. "Would that be such a bad thing?"

I thought it over. I was fifty-two and unattached. If I wanted a lover, I should be able to have a lover.

I grinned. Abby Blake had a lover.

"Now who's smiling?"

I laughed.

"How hungry are you?" he asked as he watched me start to eat my breakfast.

"Why?"

"Because I don't think I can wait until after the ball tonight to make love to you again."

I put my fork down. "Then I'm not hungry at all," I said.

Two hours later, Cole left the suite for another meeting and I spent some time gazing out a window, studying the morning sun. I was in love with more than Cole. I was also in love with Paris. How was I going to bear leaving either one of them?

I decided to pull a Scarlett O'Hara and think about it tomorrow. I'd been gone for a week; I should try calling home again. It was right that I got reconnected and found out how everyone was doing. It would be Christmas in a few days. Was I really going to spend it away from my family? Yet how could I bear spending it away from Cole?

The clock told me it was three in the afternoon in Paris, which made it eight in the morning in Willow Creek. Perfect. The grandkids hadn't even left for school yet and Natalie never went to work this early. Surely, someone would answer the phone.

When I called home, once again I got a computerized voice telling me that the answering machine was full. That meant Gwen probably still hadn't come to her senses and that Jeremy was probably still keeping the sofa anchored to the living room floor. But where were the grandkids and where was Natalie?

I looked at the phone. Maybe I should call Iris or Jo. See what they knew. Hell, didn't they have a right to know that I was in Paris and going to a ball tonight? After all, as fellow prisoners, they had a stake in this, too. The more I thought about it, the more excited I got. Yes, this was the kind of thing I had to share with them.

I called the diner.

"Jo!" I exclaimed when she answered the phone. "Guess where I am?"

"Um—can you hold on a second?" she asked. She was gone before I even got a chance to answer.

What was going on? I'd been gone for seven days now and one of my best friends puts me on hold when I finally call? While I waited I could hear all sorts of noises in the background—plates clanking, people chattering, waitresses calling in orders. It sounded like everyone in Willow Creek had decided to go out for breakfast on the same morning.

Suddenly the noises were muffled and Jo came back on the line. "Abby?" she whispered.

"Of course it's Abby. What's going on?"

"I can't really talk right now, but where the hell are you?"

"I'm in Paris! And I'm going to a ball tonight and I've got the most fantastic Dior gown!"

"Abby—have you seen the Chicago papers lately?"

"The Chicago papers? Well, no. Why? What's happening?" My heart suddenly felt as if it'd been grabbed by a bulldozer's shovel. "Are the kids all right?"

"Yes—yes. Everyone is fine. Thriving, in fact."

"Why are you whispering?"

"There are people here that I'm not sure you want—um—to know where you are. Just get the Chicago papers, hon. I gotta go—"

And with that she hung up.

I couldn't let it go at that, though. I intended to see what information I could get out of Iris, but before I could place the call, the phone rang. It was the spa downstairs, calling to remind Madame of her appointment.

Madame decided she'd better get a move on. I was getting the works. Manicure, pedicure—I decided I needed silver polish to go with my gown—the wonder bust treatment, a body scrub and the sixty-minute cocktail makeup application. There was no time to waste.

I dressed in the taupe trousers and a cream-colored cashmere sweater and headed down to the lobby. Before going to the spa, I stopped at the news kiosk and enquired about the Chicago papers. I was told that they were already sold out so I made arrangements with the concierge to have tomorrow's editions delivered to the suite.

My time at the spa was so relaxing I nearly fell asleep during my wonder bust treatment. I watched carefully, though, while the cosmetician applied my makeup. I was hoping I'd be able to recreate it myself so I bought all of the products they used.

By the time I returned to the suite, Cole was already there, his hair still wet from a shower, wearing nothing but one of the hotel's fluffy white towels wrapped around his waist.

"I was wondering where you'd gone off to. I was about to get dressed and go searching every cellar club in the Latin Quarter for you."

I laughed. "I was down at the spa, getting the works for tonight."

"Yes," he murmured, "I did think you looked even more beautiful when you just came in."

"Amazing what several hours and a few hundred euros can do."

"Come over here," he said, "and I'll show you how amazing it is what a fifty-six-year-old man can undo."

I went over to him, but mostly because I wanted to run my fingers through his long, wet hair and kiss his still damp chest.

"I have no intention of getting mussed. You're just going to have to wait until after the ball to undo me, dear," I said primly as I pulled away from him. "It's getting late and we have to drive all the way out to Versailles, remember? We should try to get there early to lend our support to Madeline and Andre."

Cole looked up at the ceiling and sighed. "One night and already she's trying to run my life."

"Oh, no—you don't have to worry about that. I'm still on strike. But I have no intention of being late for my first—and probably only—Paris ball. Now go get ready. If we don't dawdle, we might have time for a cocktail before we leave."

"Good lord, I'm having an affair with a woman who says *holy cow* and *dawdle*."

"And you said you were too old a dog to learn new tricks," I teased as I floated past him on the wings of that word *affair*. At least we were on the same page. We were both thinking of our involvement as an affair. But did that mean it would carry on once I went home? Would he want to see me when he came back to Chicago for business or to visit David? Would he want me to come to Paris sometime in the future, maybe when they broke ground for the Fontaine's museum?

My head was whirling with questions—none of them askable—or answerable—at the moment. Instead, I opened the drawer of my bedside table and took out the CD of seventies love songs I'd bought that night at the Mega-mart and slipped it into the bedroom's sound system, programming it to play song number four.

"Baby I'm-A Want You" by the pop group Bread came out of the speakers. This time there was no longing, nothing yearning to break free. There was only excitement and anticipation as I started to get ready for the ball.

Believe me, I looked a whole lot better than I had on prom night. Maybe it was the Dior. Maybe it was the makeup session. Maybe it was because I was in love. I leaned closer to the mirror to clip on the vintage crystal earrings that Olivia had helped me choose, picked up my organza evening bag, and went out into the sitting room.

Cole was waiting for me, looking handsome and dashing in a classic black tuxedo, his long silver hair drawn back from his strong face into a ponytail.

"You look incredible," he said.

"Thank you. So do you."

"Tell me who bought you that dress so I can challenge him to a duel," he growled playfully.

"Abby bought herself this dress—with the help of her friend Olivia," I said with a smile of pure pride. "She knows all the best places to go if you don't have a lot of money to spend."

"Olivia again." He sighed. "Well, I suppose if she helped you pick out that dress, then I might have to reconsider my assessment of her."

"You mean the famously arrogant architect, Cole Hudson, might be wrong about something?"

He groaned theatrically but there was laughter in his eyes. "Even worse. I think he might have finally met his match."

CHAPTER 9

I was stunned as we turned into the long drive to the Fontaine Estate. The bare branches of the trees that lined the drive met in the middle to form a canopy and they were covered in glittering fairy lights. It was like driving through a tunnel of stars. There were illuminated silver stars hanging in every window of the house and more lights entwined around the banisters and balustrades leading to the entrance. It was the most beautiful thing I think I'd ever seen. And I was suddenly scared to death.

Cole took my hand. "Abby, you're trembling again. Don't tell me that Christmas decorations set you on fire the same way I do."

"Those aren't trembles—those are shivers of fear."

Cole scowled. "Fear? Of what?"

"Cole, this might come as a surprise to you, but we don't have many balls in Willow Creek. I'm not even sure of ball etiquette."

Cole laughed.

"I mean it. My one formal dance ended in disaster and several ruined prom dresses."

He tucked my hand into his arm. "You'll do fine."

"Seriously, I think I'll just wait in the car."

Cole threw back his head and laughed with that abandoned richness I'd learned to love. And, somehow, I stopped trembling.

I slipped my hand out of his arm and drew his arm around me to snuggle up at his side.

"I thought you were worried about getting mussed?"

I shrugged. "If I go in wrinkled, maybe no one will notice when I spill something."

His held me closer. "Abby, I've spent the past week with you and as far as I know, you have yet to spill a drop of anything."

I leaned my head on his shoulder and thought about it.

"You know, I think you're right."

"We're not meant to live our lives by our mistakes, Abby, but by our triumphs."

I pulled away from him and took his strong, handsome face into my hands. This was the man I had thought was too arrogant, too larger than life. Okay, so it was true. He *could* be arrogant and he *was* larger than life. But he was also smart, wise, funny and generous. And he'd turned my strike into an adventure I'd never forget.

"What is it, Abby?" he asked me softly.

"Thank you," I said. And then I kissed him. And not once did it cross my mind that I might be ruining my sixty minute cocktail makeup session.

The driver pulled to a stop at the base of the steps leading to the mansion's main entrance. I had enough time to grab a tissue from my bag and wipe my lipstick from Cole's mouth before the driver came around and opened the door for us. Cole got out then reached for my hand to help me from of the limousine. I could hear the elegant swish of the skirt of my dress as we moved up the stone stairs of the mansion.

Madeline and Andre met us at the door. Madeline's tiny frame was covered with silver silk only a shade darker than her hair—a simple floor-length sheath with long, narrow sleeves and a neckline designed to show off an amazing choker of diamonds set in white gold. Andre was wearing black tails. He looked like a benevolent king.

"My dear," Madeline said, "you look *très* beautiful. That gown—" She leaned closer to me. "Dior?" she asked in a whisper.

I nodded happily. "Vintage," I said.

"Someday you must tell me where you came upon it, but now I'd like to introduce you and Cole to a few people."

She walked arm-and-arm with me through the immense entrance hall where a huge Christmas tree, all decorated in silver ornaments, welcomed us with the fragrance of fresh evergreen. Swags of greenery hung from large silver organza bows above every doorway and all along the banister of the grand and gracefully curved open staircase.

At the vast archway to the ballroom, we paused. There were already several couples dancing to the full orchestra playing from a raised dais farther into the room. Sparkling silver stars hung from the ceiling and more greenery, woven with wide swaths of silver organza, was wrapped around every marble pillar.

"Imagine growing up in a house with a ballroom," I murmured.

"Andre and his brothers used to ride their tricycles in here when they were children," Madeline confided as we stopped at the first group of guests.

The introductions made my head whirl. There were counts and countesses. Lords and ladies. Even a prince and a princess from countries I'd never even heard of. But there were also women with Texan accents who looked like Iris might have done their hair and men who looked like they'd be more comfortable in blue jeans than tuxedos. It was a blessing to have Cole at my side. He seemed to be totally in tune with my emotions because every time I got a little nervous or answered a question about myself hesitantly, he squeezed my hand more warmly in his.

"That's enough of that for now," Madeline finally declared, after we'd met a sheik whose name I wouldn't even try to pronounce let alone remember. "There are people here that Cole already knows and I'll leave it up to him to introduce you. But now I think we all deserve a break. And some champagne! I haven't had my first glass yet."

"Well, we're definitely going to have to do something about that," Cole said as he beckoned a waiter over. I marveled at how the waiter was able to carry a heavy silver tray of filled champagne flutes in the palm of one hand. It made me nervous just to watch his progress over to our group.

Cole picked up a flute from the tray and handed it to Madeline. Andre did the same for me, but just as he handed it to me, my heel caught in the hem of my dress and I started to trip, heading straight for the back of a woman in a dress crusted with silver sequins. Welcome to prom night, I thought in a panic. But Cole caught me with one arm around my waist as gracefully as if he were leading me into a dance. Not one drop of champagne spilled. Our gazes met, his eyes glittering into mine. After that, what could possibly go wrong? This was my night.

"Thank you," I whispered to Cole.

His arm still firmly around my waist, he leaned close to me and murmured, "Any time."

If only, I thought. *If only*.

But we were together now, and now is what mattered. But, I also had an obligation to fulfill.

"As long as we're all together," I said, "and we all have champagne, would you mind if we toasted my friends?"

"Ah, the fellow prisoners," Andre said.

"This is the perfect time, is it not?" Madeline added. "And the perfect place."

I smiled my thanks at her and raised my flute. "To Jo and Iris," I said, looking up at the silver stars glittering overhead. "Dreams really do come true."

"To dreams," Cole added.

The four of us clinked glasses and drank. I felt a lump rise in my throat as I thought of everyone I'd left back home. But I wouldn't trade this past week for anything. It had been *my* time, and I'd seized it with everything I had in me.

Andre and Madeline excused themselves to attend to other guests and Cole took me into his arms and we began to dance. Our bodies moved as well together on the dance floor as they had last night when we'd made love. As we whirled beneath those thousands of stars, I felt like Cinderella. Only better. Cinderella had only gotten a glass slipper. The look in Cole's eyes told me I was going to get a whole lot more than that before the night was over.

"You look like a gorgeous Christmas present that I can't wait to unwrap," he murmured as he held me close.

"Just don't tear the wrapping. I want to keep this dress for the rest of my life so when I'm eighty I can occasionally get it out and remember how I went to a ball in Paris on the arm of a handsome architect."

He moved his head to look into my face. "You talk as if it's over."

"It almost is."

He frowned. And then he kissed me. A sweet, soft, lingering kiss. And all the while the music played and we kept dancing.

"I think people are looking at us," I said when I broke the kiss.

"Let them."

He bent his head to kiss me again but I laughed and stepped away, grabbing his hand and leading him off the dance floor.

"We'd better find something else to occupy our mouths for a while before we get too carried away."

"Such as?"

"Such as by eating something off that lovely-looking buffet over there."

We filled small silver plates with gorgeous delicacies. We sipped glass after glass of champagne. When we finished eating, Cole took me around to meet people. I heard several languages as we moved from group to group. Cole never failed to introduce me and fill me in a on the guests' backgrounds. I couldn't have had a better escort. Everyone seemed to know him and he seemed to know everyone.

When the orchestra stopped playing, Andre and Madeline announced their plans for the Fontaine Foundation and talked about all they hoped to accomplish and how much help they would need from their many friends and fellow art lovers. Then they called Cole over to stand with them and announced that he was donating his talents to the project. As everyone applauded I felt the warmth of pride in him flow through me.

When the orchestra started to play again, Andre claimed Cole and took him over to a group of men.

"They'll be discussing business," Madeline told me. "Come.

I will sneak away from my guests long enough to give you a tour of what was once our home."

We left the ballroom and crossed the massive entry hall again. This time we went the other way and she led me to a hallway under the stairs. At the end of the hallway, she opened a door onto a small but lovely dining room.

"This was our family dining room," she told me. "So much more cozy than the formal dining room. And it is right off the kitchen. I used to love to cook for Andre and the children."

I was betting they didn't eat boxed macaroni and cheese.

She took me up a back staircase and showed me a large casual sitting room, scattered with several pieces of worn, comfortable-looking furniture. A huge stone fireplace took up nearly an entire wall.

"This is where we really lived. Not the rest of the house. Our bedrooms were on this floor, also, in another wing. But it was this sitting room and Andre's study that were the heart of our home."

I pictured younger versions of Madeline and Andre sitting there with their children at night—doing homework, playing games. Much as I had done with my girls.

"Come," Madeline said, leading me over to one of the sofas, "let's sit down for a few minutes. If I don't take these shoes off soon, my feet are certain to rebel."

I laughed. "Sounds good to me." So I joined her.

"You know," Madeline said as she gazed around, "I loved this room. No matter what any of us was involved with, we seemed to always end up here. There'd be a roaring fire and usually music playing. The game table over there would always be covered with the children's projects."

"Was it hard to leave all of this, Madeline? I mean, it sounds like there are so many memories in these rooms."

She shook her head. "I am seventy-two, my dear. My life has been through many stages—as every woman's life goes through. I've always believed in embracing those changes. Besides, we take our memories with us, do we not, no matter where we go? The past—it is beautiful to remember. But each stage of life has its own richness—its own rewards. Andre and I are very happy in our Paris apartment. We are like newly-weds, almost. Discovering the city again. Discovering each other again."

"You're so lucky to still have each other," I said. "What will happen to these family rooms now that the rest of the house will be open to the public?"

"You know, I have never really thought about it. I do not think our children would care to stay here anymore—and Andre and I have learned to prefer Paris." She shrugged her thin shoulders. "I suppose they will sit here, empty."

"That seems like a shame—and kind of a waste. Maybe you could turn them into a luxury apartment. Rent it out to honey-mooners or visiting dignitaries or really, really rich art lovers." I shrugged. "I don't know—there might be a lot of people who would want to experience living in a place like this for a short while. It would be another way to earn money for the foundation."

"Abby! That is an excellent idea!" She took my hands in hers and squeezed them. "See? I knew you were a woman full of wonderful ideas. I do hope you'll give serious consideration to coming to work at the foundation. We can use someone with fresh thoughts."

When I didn't say anything, she added, "I think Cole would want you to stay, too."

"What makes you say that?"

"You have become lovers, have you not, since I saw you yesterday?"

I looked at her in astonishment. "How could you know that?"

She shrugged. "There is something new in the way he touches you. In the way you move together. In the sound of his voice when he speaks your name."

"And what gave me away?"

"Your eyes. You can always tell from a woman's eyes if she is looking at the man she loves."

"I never said I was in love with him."

Her laugh rang like tiny bells. "You don't have to say it, Abby. I am a woman with a heart. I can see it."

"Being with Cole this week has been terrific, but there could never be anything lasting between us."

"Why ever not?"

"Because I'm from Willow Creek, Wisconsin."

"Nonsense. I come from a town in the countryside that you've never heard of. That no one has heard of. What does where you are from matter? It's where you end up that counts. Which reminds me—oh, how could I have forgotten this long? I have something exciting to tell you! Andre and I have discussed it and we have decided that we are going to do what we can for your Olivia. It will take too long for a grant to help her, but we have decided to personally mentor her."

"Oh, Madeline—you have no idea what that means to me! Have you told Olivia yet?"

"I sent a courier over to her rooms with enough money for

her rent and to get her phone reconnected along with a note telling her of our decision."

I sniffed.

"Oh, my dear, do not cry! You will ruin your makeup. Besides, if I take you back to the ballroom with red eyes, Cole will be very displeased, I think."

"I'm so very grateful. You've been wonderful about this, Madeline."

"Nonsense. It is what I love to do. And lucky for me, I have a rich husband, which allows me to do it. Now, come. I must return to my guests."

We slipped our shoes on and walked arm-and-arm back to the ballroom.

When we arrived, Madeline was immediately swept away by guests and I found an empty spot near a series of arched glass doors that overlooked the gardens. I was glancing around the ballroom, hoping to spot Cole. I was so excited for Olivia and I couldn't wait to tell Cole about Madeline and Andre's decision.

Suddenly, someone grabbed my hand and pulled me behind a pillar.

"Where on earth have you been?" Cole demanded. "I was beginning to worry that you'd run off with a man with a bigger plane than mine."

"Madeline was showing me the family's quarters," I said.

He was examining my face. "You look too much like the cat who swallowed the canary for me to buy that explanation."

"Well," I said, trying to hold down my excitement, "it's true. That's where we were. But—"

"Aha—I knew there had to be a *but* coming."

I threw my arms around his neck. "Oh, Cole, Madeline just told me that she and Andre are going to mentor Olivia. She'll be able to stay in Paris and study, after all."

"So, your tenacity has paid off once again. And now I think I'd better go check out that buffet table again."

"What for?"

"To see if they have any crow. It seems I'm going to be eating some."

"I'd rather you danced with me instead."

"Ah, tenacious and forgiving," he said as he took me into his arms and we began to sway to the music. "I always knew you were a rare one, Abby."

I laughed with pure joy but he caught my open mouth with his. When he'd thoroughly kissed me he said, his voice husky with the desire that I was feeling in my lower belly, "Let's get the hell out of here. We have better things to do."

"Isn't it too early to leave? I mean, you're sort of the guest of honor."

He raised one of his dark brows. "Don't tell me the newly irresponsible Abby Blake is going to turn responsible again."

"I wouldn't dream of it," I said.

"I want you, Abby," he whispered, his mouth at my ear. "I want to take you out of here," he said while the band played something perfectly staid and classical, "and have you in the back of the limousine."

My breath caught in my throat.

"I want to hear you cry out my name as we drive under that canopy of lights," he murmured against my throat before he pressed his mouth against my pulse.

The muscles in my lower belly actually quivered.

"And I want to make sure that you never, ever think of Neil Diamond when I'm inside of you."

I burst out laughing and so did he. Then we went and found our host and hostess, bid them good-night and headed for the limo.

Where he *did* have me in the backseat. Where I *did* cry out his name under the canopy of lights. And where I thought of no one—or nothing—but Cole.

By the time we got back to the hotel, we were hungry for each other again. We barely made it to the suite before we started undressing each other in the golden glow of the table-top tree.

"You're not on Viagra or anything, are you?" I asked breathlessly as he pulled my gown off my shoulders.

He laughed. "No, I'm on *Abby*. Or I'm going to be—very soon."

I laughed, too, but then he ripped off my strapless bra and covered my breasts with his hands and I stopped laughing and started breathing heavily. He lowered his head and while his mouth did amazing things to my newly firmed breasts, I said, "It's—um—it's that you're so—well—"

He nipped one of my nipples and I squealed with pleasure and started to tear off his shirt.

"*Hot for you*, I believe is the clinical term for it."

"Works for me," I said breathlessly as he dragged me down to the floor.

We soon learned there were drawbacks to trying to make love on the floor when you're over fifty. Especially if you've just done it in the backseat of a limo while dressed in formal wear.

Cole got to his feet. "To my bed," he said as he held out his hand.

I put my hand in his and he pulled me up.

I'm sure if I would have thought about it, I would have chosen to grab something to cover up with. But my mind was too filled with the sight of Cole, totally naked, in the glow of the nearby Christmas tree. He might be fifty-six, but he was a magnificent fifty-six.

Of course, while I'd been looking my fill, he'd been doing the same thing. When our eyes met, his silver ones were gleaming.

"You don't even have any idea how beautiful you are, do you?"

"Show me," I whispered.

He led me to his bed. And everything he did and said to me there made me feel like the strongest, most beautiful woman in the world.

While I lay in his arms afterwards, my stomach growled.

You can take the girl out of Willow Creek, I thought— "Sorry," I said, "but all those little things we ate at the ball didn't exactly fill me up. I'm starving."

"Why didn't you say so?" Cole reached for the phone.

We ordered nearly everything on the late-night menu. There were paper-thin crepes with strawberries and whipped cream. There were medallions of tenderloin crusted with cracked pepper and topped with a butter-rich blue cheese sauce and served with stalks of grilled asparagus. There was a terrine of layered pâté and vegetables served with the inevitable crusty baguette and there was a footed plate filled with beautiful miniature pastries.

I looked at the feast and said, "Maybe we should have told them to send up silverware for six."

Cole frowned. "Whatever for?"

"So they wouldn't think that only two people were going to pig out on all this."

Cole's mouth quirked. "You're the woman who cried out my

name in the back of a limousine a few hours ago. What do you care what people think?"

I gasped. "You know it never occurred to me that the driver could hear us!"

Cole shrugged. "We did the guy a favor. Now he's got a good story to swap with his cronies back at the limo garage."

"Hmm, then I guess we gave them a good story down in the hotel kitchen, too, so we might as well dive in."

We spread out a picnic on Cole's bed—me wearing his flannel pajama top, he in the bottoms—turned the television on and watched an old romantic comedy, dubbed in French, while we ate.

"You know, I think this movie might be better in French," I said before Cole fed me a forkful of tenderloin.

"That might be because you don't understand a word of the dialogue."

"That would certainly help with this bomb."

I grabbed the remote and turned the television off then took my time choosing a pastry.

"Something on your mind?" Cole asked as he lay down and put his arms behind his head.

I bit into a small cake covered in pink fondant. It was creamy chocolate inside. "Mmm, here, try this."

Cole opened his mouth and I popped what was left of the cake in. While he chewed, I ran my hands over his chest. Hmm, and here I thought I didn't particularly like men with hairy chests.

"Abby?"

"Yes?"

"Something's on your mind, isn't it?"

"Aside from you?"

He laughed. "Aside from me. You were off with Madeline for quite a while. What did you talk about? Other than Olivia's good fortune, that is."

"And her talent. Don't forget her talent."

"I will never forget her talent again. And I'm sure if I ever do, you'll happily remind me."

I smiled and lay down next to him. It had been years since I'd been naked with a man. I never would have dreamed that I could be with a man like this and feel so comfortable, so free. I felt his fingers in my hair, massaging slowly near my scalp.

"Madeline," I said, "offered me a job with the foundation."

His fingers stilled on my scalp. Did I just make a big mistake telling him? And especially under these circumstances—naked and tangled?

"What did you tell her?"

"I told her I didn't know. That I had to go home first and see how my children were doing."

"You have to let go of them sometime, Abby. They're adults now."

I raised myself on my elbow. "Oh, is that why you flew to Willow Creek to try to get my daughter to go back to your son? Because you'd let go?"

For a moment, I thought I'd blown it, but Cole laughed and said, "Touché."

I grinned and popped another pastry into my mouth.

"That's it," I said, "I'm stuffed."

"Not too full for another round, I hope," Cole said.

My eyes widened. "You can't be serious?"

"Sorry," he said, his mouth twisting into a half smile. "I can't seem to get enough."

Like that was anything to be sorry for. Because, suddenly, I wanted more, too.

"I'll have to get on top this time," I said, worried about how my belly full of French food would handle another romp.

"A sacrifice I'm more than willing to make," he confessed.

I didn't go back to my own room at all that night.

When I woke up I was alone in Cole's bed. I checked the sitting room. He'd already left to run some errands, his note said, but I didn't mind because his note also mentioned a few of last night's activities that he'd especially enjoyed. In case I needed another reminder, my lovely vintage Dior gown was draped across the arm of a chair like it'd been tossed there by an impatient lover. Which it had. Cole's tuxedo hadn't fared much better. I laughed with joy as I went around the sitting room picking up bits and pieces of our clothing.

I went to my room to brush my teeth and wash my face. I pulled Cole's pajama top off and slipped into my robe. Then I ordered breakfast. Room service assured me that it would be at least a half hour wait so I dashed back to my bathroom and took a quick, hot shower.

I ached from head to toe and the multisprays of hot water felt good on my muscles. When I thought about why I ached, my body ripened again, swelling with brand-new desire.

"Unbelievable," I murmured as I let hot water pour on my face.

Nothing, for me, had ever been this way before. It felt so wonderful to just be alive.

I was towel-drying my hair when there was a rap on the door. I opened it and the waiter came in with a large tray full of covered dishes that he spread out on the dining room table for me. As he left, he picked up some newspapers outside the suite's door and handed them to me with a smile.

I put the papers aside and poured myself some coffee and slathered butter on a brioche. I felt both relaxed and tired—but the good kind of tired. The kind that comes after something special. Like a ball in Paris and making love with a world-famous architect all over the place, I thought with a smile.

"Abby," I murmured, "who would have thought the first time you ever did it in the back of a car you'd be fifty-two years old?"

Gently laughing to myself, I picked up one of the papers and that's when I noticed it was the *Chicago Tribune*. Suddenly, I remembered the odd conversation I'd had with Jo the day before.

Between bites of brioche and sips of coffee I started to read the headlines of one of the two Chicago dailies. Politics. Crime. The economy. And me.

Me?

I put down the brioche and picked up the newspaper for a closer look. It was a picture of me and Cole dancing at the ball last night. I felt immediately relieved. After all, Cole was a well-known Chicago architect involved in a newsworthy project. It wasn't so odd for the paper to have picked up a wire service photo to fill a gap in a slow news day.

And then I read the caption beneath the picture.

Is This Abby Blake Dancing With One Of Chicago's Premiere Architects At A Ball In Versailles?

My gaze swung to the headline for the small article that went with the picture.

Did Striking Mom Run Away To Paris?

"Holy cow," I muttered as I started to read the article. It was all there. How I'd gone on strike against my family and how I'd disappeared one day, leaving a note that I was going to Chicago. A lump rose in my throat as I read about how my daughters had put a personal ad in both Chicago papers that read, in part,

Mom, please come home for Christmas.

Oh, my God, I wondered, what must people be thinking of me?

I picked up the second paper to find a picture of me at the Willow Creek Fourth of July picnic last summer. The headline to the accompanying story read:

What Would Make "Perfect Mom" Run Away?

Perfect mom? Who was claiming that? I certainly wasn't claiming perfection. But as I started to read the story I found out that that was how Gwen and Natalie had referred to me in an interview on one of the Chicago television stations. When I turned to the page where the story was continued, there was a picture of Gwen and Nat—Nat looking teary, Gwen looking stoic, their arms around each other. Supporting each other.

"Our entire family was going through a tough time," Gwen was quoted as saying. "My mother, like a lot of women, just felt taken for granted."

There was also a smaller picture. I recognized my front porch—still in need of painting—and an angry-looking Nat, flipping the bird at a group of reporters and cameramen crowding around her. Of course, the offending digit was blurred, but the message came across loud and clear.

The article went on to say how the population of Willow Creek, Wisconsin, had swollen recently because of all the reporters and photographers who'd flooded the town after the wire services picked up the poignant story of a middle-aged woman who had gone on strike against her family at Christmas.

"You can't even find a parking spot in front of Dempsey's Diner," complained a citizen who wished to remain anonymous.

Talk about cringe-worthy. I scanned the rest of the article, coming to a dead stop when I saw Jo's and Iris's names. They both agreed that I hadn't done anything that most women probably wished they'd had the guts to do. Yet another anonymous source was quoted as saying that I'd been a troublemaker since high school, where I'd single-handedly ruined the junior prom for the class of 1972. There was mention that one of my clients was being audited by the IRS, and speculation about whether that had anything to do with my disappearance. I read on. Holy cow—it was Ivan Mueller who was being audited! He was probably a nervous wreck over it, too. Guilt was piling on top of guilt. I ran to the phone and tried to call home. This time a recorded voice told me that the number had been changed to an unlisted one.

I felt terrible. I'd had no idea what I'd started when I'd taken off that day. I couldn't even imagine what Gwen and Nat were going through—or my grandchildren! The way Willow Creek hung on to its small-town anonymity, I was betting that the whole town was mad at me and my kids and grandkids were probably paying the price. As far as I was concerned, the faster I got home, the better.

I called the concierge and asked him if he could book me on the next flight to Chicago. Then I packed, but since I had more clothes than I did when I came, not everything fit into the Louis Vuitton. I already had two shopping bags of Christmas presents I'd have to carry on so I decided I was going to have to leave the Dior gown behind. Maybe Cole would ship it to me in Willow Creek.

Cole. Where was he? I went to the phone again and dialed his cell number. When the cell started to ring, the sound came from Cole's bedroom. I put the receiver down on the desk and went to investigate. He'd left his cell phone on the charger. I had no idea where he was or how to get in touch with him.

The concierge called to let me know that he'd booked me on a flight that was leaving in four hours.

"How long will it take to drive to de Gaulle Airport?" I asked.

"At least an hour, Madame. And they suggest you check in at least two hours prior."

I looked at the clock. "You'd better order me a taxi right away, then."

I thanked him, hung up and went to get dressed.

My hand hovered above the remaining garments in the closet. The jeans and sweater I'd been wearing when I'd arrived in Paris—and the winter-white Ralph Lauren suit. With only a moment's hesitation, I chose the suit and threw the jeans and sweater into my suitcase. I had to practically sit on it before I could get it zipped, but it was hard enough leaving the Dior gown. I couldn't bear the thought of leaving anything else behind.

But I'd be leaving Cole behind. I would have gladly emptied my suitcase if I could stuff him inside and take him home with me. Would a larger-than-life man fit in the Vuitton—or in Willow Creek? In all the whisperings of the night before, we had never talked about forever.

After I was dressed, I sat at the antique writing table in my room, drew a sheet of the hotel's stationery out of the drawer and started to write a farewell note to Cole. I'd barely begun to explain things when the bellman came to help me with my luggage. My taxi had arrived.

I asked him to wait and hastily finished the note to Cole, took it to the dining table in the sitting room and put it on top of the Chicago papers, open to the pages that I hoped would help explain everything. I grabbed my coat and was almost to the door when I ran back and added

Thanks for being my Prince Charming. I'll never forget our time in Paris.

There wasn't even any time to cry.

I checked in at de Gaulle, found out where my gate was, then got myself a cup of coffee and chose a place to sit and wait. I was wondering if I should try to call someone else in Willow Creek to tell them I was coming home when an angry voice above me growled, "You were just going to leave without talking to me?"

I looked up. Cole was standing over me, one of his mightiest scowls on his face.

"I left a note."

"A note! After what we've shared?"

His voice was booming and people in the airport were starting to notice us.

I stood and put my hand on his arm. "Cole, it's time for me to go home. Time for me to end my strike and face my family—face my life."

"And what about me? Is there no place for me in your life?"

I stared for a moment, unsure if I'd understood. Unsure if I'd heard him correctly. "Cole, what are you saying?"

He shoved one hand into his trouser pocket and pushed one hand into his hair and started to pace in front of me. Finally, he stopped and took me firmly by the shoulders. "What I'm saying is I want to be a part of your life. An important part."

I was shocked.

"Well, don't look so dumbfounded. Surely you must know I love you."

I burst out laughing.

"She laughs," he said in exasperation.

"It's just that—well, it's just so *Cole Hudson* of you to blurt something like that in the middle of a crowded airport when I'm about to board a plane."

He looked away for a few beats, then looked me right in the eyes. "Maybe it's fear, Abby," he said softly.

"Fear?"

"Fear of losing you. Look, I know you don't want to be needed, but I need you, Abby, and I want you."

I smiled. "That's the second line in the song."

"What?" he asked impatiently. "What song?"

"Right after they sing about want, they sing about need. Maybe one isn't possible without the other." I shook my head, knowing I wasn't making any sense. "There's no time now. I'll have to explain it to you later."

"Does that mean you'll come back to me?"

"Oh, Cole. I don't know what to tell you. I don't know what will need fixing or how many people I've hurt—"

My flight number was announced over the loudspeaker.

"All right. I know you're going back to uncertainty. But we can't leave it like this. Unless I'm wrong, of course."

"Wrong about what?"

"Wrong about the fact that you love me, too."

I smiled softly at him and took his face into my hands. "You're not wrong, Cole. I love you."

He gathered me to him and kissed me then, a long, lingering kiss, right there in the middle of Charles de Gaulle Airport.

Above the beating of my heart in my ears, I heard them announce last call for boarding my plane.

"Cole, I've got to go."

He cupped my cheek. "I know. I'm afraid that when you go back there they'll suck you up again and there will be nothing left for me and I'll have to face living with those pink walls all by myself."

"You're taking the apartment?" I asked in astonishment.

"That's where I was this morning, Abby, looking at it again. You were everywhere. You belong in that apartment, Abby. With me."

My eyes filled. "I don't know what to say—"

"Just promise me this—promise me you'll think about coming back to me."

"I promise," I said, the tears building in my throat.

"If you want to try—if you think we have a chance—meet me under the Eiffel Tower at midnight on New Year's Eve."

That's when the tears did start to fall. I gave him a quick, hard kiss and started to run for my gate. I barely had time to look back. But when I did, he was still standing there, watching me go.

CHAPTER 10

It was the day before Christmas Eve and Chicago's O'Hare Airport was crowded with holiday travelers. People scarfing down food between planes. People picking up last-minute gifts in the shops. People drinking, for whatever reason, at the bars. My stomach was aflutter with reentry nerves. I decided I'd be one of the people drinking at the bar.

I hadn't thought about what to order but when the bartender came over I immediately asked for a martini, straight up, with two olives.

I don't think I'd had a martini since Charlie had died. I remember how sophisticated we felt the first time we'd ordered martinis at a restaurant we couldn't really afford to celebrate our first anniversary. We'd nearly spit them out when we'd tasted them. But we refused to give up even that small piece of hard-won sophistication and eventually they became an acquired taste. What had made me order one now?

I suddenly caught sight of myself in the mirror behind the bar. The woman looking at me had a sheen of sophistication that the Widow Blake of Willow Creek never possessed. Is this what I would have ended up looking like if I hadn't moved back to Willow Creek? If Charlie and I had stayed in Milwaukee, would we have kept acquiring the kind of sophistication that was associated with martinis? Those were the days when you had six choices. Gin or vodka. Rocks or straight up. Twist or olives. We were now in another century and martinis came in hundreds of varieties.

Not even ordering a martini was easy anymore.

Choices. Boy, I'd made some dillies lately. What would Charlie have thought of my choices? And what would he have thought of Cole? It was impossible for me to guess because people change. People grow. I had no way of knowing what Charlie, had he lived, would be like now.

My martini came and I took a fortifying gulp. I couldn't think of Cole. There were too many other things to think about. Like were the good citizens of Willow Creek going to run me out of town for turning their tourist-free oasis into a media circus? And had I scarred my daughters for life? They already carried abandonment issues because of losing their father at an early age. Now I'd run out on them and in front of the whole damn world, too.

Not that they were little kids anymore, I reminded myself. They were adults who *should* be able to take care of themselves. The thing is, I'd learned the hard way over the years that when you think the really tough years of parenting are over, the real problems are only beginning. A bad report card, a school yard fight, skipping a class, all turn out to be nothing compared to a daughter losing her home or leaving her husband.

Hadn't I always told Natalie and Gwen that running away from their problems never solved anything? And isn't that exactly what I'd done—run away from my problems?

No, I told myself firmly as I finished off my martini with no urge whatsoever to spit it out. I hadn't been running away from anything. I'd been running toward something. I hadn't known

exactly what at the time, but in the end I'd found Cole, I'd found
Paris and I'd found myself. The self that had just started to
emerge all those years ago before I'd returned to Willow Creek
as soon as an excuse presented itself.

Was I going to be able to hang on to myself and still do the
right thing by my children? And what about my business and
my clients? It wasn't as if Willow Creek were overrun with free-
lance bookkeepers and accountants. Poor Ivan Mueller, one of
the most nervous people I'd ever met, was facing an audit and
his bookkeeper was missing.

I popped the last olive in my mouth. I was still a thirty-
minute plane ride from Willow Creek, but I could already feel
responsibility rushing at me like an incoming tide.

I looked at the clock over the bar. It was time to catch my
plane—the one that would land me at the little airport near Willow
Creek. Back where it all started. But was it back where I belonged?

My station wagon was no longer at the airport where I'd left
it. Which was probably a good thing. Otherwise it would be
buried under a few feet of snow. Willow Creek was definitely
going to be having a white Christmas. It had just turned dark—
that period right after sunset when the sky is so deep blue that
the moonlight tints the snow. The air was crisp and cold and I
could see my breath coming out in clouds.

In Paris, I thought, it might be raining. Gently. That was
one of the things I'd learned—the rain in Paris always seemed
to be gentle.

I started for the small terminal, wishing my new boots didn't
have such high heels as I battled wind and trudged through
snow. Honestly, I don't know how Iris trotted around all winter

in these things. I was just wondering who I could call for a ride home, when I recognized Ernie's taxi dropping someone off.

"Abby Blake? That you?" he asked after I tapped on his taxi's window.

"It's me, Ernie. Can you give me a ride home?"

"You betcha," he said, popping his trunk so I could stow the Vuitton and my shopping bags inside.

I slipped into the front seat with him.

"I hardly recognized you, Abby," he said, not bothering to take the unlit cigar out of his mouth. "You sure look different. Is it true you been in France?"

"Yes, Ernie, it's true."

"Well, hell's bells, woman, why didn't you let people know you were coming back so folks could give you a proper welcome?"

I grimaced. "You mean like toilet paper my house or egg my car?"

"Hell, no. Why'd anyone do that? The whole damn town is making money off of your strike. Those news guys from New York City are big tippers, but—"

"Wait a minute," I interrupted. "News guys from New York City?"

"Yeah. Caused quite a stir when they arrived in town. 'Course when that talk show lady from Chicago sent a couple of producers around asking questions everyone really went nuts."

"Seriously?" I croaked.

Ernie laughed and I marveled anew at how that ubiquitous stogie managed to stay put.

"You got no idea what kind of stir you been causin', do ya?"

"I found out this morning. The Chicago papers said the town had become a media circus. I guess I assumed that it was just the Chicago and Milwaukee media they were talking about—and I figured everyone would be as angry at me as a January blizzard because of it."

"Hell, no. Well, okay, there's always a few folks who put everything down. But most of us are busier than we've been in years. The motels on the highway are full. Dempsey's has started staying open later. Stores are sellin' out of everything. Lots of folks are gonna have one heck of a Christmas 'cause of you, Abby."

I was still trying to process this when we turned onto the street where I lived. The first thing I noticed was that all the bare branches of the barberry bushes lining the porch were glittering with multicolored lights. There was a wreath on the door and an electric candle at every window. Apparently, Christmas had arrived despite my absence. But it looked like something else had arrived, too.

I leaned forward, peering out the taxi's window. Vans clogged the street. CNN. MSNBC. FOX NEWS. The front yard of my old Victorian was crammed with people. I don't think I recognized any of them. Oh, wait—was that the woman from Channel Twelve News? And that gray-haired guy looked an awful lot like that reporter from CNN.

"This is amazing," I said. "I had no idea it was this bad."

Ernie cackled. "You're the holiday story of the year, Abby. Even *People* magazine sent a writer to interview Iris and Jo."

My mouth dropped open. "Holy cow—Iris must have loved that."

"Yeah, her head's gettin' bigger than her hair."

I laughed, which was one thing I didn't think I'd be doing that day.

"How long has this been going on?" I asked, indicating the mess of equipment and people on my snow-covered lawn.

"I'd say it started right after your girls put that personal ad in the *Tribune*."

I groaned. How could I have done this to Gwen and Nat? And how the heck was I going to get out of Ernie's taxi and walk through that sea of vultures? I'd brought it all on myself, though, hadn't I? It was time to face the music, even if I didn't feel like dancing. I took a twenty out of my purse and handed it to Ernie.

"Hey, this one's on me, Abby. I've had the busiest season of my life. In fact, I'd be honored to carry your bags in for you."

I jumped at the offer. "Would you, Ernie? I'd be forever grateful." Running the media gauntlet by myself looked daunting at the very least.

A few people noted when Ernie got out of his taxi, but the stir didn't start until Ernie yelled, "Here she is, folks! Abby Blake has returned from Paris, France!"

Oh, brother. I did my best not to hold it against him when the photographers and reporters started to rush the taxi.

"Gang way! Gang way!" Ernie yelled as he pushed his way through the crowd.

It was surreal to have all those microphones shoved into my face.

"Abby, what made you come back?"

"Abby, what made you leave?"

"Abby, what designer are you wearing?"

"Abby, are you back for good?"

Well, that was one question I couldn't answer even if I'd wanted to.

Ernie elbowed his way past people, pulling the Vuitton behind him, clearing a path for me.

"Abby, can you tell us why you'd go on strike at this time of year?" a woman reporter called out as I started to climb the stairs.

A few pithy answers came to mind. Insanity? Selfishness? Nervous breakdown? When I reached the porch, I stopped and turned around. "No comment," I answered.

Just as I headed toward the house, I noticed movement at one of the curtains in the living room and then the front door was flung open

"Grandma!" Ashley yelled.

I bent and she ran to me and threw her welcoming little arms around my neck.

"Ashley, baby," I said as I lifted her and carried her into the house, keenly aware of the cameras flashing as I shut the door, "how is my girl?"

"We might be on TV, Grandma!"

"TV?"

I didn't have time to say more because the two boys came running down the staircase.

"Grandma!" Tyler yelled. "Did ya see all the cool news trucks outside?"

"Did you see the cameras?" Matt asked. "I want to be a cameraman when I grow up."

"Grandma, where's that pretty dress I saw you wearing in the paper? The one you were wearing in Paris when you danced with Uncle David's daddy?" Ashley wanted to know.

"Wouldn't fit into my suitcase, pumpkin," I said before I turned to Ernie and thanked him for his help. Just before he left, I shoved the twenty into his jacket pocket.

"Mom?"

I put Ashley down and unwrapped her arms from my neck, then straightened to find both of my daughters standing in the doorway to the dining room. I was frozen still, not at all sure of the reception I was going to get. The grandkids were young enough to be excited by it all, but Nat and Gwen—I had no idea what they were feeling at that moment. I tried to brace myself for anything that might come out of their mouths.

Gwen was the first to speak.

"Is that coat a Ralph Lauren?" she asked in an awed tone.

I started to laugh, but Nat pushed Gwen aside and charged toward me.

"What the hell were you *thinking?*" she demanded. "Have you any idea of what you've put us through?" She put her hands on her hips. "Don't you know how worried we've been?"

It was such a parody of what I'd said to her over and over again from the time she was about fourteen until she'd become a mother herself that all I could do was walk up to her and pull her into my arms.

"I'm sorry, baby. I'm sorry you were worried. I guess I was only thinking of myself for a change."

She stood stiffly in my arms for a moment, then she threw her arms around me and let out a sob before she said, "I'm sorry, Ma. I'm sorry for everything I ever put you through."

How typical, I thought, that it was tough Natalie who was crying in my arms while Gwen was busy checking my outfit.

"My God, is this cashmere?" she asked when she touched the sleeve of my coat.

"Wait until you see the suit I'm wearing," I said.

Nat pushed out of my arms. "How can you two talk about clothes at a time like this?"

I took my beautiful, defiant daughter's face into my hands. "I'm sorry, Nat. I'm so sorry you were worried."

She pointed a finger at me. "I swear, if you say *paybacks are a bitch* I'm going to start screaming."

"I didn't do it to pay anyone back or anything remotely like that. I did it for myself."

Nat dashed at an errant teardrop on her cheek. "Okay, *that* I get. But I'm still pissed."

"I did try to call a few times, but the answering machine was full and no one was picking up. And then all of a sudden, the number was changed."

"We finally gave up trying to respond to all the phone calls," Gwen told me. "It was either go totally insane or change the number."

I released Natalie and slipped out of my coat.

"Ohmigod," Gwen gushed. "That suit!"

"Ohmigod," I mimicked, "that tree!"

"Isn't it pretty, Grandma?" Ashley asked.

"Uncle David took us out to cut it down ourselves," Matt said.

"Uncle David?" I asked, raising a brow at Gwen.

Gwen blushed.

"Does this mean you're still together?" I wanted to know.

"I think after Christmas, I'll be going back to Chicago."

"Gwen, that's great," I said as I pulled her into a hug. "I think it's the right thing to do. Now let's have a look at that tree."

We crowded into the living room.

"Daddy held me up and I put the star on the top myself," Ashley said.

A silver star. I smiled. "Ashley, it looks beautiful."

"Mom made us hang all those dumb ornaments we made when we were younger," Matt complained.

I put my arm around his shoulders and drew him close to me. "Those ornaments aren't dumb to me, kid. Every one of them is a treasure."

Matt allowed me to kiss the top of his head, which was getting closer to my shoulder all the time, before he tugged away. That's when I noticed that the rest of the room was decorated, too. My crystal tree collection was on the coffee table. All the different candle sticks I'd found in antique shops over the years scattered around the room and holding snow-white tapers. The hammered-tin baskets I always put out at Christmas for potpourri were filled. It was all there.

"The room looks beautiful," I said.

"We wanted you to have a Christmas to come home to," Gwen said.

"It's more than I deserve."

"Oh, bull," Natalie said. "You deserve this and more."

Gwen went over to the window and pushed aside a curtain.

"I see the mob is still out there." She sighed a little theatrically. "They're probably waiting for me to appear to make a statement. I think I'll go freshen up a bit first, though."

Gwen ran upstairs and I looked at Nat. "She's going to make a statement?"

Natalie rolled her eyes. "Gwen has become the family spokesperson. She gives daily press conferences, Ma. But I gotta tell you, this is one time I don't mind that Gwen has found a way to make it all about her."

I laughed.

"I'm serious," Nat said. "She was born for this moment."

Gwen came flying down the stairs, her face glowing with an application of blush, her lashes darkened with expensive mascara, her hair looking silkier. "I think this occasion calls for me to have my husband at my side, don't you? I mean, I think it would look better. A united front."

"Well, if you want a united front, I could go out there with you," Nat suggested, winking at me over Gwen's head.

Gwen reacted swiftly. "If you even *dare* to come out there, I swear—"

"Hey, chill, sis. I was kidding. I've already made my statement to the press."

"Yes," I said drily, "I believe I saw a picture of your—um—*statement* in a Chicago paper."

"I've never been so embarrassed in my life!" Gwen exclaimed.

"I doubt that," Natalie drawled. "Seems to me you embarrass yourself quite a bit."

"See? It's those kind of statements that make me prefer to have my husband at my side," Gwen said haughtily as she headed through the living room toward my office.

"Is David here?" I asked, my heart beating a little faster at the thought of Cole's son being in the next room.

Nat nodded. "He came last night. He's been real supportive, Ma. I think she might be starting to see how lucky she is."

"Well, thank goodness one good thing came out of my going on strike."

Just then the door to my office opened and Gwen came out with David.

"Abby," he said as he gave me a hug. "I'm glad you're all right. I'm glad you're back."

"Thanks, David." I tightened the hug. This was Cole's son I was holding in my arms. "I'm glad you're back, too."

I watched as Gwen and David went out the front door to face the press.

"Will they be okay out there with that mob?" I asked Natalie.

"Are you kidding? Gwen is having the time of her life. Check this out."

Natalie went over to the television in the living room and turned it on, switching the channel to a cable news show. And there was Gwen, at the railing on our front porch like she was a queen giving an audience to her subjects, with David at her side. She looked radiant. She also looked as if she'd been handling the press all her life. She made a statement that was quite dignified. She said the family wasn't prepared to take questions yet. She said that she hoped that now that her mother had returned for Christmas that they would all do the same thing—return to their families for Christmas.

I shook my head. "She's amazing."

"Hey, you turn a camera on her and she performs," Nat said. "You might want to hire her as your agent, Ma."

"My agent? What would I need an agent for?"

"To help you sort through all the offers pouring in. *Larry King*. *Geraldo*. *Oprah*. *The View*."

I buried my face in my hands and groaned. "Can't things go back to normal?"

"Ma, I get the feeling nothing is ever going to be normal around here ever again."

I took my hands away from my face and looked at Natalie. She had no idea how right she was.

* * *

A few hours later, after we'd dined on hot dogs and canned beans and the grandkids were in bed, all but a few of the die-hard press had given in and left for the night. I was sitting in the living room gazing at the Christmas tree. It was hard to believe that that morning I'd been sitting in a luxurious suite in Paris eating brioche after a night of making love with Cole Hudson.

Nat came in carrying a tray full of cups and a pot of steaming hot chocolate followed by David and Gwen, who were each carrying a small plate of Christmas cookies.

"These look fantastic," I said as I chose a green frosted tree from one of the plates while Nat filled the cups and passed them around. I noticed that she'd unearthed the Christmas dishes—the ones she'd always told me were a waste of time to unpack for a couple of weeks to just pack them up again.

"Ashley and I searched all your recipes looking for the ones you usually make," Gwen said.

"You and Ashley baked together?" I asked in astonishment.

"Yeah," Nat answered, "you should have seen the mess they made of the kitchen. Jeremy took pictures but we haven't had them developed yet."

"Where is Jeremy, anyway?" I asked.

"He should be back soon," Nat answered. "He's over at Ivan Mueller's house, trying to convince the poor man that he's not headed for federal prison."

I almost choked on my cookie. "What?"

"Ma, you'd be so proud of Jeremy. It turns out he's good with numbers. He really picked up the slack with your clients after you took off."

"You're kidding?"

"It's true," David agreed. "I think he has an affinity for accounting. And you know how good he is with people. Everybody loves him. I'm going to help him choose some online courses in accounting and tax prep."

The front door swept open and Jeremy called out, "Hey, what happened to all the vultures that were out on the front lawn?"

Then he came into the living room and saw me.

"Abby! You're back!"

He hurried over and pulled me up into a hard hug. I hadn't seen such enthusiasm in him in months. He looked healthier, too.

"Nat's just been explaining to me how you stepped in for me," I said. "I guess I owe you one."

"Get real. I'm the one who owes you, Abby. You put a roof over our heads when we needed it. You told me off when no one else would. You—"

"Hush," I said, fighting back tears. "You're family."

"How's Ivan doing?" I asked after everyone sat back down and Gwen had poured Jeremy a cup of hot chocolate.

"He's a nervous wreck. I keep telling him everything is going to be okay. He'll sail through that audit. His records are impeccable." He grinned his old Jeremy grin. "So are yours."

David asked him a question and I watched my two sons-in-law talk business. I especially watched David, hungry for any sign of his father in his features. He was handsome, yet in a very different way than Cole. He was what we would have called a preppy back when I was in high school. There was evidence of prematurely gray hair, but other than that there wasn't much resemblance to the passionate, over-the-top man who was his father.

It was almost shocking how much I was missing Cole that night, even though I was surrounded by my family. This time I knew what I was missing. I knew what the restlessness was. What the longing was. And I'd found the man—the life—that could fulfill them both.

I looked at my daughters and their husbands and wondered what they would make of Cole and me. How was I ever going to break it to them? And did I have the guts to leave them all once again and take a chance on a brand-new life?

I sat in my kitchen the morning of Christmas Eve, buttering toast and wishing I could crawl back into bed.

"Mom, you're going to have to make a decision about this," Gwen nagged, "or these people are never going to go away."

"I gotta say I agree with Gwen on this, Ma," Natalie said. "The only way we're gonna send those idiots home in time for Christmas is if you talk to them."

I took my toast over to the table. "I wouldn't know what to say at a press conference. I mean, who knows what they'd ask?"

"Mom," Gwen said, "if you could handle being with David's father for a week, I think you can handle the press."

I sipped my coffee and kept my mouth shut. Gwen was not going to be happy when I told her that the way I'd handled being with David's father for a week was to fall in love with him. I still hadn't decided when I was going to broach that subject with her—or with anyone else.

I nearly jumped when the phone rang. "I don't even know our new phone number, yet," I said. "Who could be calling?"

"I'll get it," Gwen said importantly as she rose from the kitchen table.

"Man is she in her element," Nat muttered. "Next thing you know she'll be writing a book about the whole thing and making it into a Lifetime movie. And guess who will be playing Gwen?"

I laughed. "Gwen. Who else?"

"Mom? It's Jo. Do you want to talk to her?"

"Oh—absolutely," I said, eagerly grabbing the phone from Gwen.

"I gotta find out from CNN that my best friend is back home?" Jo asked as soon as I'd said hello.

"Oh, Jo! There hasn't been time to get in touch. Last night, when I got home, the place was crawling with the media and then with the kids—"

"Shut up, girlfriend. I'm only teasing. I'm willing to forgive all as long as you come over to the diner this afternoon and tell me everything."

I took the cordless phone into the living room and peeked around the curtains. The circus had returned.

"Jo, I'd like nothing better. However, I don't know how I'll get through the crowds of reporters surrounding my house."

"Maybe they'd go away if you talked to them," Jo suggested.

"Gwen thinks I should give a press conference. Make some kind of statement. But I don't know where to begin. I mean, what do I do? Invite them all in for coffee?" I asked dubiously.

"Do it here," Jo said.

"At the diner?"

"Sure. Why not? Get Gwen to make an announcement that you'll be giving a statement at Dempsey's this afternoon. That should get most of them off your lawn."

"Yeah, but then they'll be in your diner."

"Exactly—and they'll be buying lots of coffee and donuts and leaving lots of tips."

I laughed.

"Hey, I'm not kidding. I think I made enough in tips alone to buy my cappuccino machine."

"And what does Mike have to say about that?"

"Ha! He's starting to see things my way. Some of those media types from the West Coast are vegetarians. I've already had to put a few pasta dishes on the menu. The cash register never stops ringing and Mike couldn't be happier."

"All right. I'm game if you are. Fire up the deep fryer and I'll see you around two. Oh—and call Iris for me, would you? I'd like her there, too."

There was a pause. "Uh—Iris? Yeah—sure. I'll call her."

"You sound less than enthusiastic. Is Iris okay?"

"Uh—yeah. Far as I know. I'll give her a call."

I still thought Jo sounded odd, but I let it go. I hung up the phone and I went back into the kitchen. "Jo says we should have the press conference down at the diner. What do you think?"

"Hey, whatever gets them out of here," Nat said.

Gwen frowned. "Isn't there someplace with more—um—"

"Classy?" Nat asked sarcastically. "You *were* going to say classy weren't you?"

Gwen sighed. "All right. All right."

"Well, hell, Gwen, Jo is one of Ma's best friends."

"I'm sorry, okay?" Gwen said impatiently. "The diner will be fine. Just fine. I'll go get ready to make the announcement."

"I just thought of something! It's Christmas Eve. What are we going to do about dinner? It's too late to thaw a turkey."

"We've got it covered, Ma," Nat said. "Gwen is making lasagna."

"Lasagna?"

"Well, Nat and I drew straws and I got Christmas Eve dinner. I'm very sorry, but lasagna is the only thing I know how to make," Gwen said in a huff before she swept out of the room.

"Don't worry, Ma. I bought a ham and sweet potatoes for Christmas dinner."

I shrugged as I refilled my coffee cup. "Nothing wrong with lasagna on Christmas Eve. Besides, I've got bigger things to worry about. I only have a couple of hours to write my statement. I'll be in my office."

Later, dressed in my Ralph Lauren taupe pantsuit, I left for the diner for my first—and only, I hoped—meeting with the press. Boy, could I use a dose of Cole's arrogance right now, I thought as Gwen, Nat and I piled into the station wagon.

"I don't know why we couldn't take my car," sulked Gwen, who owned an Audi. "David's would have been even better."

"Duh," said Natalie. "David had to go back to Chicago for the day, remember? He won't be back until late this afternoon."

"Well, he could have taken my car, and we could have kept his. Those reporters would have shown some respect for a BMW."

"Just get over yourself, okay?" Nat shot back.

"Hey! I could use a little support over here," I said from behind the wheel. "I'm scared to death."

"Nothing could be scarier than spending a week with my father-in-law," Gwen shot back.

I bit my tongue and wondered what this headstrong daughter of mine would say if she knew how much I wished Cole was with me right now?

I drove a circuitous route to the diner so we could park in

the narrow dead-end alley behind the place and thus sneak in the back door. Jo and Mike had admirably held the press at bay by locking the front door as soon as the lunch hour rush ended. As we entered through the back door that led directly into the kitchen, my salivary glands went into high gear.

"Paris has nothing like your donuts, Jo," I said as we flew into each other's arms.

"Oh, lady, am I glad to see you," Jo said before holding me at arm's length. "And just look at you. You look so—so sophisticated," she ended with a sniff as she dashed away a tear. "Much too sophisticated for this town."

"Yeah," Mike agreed as he came from the kitchen, wiping his hands on his white apron, "how ya gonna keep 'em down on the farm after they've seen Pareeee?"

I grinned. "Mike, you could keep me down on the farm with a cup of your coffee." For now, anyway, I added in my mind.

"Comin' right up." While he poured my coffee, he said, "The wife here already has her tip money earmarked for one of those fancy coffeemaker things. Aw—I can never remember what they're called."

Jo patted him on the cheek. "Honey, you don't have to know what it's called. You just have to learn how to use it."

"No way. Making fancy coffee is woman's work," Mike said, winking at me as he handed me a filled cup.

I took a grateful sip then asked, "Where's Iris?"

Jo and Mike exchanged a look.

"She can't make it. Said something about having a full appointment book for the day—or something."

"Is something wrong? A press conference seems like Iris's sort of thing."

Jo just shrugged then got busy wiping off the already immaculate counter.

One of the reporters outside rattled the doorknob and I looked at my watch.

"How are we going to do this?" I asked.

Apparently, Gwen had it all figured out. I just followed her orders and at two o'clock, Mike opened the door and the media swarmed in. I was sitting, after slight protest, on top of the counter, next to the pie keeper. I felt a little silly, but it was the only way we figured we could get everyone in and give everyone a clear view of me while I gave my statement. My two daughters and Jo stood behind the counter on either side of me. I'd never needed their support more than I needed it now. Frankly, I could have used some of Iris's wisecracks at the moment, too, just to break the tension I felt in my shoulders.

"Go ahead, Mom," prodded Gwen.

I took a deep breath. "Hello, I'm Abby Blake." And the cameras started flashing and the questions started coming.

I held up my hand. "Please!" I yelled over the din. "I've agreed to make a statement but I won't be answering questions at this time. I think this is the best way for us to all be sure that we get back to our families for Christmas Eve, don't you?" I asked ingenuously. How could they argue with that?

"I'm sure the number one question on all your minds is *why*? So that's the one question I'm going to answer." I took a moment to look at the sea of faces, all focused on me, all silently waiting for what I was going to say. Like it mattered. But maybe it did. I couldn't be the only woman who'd felt the way I had on that day I'd begged Cole to take me with him.

"I went on strike against my family because," I said as cameras flashed and minicams whirred, "like a lot of women my age, I felt both taken for granted and overlooked. So I decided to take a stand. I ended up in Paris purely by accident. But I always intended on coming home again. I love my family. I'm very proud of my daughters and always have been. What I needed was some time for myself. Now, before I return to my family to begin our holiday festivities, I'd like to add that if any of you women out there *of a certain age* are feeling the same way I was, I suggest that you discuss with your families how you feel and then get on the phone to a travel agent and plan a solitary vacation of self-discovery. That way, you won't have to make anyone worry—and you also won't have the press camping out on your lawn when you get back."

There was laughter from everyone, then applause from the women reporters and photographers who were there.

I held up my hands. "One more thing! There are some of those fantastic Dempsey donuts fresh from the fryer and the best coffee you'll find in Wisconsin. So buy up, then have a safe trip home and a wonderful holiday."

Mike helped me down from the counter. I headed directly for the kitchen and while I heard Gwen announce that any offers for interviews should be submitted to her, Nat whisked me out of there before anyone noticed.

That night we had a Christmas Eve dinner of tossed salad, lasagna and garlic bread and played board games with the kids. And then, instead of telling the story of "The Night Before Christmas," I told the story of how I ended up in Paris.

"—and when I woke up, I expected to be in Chicago, but I was in Labrador, Canada, instead."

"Canada! Wow!" Matt said. "And then what happened?"

"And then I had to try to talk David's daddy into taking me to Paris with him."

"You mean Cole was going to leave you there?" Gwen demanded. "Just abandon you in the middle of nowhere?"

"Well, he definitely wasn't happy to have a surprise passenger, but he wasn't technically deserting me. He had arranged for a pilot to fly me to Chicago the next morning. But I figured, why not go on to Paris? First, we had to fly to Iceland to refuel again. And the coolest part about that is I got to sit in the copilot's seat and watch Cole fly."

"Did he let you take the controls?" Matt wanted to know.

"No. And I didn't ask to, either. I was just happy to be sitting up front where the action was."

I decided that I'd save the tale of how I thought we were going to crash head-on into a 747 for another time.

"That is so cool, Grandma!" Tyler exclaimed. "Did you see any reindeer?"

Matt elbowed him. "They don't have reindeer in Iceland!"

Tyler elbowed him back. "How do you know? You don't know everything!"

"Actually," I said, "I don't know if they have reindeer in Iceland. Maybe tomorrow we can look it up on the Internet. As it turned out, I hardly saw anything at all. Iceland only has about four hours of daylight this time of year."

"Cool!" exclaimed Ashley. "We could have the tree lights on almost all the time."

"Forget Iceland," Gwen said. "Tell us about Paris. Start with the Ralph Lauren."

"Cole bought it for me. He said I'd be doing him a favor to

accompany him to some functions he had to go to and since I didn't have anything dressy with me—"

"Well, at least you got something out of having to put up with him," Gwen murmured.

Should I tell them now, I wondered? Natalie was looking at me speculatively. So was David. Gwen seemed oblivious and Jeremy was wrestling with the boys.

"Did David's daddy buy you that pretty dress you were wearing in the paper, Grandma?" Ashley asked.

"No. That I bought myself at a secondhand store, believe it or not."

"Oh, Cole must have loved that—you going to a ball with him in used clothes."

"Gwen," David admonished.

"What? You know how he is."

"Actually," I said, "he told me I looked beautiful in it."

For a moment nobody said anything. Then Ashley threw herself into my arms. "You did look beautiful in it, Grandma!"

"Thank you, pumpkin," I said as I hugged her hard.

If I went back to Paris, I would miss seeing my grandchildren grow up. Oh, I'd come back often enough—and they'd all come visit me. But it was the day-to-day things I'd miss. The drawings and arithmetic papers brought home every week and hung on the refrigerator with magnets. The way they smelled after coming in from jumping in piles of leaves in the yard in October. The snow angels and snowmen they'd make on the front lawn.

But if I didn't go back to Paris, I would miss Cole—and myself. Myself most of all.

"What's the Eiffel Tower like?" Nat asked.

"You can't believe how huge it is. We had a view of it from

the balcony of our suite." Gwen gave me a sharp look so I started talking about the lights along the Champs-Elysées and the huge obelisk in the Place de la Concorde.

I kept glancing at the telephone, wondering what Cole was doing and hoping he hadn't spent Christmas Eve alone. It gave me such a secret thrill to have his son here with us, though, and I kept hoping that David would decide to call his father to wish him a Merry Christmas but he never did.

We tucked the kids in around ten, waited for them to go to sleep, then crept around the house gathering all the hidden presents. We put them under the tree. I sat back and watched Jeremy and David put a train set together for the boys and a doll-house for Ashley.

Natalie and Gwen were wrapping a few last minute things, laughing about Christmases past and singing along to the holiday songs on the radio.

Around midnight, I wished everyone a Merry Christmas, pleaded exhaustion and told them I was going to bed.

There were good-night kisses all around.

"We're glad you're home, Mom," Gwen said as she stood by her sister's side.

"I am, too," I answered.

But after I'd slipped into the narrow bed in the maid's room, I couldn't sleep. I felt so torn. I hadn't been lying. I *was* glad I was home. But a big part of my heart now lived somewhere else.

Later, when I was sure everyone was sleeping, I crept into the living room, picked up the cordless phone, curled up on one of the sofas and called Cole's cell phone.

"Cole Hudson," he answered sleepily on the fourth ring.

"Merry Christmas," I whispered.

"Abby," he said. "God, I miss you."

"Me, too," I said.

"I'm surprised you called. I thought you wanted time to think."

"I do. I just couldn't go to sleep without wishing you a Merry Christmas."

"Merry Christmas, baby."

I savored the sound of his voice when he called me *baby* for a moment, then asked, "What did you do for Christmas Eve?"

"I spent it with Andre and Madeline."

I smiled. "I'm glad."

"What about you? How is everything going?"

"Well, I gave a statement to the press this afternoon and I'm getting requests for interviews."

He laughed that rich, warm laugh.

"It's insane, Cole. It's like I'm the holiday story du jour. Surely there are more important things going on in the world."

"Your fifteen minutes will be up soon enough."

"I certainly hope so."

"Come back to me. I'll let you hide out in my apartment with the pink walls."

"My granddaughter, Ashley, would love those pink walls."

"Lord help me, I'm in love with a grandmother."

"Listen, if things keep going the way they are, you might be a grandfather before you know it."

"What's happening? I tried to call David in Chicago but I got his machine."

"That's because he's here. And after Christmas, Gwen is going back to Chicago with him." I paused briefly, then asked, "How do you feel about that?"

"If it makes my son happy, I'm all for it."

I laughed softly. "That's a switch."

"I've now had the experience of being in love with one of the Blake women. It changes my perspective somewhat." He sighed hugely. "Abby—I should be there."

"I don't see you spending Christmas in Willow Creek."

"Hell with Willow Creek. It's you I want to spend Christmas with. Just tell me, have you decided where you're spending New Year's Eve?"

I had no answer. "Let me get through Christmas first, Cole. I mean, I haven't even told anyone here about us, yet."

A long silence. Then, "Are you sorry about what happened between us?"

"God, no! Of course not. It's just that, I don't know how everyone is going to take it."

"You mean you don't know how Gwen is going to take it, don't you?"

"Okay. Mostly Gwen. Aren't you worried about how David will react?"

"I'm not worried at all. David loves you. I think he'll be very supportive. But I'm well aware that Gwen doesn't love me. She isn't going to like it." There was another pause, then, "You can't let your children decide your life for you, Abby."

"I know that. And there are other things I need to think about, too."

"Is one of those things you have to think about whether you love me or not?"

I smiled gently. "No, Cole. I already know I love you."

"Good. Because I sure as hell love you. Just remember, Abby, I'm not a patient man."

"I'm not exactly feeling very patient myself right now," I said.

"Have you looked in your coat pocket?"

I frowned. "My coat pocket? Why?"

"Because I slipped something in there at the airport. Merry Christmas, Abby," he said. And then he hung up.

My coat pocket? Where was my coat? Hall closet, I thought as I ran to take a look. Yes! It was hanging there. I felt in one pocket. Nothing. Then I felt in the other and drew out a small box wrapped in silver paper.

I felt almost giddy as I ran back to my room off the kitchen. I shut the door, sat on the bed and started to unwrap Cole's gift.

There was a velvet box under the silver paper. I opened it to find a pair of pearl earrings and a pearl bracelet. They shimmered beautifully in the light of the bedside lamp. There was a small card, like the kind you get with flowers, tucked inside the box. I took it out and read it.

Now everything about you is real, it read. *Love, Cole.*

I kissed the card and put it neatly back into the box. The box I put under my pillow where I could feel it against my cheek and, finally, I fell asleep.

CHAPTER 11

It seemed as if I'd barely slept when I felt someone staring at me. I opened one eye to find all three of my grandchildren standing by the side of my bed, looking down at me.

"Are you awake, yet, Grandma?" Ashley whispered. "'Cause we can't get up until you're awake."

I opened my other eye. "It looks like you're already up to me." I threw back the covers of the narrow bed. "Better hop in here quick before you get caught."

All three of them crowded in, even Matt, who, most of the time, acted as if he was too old for such foolishness.

"Where are your parents?"

"They're still in bed, too," Matt chimed in. "But I don't think they're really sleeping."

Tyler shook his head. "Daddy's not snoring, so I think he's pretending."

"Well, let's give them a few minutes, then we'll get up and start making breakfast. I hope someone remembered to buy the cinnamon rolls!"

One of the Blake family traditions, and there weren't that many of them, was baking those tubes of chilled cinnamon rolls for Christmas breakfast every year. It was a tad corny, but it worked for us.

"This is so low-class it's not even on the map," Gwen would invariably complain but it never kept her from devouring at least three.

Now Ashley nodded. "Mommy got some from the store."

I was relieved out of all proportion. For one thing, I'd feel responsible if the tradition had been broken. For another, I saw it as a good sign that Natalie had remembered to get some. Instead of the passing of the torch, it was sort of like the passing of the chilled tube of dough.

There was a gasp from the maid's room door. "What are you guys doing down here in Grandma's room?" Natalie asked. "I've been looking all over for you. I thought maybe Santa had kidnapped all of you in exchange for the presents under the tree!"

"Aw, Ma," Matt said. But Ashley and Tyler giggled gamely.

Jeremy stuck his head around the door. "You guys didn't wake Grandma up, did you?"

All three kids shook their heads wildly.

"Good. 'Cause I'd hate to have to give anybody a spanking on Christmas morning."

As if Jeremy had or would ever spank any of the kids. He was as good a dad as you could hope for. It was such a pleasure to see him back to being himself again.

Gwen and David crowded into the doorway. "Merry Christmas, everyone," Gwen said sleepily.

"Merry Christmas!" various people shouted.

Pretty soon, everyone had crowded into the tiny maid's room, Gwen taking the rocking chair, Nat perching on the end of the bed and Jeremy and David sitting cross-legged on the floor.

"Grandma," Ashley said, "my teacher says that people travel so they can learn things. What did you learn on your trip to Paris?"

Oh, boy. Out of the mouths of babes. I didn't think I should say that I learned I was still capable of falling in love—not before breakfast, anyway. Instead, I said, "I learned that people are pretty much the same everywhere. And I learned that I haven't always been brave in my life."

"Huh," scoffed Gwen, "flying off with my charming father-in-law would certainly count for bravery in my book."

I stole a quick look at David. I could see that he was getting slightly fed up with Gwen making jabs at his father whenever an opportunity arose. I decided maybe it was time to get out of bed.

"Come on, you guys. Let's get those cinnamon rolls in the oven."

"I'll start the coffee," Nat said.

The kids all jumped out of bed. I followed more slowly, pulling my robe on over my pajamas and running my hands through my hair. When everyone had left my room, I slid my hand under my pillow and drew out the box. I opened it and read the card again. How I would love to show everyone the gift and the card and then they would all know. It was even getting harder to not come to his defense every time Gwen said something. But it was Christmas morning and, for once, everyone was on their best behavior. I didn't want to spoil it. Because when the truth came out, I knew Gwen wasn't going to make it easy—for anyone.

The kitchen was soon filled with the yeasty aroma of the rolls baking in the oven. It made me think of Paris—of the *boulangerie* across from the apartment I'd chosen for Cole.

This was no way to spend Christmas, I thought. Part of me here, part of me there. Focus, Abby, I told myself.

The oven timer went off.

"Okay—who wants to help me frost those rolls?" I asked with all the enthusiasm I could muster.

"Me! Me!" Ashley squealed.

Ashley got almost as much frosting on herself as on the rolls, but soon I was carrying a plate of them into the living room, followed by Gwen with coffee for the adults and Natalie with hot chocolate for the kids.

David and Jeremy were busy teasing the kids, getting them all fired up about the gifts under the tree. They weren't allowed to open anything until all the adults were fortified with caffeine and everyone had eaten at least one cinnamon roll. It raised the frenzy quotient and I guess that was the point. The older my grandkids got, the more important it seemed to keep some of the magic of the holiday alive in them. Matt already didn't believe in Santa. Tyler wasn't sure. Ashley, bless her, was still a firm believer.

"Now?" Matt, being the oldest, finally demanded.

It was also tradition that the kids were allowed to rip through two presents each before they had to start handing them out to everyone else. Thus, allowing them to be totally selfish for about twenty minutes toward the close of every year.

"Now," I said.

I watched Jeremy and Natalie watching their kids. Natalie trying to hold back her giggles and Jeremy throwing his head back with abandoned laughter. And I felt a stab of both warmth and pride. Along with, I must admit, a small underlying morsel of envy at the time they'd already had together that Charlie and I missed. Did I want to risk missing any time with Cole?

When the kids had opened two gifts each, they crawled under the tree and chose a gift to distribute to each of us. Ashley chose a gift for Nat from Jeremy and one for Gwen from David. Matt and Tyler dived in and picked gifts from themselves for their dad and their uncle.

Jeremy made a big deal of the monogrammed handkerchiefs while David tried not to laugh at the outrageous tie the boys had chipped in for with their allowances.

Gwen unwrapped a sapphire-and-diamond ring from David while Nat unwrapped a lovely pair of sterling silver earrings from Jeremy. Both of my daughters were equally excited, equally grateful.

Next, the grandkids presented their gift to me—a bottle of my favorite bath oil. I opened it and took a big, appreciative sniff. Then there were hugs and kisses all around.

Both couples had chipped in for a gift for me. A digital camera.

"So next time you run away, you can e-mail pics," Nat said.

Everyone laughed, except for Ashley, who climbed into my lap and asked, "You're not going to ever run away again, are you, Grandma?"

"Don't worry, pumpkin. From now on, I promise not to go anywhere without telling everyone before I leave."

Finally, it was time for me to distribute the gifts I'd bought in Paris. The kids seemed happy with their marionettes, especially after I told them the story of how I'd met the man who made them and of some of the really wild puppets he had in his shop.

"I made friends with a young artist in Paris," I told them. "Her name is Olivia. She knew the puppet maker and took me to his shop when I told her I wanted to bring something special back from Paris for my grandchildren. Each marionette is unique. No two alike."

"So nobody else has one like this?" Matt asked as he held up his pirate.

"That's right."

He grinned. "Cool."

The kids needed help figuring out how the marionettes worked since there were no batteries or microchips involved but soon got the hang of it.

Nat and Gwen loved the scents I'd given them and were interested to hear all about the perfumery. Jeremy and David immediately put on their berets and matching scarves and we all agreed that they looked dashing.

"You all have Olivia to thank. I never would have found the puppet maker or the perfumery without her. She ended up showing me quite a few things in Paris I wouldn't have seen otherwise."

"Did she go home in time for Christmas, too?" Ashley wanted to know.

I shook my head. "She doesn't get along with her mother."

"Wouldn't that be awful," Gwen said, "to not get along with your own mother?"

Nat and Jeremy and David looked at each other, then burst out laughing.

"What?" Gwen asked.

"You're always disagreeing with Mom about something," Nat said.

"Oh, I am not," Gwen insisted.

"Whatever." Natalie grinned.

"Um," I interrupted, "I think it's time for the kids to open their presents from Santa."

Later that afternoon, the grandchildren were off concocting a play for their marionettes while the Blake women gathered in the kitchen to start Christmas dinner.

"I can't believe we're still making that tacky green bean casserole," Gwen said.

"Oh, shut up," Nat shot back. "You'll end up eating more helpings of that junk than anyone else."

I smiled as I listened to Gwen and Nat exchange wisecracks as they debated what kind of glaze to put on the ham. Some things would never change.

Jeremy and David could be heard from the living room, shouting at the football game on TV.

The only thing missing, for me, was Cole.

The doorbell rang and my heartbeat went into overdrive. Could it be?

Gwen and Natalie looked at each other, then at me.

"Um—Ma," Natalie said, "we sort of forgot to tell you something."

My heart leaped into my throat.

"We invited Iris for Christmas dinner."

I felt a shot of guilt at how disappointed I was.

"That's great. Very thoughtful. I'm proud of you," I said in a pitiful attempt at recovery. My daughters didn't seem to notice.

"Otherwise, she would be alone," Gwen whispered with a look of horror on her face that only someone who held the complete conviction that she'd never end up alone on a holiday could possibly feel.

I went to answer the door and found Iris stamping out a barely smoked cigarette on my porch.

"Iris! What the heck are you ringing the doorbell for? Come on in!"

She teetered past me on stiletto-heeled boots, a large metallic bag brimming with gifts swinging from one arm.

"Merry Christmas!" I exclaimed. "I'm so glad the girls invited you for dinner. I missed you at the news conference."

She tossed her hair in a gesture that was reminiscent of how she acted when she was pissed off at anyone when we were teenagers. "I'm surprised you noticed I wasn't there."

I frowned. "Of course I noticed."

"Now that you're cavorting with lords and ladies I figured I wouldn't be missed."

I burst out laughing. Iris, however, didn't. Instead she walked past me and into the living room.

"Hey, rug rats!" she exclaimed. "Auntie Iris has gifts!"

The kids crowded around her. I watched for a moment, puzzled. Something was going on with Iris. I wondered if the guy in Milwaukee had turned out to be a loser. I'd have to find the time to ask her about it later. Right now I wanted to get back to the kitchen and make sure Gwen didn't win out with her fig glaze. Figs, as far as I was concerned, only belonged in Newtons.

Christmas dinner was a raucous affair. Between the grandkids making various noises and ploys for attention, the sisters waging a good-natured war over how the table should have been set, and Iris flirting heavily with both Jeremy and David, not much was required of me. I'm not even sure anyone noticed that half my mind was occupied with something—someone—else.

Time and again I thought about slipping away and calling Cole. Then I'd remembered how he didn't expect to hear from me, since I'd told him I needed time. I'd feel an utter fool if I kept breaking my own rules. Besides, he might feel free to start calling me. Listening to that deep voice over the phone every day would definitely sway my decision. This decision had to be made on logic, not on emotion.

Didn't it?

Right. This from a woman who'd slept with a box of pearls under her pillow. Pearls from her lover, no less. I expected logic from this woman?

Yes, I told myself emphatically, of course I did. After all, wasn't I too old to chance making a mistake? I'd spent so much of my life following the well-worn path of least resistance. True, it wasn't the path I'd originally planned to set out on, but wasn't fifty-two too old to begin walking in another direction? The job offer from Madeline excited me, but it was also scary. Was it too late to begin a new career?

When Matt, Tyler and Ashley were exhausted enough to be led up to bed by their equally exhausted parents and Gwen and David slipped off to be by themselves, I thought Iris and I would finally have a chance to talk. To my surprise, she grabbed her coat and headed for the front door.

"It's been real," she said and I swore I could see the same chip on her shoulder that had been there in 1972, when she'd been caught skipping chemistry to try to create some of her own under the bleachers with a guy who was supposed to be going steady with the head cheerleader. She wasn't going to let anyone think she gave a damn.

"Iris—wait."

Her hand already on the doorknob, she turned. "Yeah?"

"Why don't you stay and have a glass of wine with me. We haven't really had a chance to talk all evening."

She hesitated and I thought for a moment she was going to say no. Then she shrugged and said, "Yeah, I guess I could stay for a little while."

I brought us each a glass of wine and we sat in the living

room with only the Christmas tree lights to keep us from being in the dark.

"Iris, what's wrong?"

"What do you mean?" she asked without looking at me.

"I don't know—you're acting different."

"You're the one who's different."

"How so?"

"Take a look at how you're decked out, for one thing."

I was wearing the organza shirt with the black trousers and my black suede pumps.

"Cole took me shopping."

She raised a perfectly plucked brow. "Cole? Sounds pretty chummy."

I set my glass of wine on the coffee table. "You're pissed off about something, aren't you?"

She tossed her head again. "What was your first clue?"

I was starting to lose patience with her petulance. "Iris, what the hell is wrong with you?"

She jumped to her feet. "What's wrong with *me*? You take off for parts unknown without so much as informing your best friends. You think we didn't worry? You think we didn't wonder where the hell you were and why you'd left?"

"Jo never said anything about—"

"It's like I didn't matter at all to you."

I rose to my feet and tried to reach out to her but she shrugged off my hand.

"What you're saying isn't true," I said earnestly. I might as well not have spoken.

"And look at your hair! Your makeup! I've been trying to give you a makeover for years but, no, you had to go to Paris to have one. Like Iris's House of Beauty isn't good enough for you."

"That's not the way it was at all. It's not that I didn't want *you* to give me a makeover. I just never took the time for myself. In Paris, that changed. I started to feel things I hadn't felt in a long time. There are things I need to tell you—"

"Huh—then isn't it odd that you didn't even bother to call when you got back? I had to turn on the TV to find out my so-called best friend was back in town."

"I'm sorry. There just wasn't time—"

She nodded her head once. A very decisive nod. "Right. Well, maybe now I don't have time."

She grabbed her coat and headed for the front door.

I was right behind her.

"Iris, please. I've got some decisions to make. I need my friends."

"Seems to me you've gotten pretty good at making decisions all by yourself."

"Please, Iris. Tomorrow is our usual Friday to get together. Why don't we meet at that Mexican place again? Tequila shots on me," I added, hoping to entice her into softening a little.

"Yeah, like you're going to want to do shots with a small-town beautician after you've sipped champagne with famous architects and wealthy Frenchmen."

"That's exactly what I want to do," I said emphatically. "Are you going to be there?"

She shrugged. "Can't say. I'll check my social calendar."

She swept out the front door. I closed the door after her and leaned against it. Of all the people who I'd thought might be angry or hurt over what I'd done, Iris was the last person I would have suspected. She was the independent one. The one who never wanted to be needed.

I went back into the living room and sat on the sofa. I gazed at the tree for a long time, remembering Christmases past when Charlie was still with us. I realized now that we'd been happy then, despite everything. Happy because life was full of promise, full of possibilities. It had never been Willow Creek holding me back. After Charlie died, the promise and possibilities had started to wither inside of me.

I wanted those feelings back again. But what would be the price? Was I going to lose one of the best friends I'd ever had? And how could I be sure that it'd be worth it?

"Mom, I really think you should hold out for Oprah," Gwen said at breakfast the next morning.

"I somehow think this story isn't Oprah's thing."

"Well, she did send some producers to check into things."

"Tell you what, honey, we'll save Oprah for after the book you're going to write."

Gwen gasped. "Who told you that? I never said I was going to write a book—for sure, anyway."

"Whatever," Nat said as she poured herself another cup of coffee.

"No point in getting all worked up about this," I began. "I've already decided that I'm not giving any interviews."

"Mom, I think you might want to discuss this with an entertainment lawyer," Gwen said.

"Nope. I've made up my mind. My life is not for public consumption. I've made a statement and that's all anyone is getting—for now, anyway."

"There go Gwen's chances for stardom," Nat muttered while she slathered a piece of toast with peanut butter. "Pity. She'd probably already decided on which outfit for her appearance on Oprah."

"Do you always have to be this way?" Gwen demanded.

Nat pointed an accusing finger. "Just get off Ma's back, okay? Let her do what she wants."

Gwen thought it over for a few seconds. "I suppose she does deserve that, at least, after spending a week in a foreign country with Cole Hudson." Gwen shuddered. "I can't even imagine. The man is so disagreeable, he'd even ruin Paris."

"He ruined nothing," I said, perhaps too sharply. "It would do you good, Gwen, to remember that Cole is the father of the man you love."

Gwen and Nat looked at each other.

"Whoa," Nat said. "Where did *that* come from?"

"Gwen should consider that Cole Hudson must have some redeeming qualities if he was able to raise a caring, thoughtful, creative son like David. That's all. Now, if you'll excuse me," I said before anyone could ask any more questions, "I'm going to take a shower. I'm meeting Iris and Jo in a while."

"Iris isn't coming, is she?" I asked Jo. We were already on our second margaritas and there was still no sign of her.

Jo sighed. "No. I don't think she's coming. She's been pretty upset about your leaving the way you did."

"I was worried about how the kids would handle my taking off, but I never dreamed that Iris was the one who would be so hurt by it. You think it would help if I called her?"

"I think maybe what you need to do is give her time."

"That's the thing, though. That's why I wanted to talk to both of you. I may not have much time."

"Ohmigod," Jo exclaimed. "What's wrong? Are you sick? Did you go to Paris to see a doctor?"

"No!" I quickly assured her. "No—no. Nothing like that at all."

Jo settled down. "Okay—I give. Why wouldn't you have the time to set things right with Iris?"

"Because I might be going back to Paris."

"I knew it!" Jo slapped her hand on the table. "You met someone over there, didn't you?"

I took a deep breath. "Well, not exactly."

"You met someone at O'Hare?" Jo asked dubiously.

I chuckled. "No—it's someone that I knew from before."

Jo scrunched up her nose in puzzlement. "The only person involved in this that I can think of that you knew before is—" Her mouth dropped open.

I nodded. "I'm in love with Cole Hudson."

Jo gasped. "*Cole Hudson? The* Cole Hudson? Gwen's father-in-law?"

I nodded. "Weird, huh? And—even weirder—he says he's in love with me."

"And this is a problem because…?"

"Well, other than I'm not sure Gwen can handle it, Cole will be living and working in Paris for at least a year."

"And he wants you with him?" Jo asked.

I nodded. "If I want to give us a chance, I'm supposed to meet him under the Eiffel Tower on New Year's Eve at midnight."

Jo slid down into her seat like the wind had been knocked out of her. "That is the most romantic thing I've ever heard. Are you going to do it?"

"I don't know—that's one of the reasons I wanted to talk to you and Iris. I don't know what to do."

"Go for it," Jo said.

"There's more. I've been offered a job in Paris, too. Working for a foundation that will be awarding grants to artists."

"Go for it," Jo repeated.

I compulsively shoved stale chips into my mouth.

"I don't know. It would mean deserting my family again."

"Um, girlfriend," Jo said, "haven't you noticed something?"

I frowned. "What?"

"The kids have done just fine without you. In fact, they're finally all getting their acts together. I think your time has finally come."

Was it possible, I wondered?

"I don't know what to do. I mean, what if none of this is real?"

"What the heck does that mean?"

"Well, doesn't it strike you as a little weird? A few weeks ago, Cole and I couldn't stand each other."

"In my opinion," Jo said, "love is always weird. I mean, I ended up marrying Mike Dempsey, thus dooming myself to a life of frying donuts and making coffee—in Willow Creek, yet. Now that's devotion. But who knows where it came from? Was it perhaps the knowledge that no matter how much weight I gained over the years, Mike would still be able to lift me and carry me off to bed? Or was it something as simple as his dimples?"

"Can it be that simple?" I asked.

"I think it really can be something that simple," Jo said with conviction. "Love is an irrational emotion. Why look for rational reasons?"

I sighed and dipped a chip into guacamole. This was a

decision I was going to have to make on my own. And, somehow, I was going to have to make my peace with Iris. But before I could do that, there was something else I had to do. I had to tell Nat and Gwen about Cole and me.

When I got home Jeremy and David were loading Gwen's pink luggage into her car. That meant it was now or never. I almost chose never, but then the guys noticed me and waved and it was too late to turn around and head for another margarita.

"Hi, guys," I said as I got out of my station wagon.

Jeremy slammed Gwen's trunk shut. "Hey, Abby."

"It looks like you and Gwen are going back to Chicago," I said to David.

"Yeah, and it's a good thing we've each got our own car. Do you think you could teach your daughter to travel any lighter?" David asked with a wry grin. "According to Dad, you're an extremely economical packer."

My heart tripped. "You've spoken to your father today?"

David nodded. "I called him to let him know I'd be in Chicago today."

"Did he say anything—um—interesting?"

"About what?" David asked as he stowed his one black carry-on bag into his car.

"Oh—just anything. You know, anything unusual?"

Jeremy and David shared a look and I started to wish I'd kept my mouth shut.

"What's up, Abby?" David asked.

"I need to talk to both of you, and to Natalie and Gwen," I said. "Right now, if you don't mind, before you leave and before I lose my nerve."

David touched my arm. "Abby, are you all right?"

"Yes. Ah, no, I'm nervous as hell. Just come inside, okay?"

I started for the house and Jeremy and David followed.

My daughters were in the living room, sorting through gifts. Gwen was carefully putting hers in a Neiman Marcus shopping bag. They seemed to be getting along—for the moment, anyway.

"Girls, could you please come sit down. There's something we need to discuss."

They both looked up. "Something wrong, Ma?" Nat asked.

"Ah, no, not really. There's something important I need to talk about with all of you."

I sat down on one of the sofas and Nat and Gwen joined me—one on either side. Jeremy and David sat on the sofa across from us.

The time was here and I had no idea how to begin.

"It's about Cole and me," I finally said.

Gwen put her hand on mine. "Mom, this might not be something you want to air in front of David. After all, as you reminded me, Cole is his father and—"

"Oh—it's not something *bad*."

"Oh," Gwen said, sounding slightly disappointed. "Then what about Cole and you?"

I took a deep breath and studied each of them in turn. All four of them were staring at me expectantly. I decided that the only way to do it was to just say it.

"Cole and I are in love and we want to be together."

I swear, it was so quiet you could hear needles dropping off the Christmas tree. And then all of a sudden, Nat grabbed me into a hug. "Ma—that's great!"

"I'm speechless. Absolutely speechless," David said, but he was grinning ear to ear.

"Well, what can I say—the man's obviously got great taste in women," Jeremy stated before he came over to join me and Nat in the hug.

"Are you people out of your mind?" Gwen screeched as she jumped to her feet. "Did you hear what she just said?"

"Yes," said David, "she said that she's in love with my dad and he's in love with her and that they want to be together. I find that pretty miraculous."

"Miraculous?" Gwen gasped. "I think *insane* would be a better word."

"Look," I began, "I know this comes as a shock, but—"

"A shock? Mother, do you have any idea what this will do to my life? My father-in-law will be here for every holiday, for every—"

"Well, not exactly," I interrupted. "At least not right away. Cole has to be in Paris for at least a year and he wants me to join him there."

"So just like that," Gwen said as she snapped her fingers, "you're going to leave us again and go live in Paris with a man that I absolutely loathe."

David shot to his feet. "Hey, that's my father you're talking about, Gwen."

"Yes. And that means you *have* to love him no matter what— just like I have to love my mother no matter what."

I stared at Gwen. I wasn't sure I wanted to ask her to clarify that statement. Natalie had no such compunction.

"What the hell is that supposed to mean?" she demanded of her sister.

"I only meant that Mother is far from perfect, but I love her, anyway."

"If we're talking about perfect," Nat said, "maybe we should talk about how far from perfect you are."

"Or maybe," Gwen countered, "we should talk about why you're so willing to let our mother cross the Atlantic to end up miserable."

"At the very least," David asked, "don't you think your mother has a right to decide what would make her happy?"

"How could that arrogant, angry, *rude*—"

"That's only one side of him, Gwen," David insisted. "You just never wanted to look any further."

"He's right, Gwen," I told her. "There's so much more to Cole than I ever thought there was. He has so much to offer a woman—"

"I don't want to hear this! I *can't* hear this! Mother, this is the man who less than two weeks ago called me a spoiled brat!"

"You were *acting* like a spoiled brat, Gwen," David pointed out.

"Just like you are now," Nat added. "As usual, everything is always about you."

Gwen gasped. "How dare you!"

"She dares," David said, "because it's the truth. Everything *is* all about you. You can't even see that maybe your mother could be happy in Paris with my father and that maybe you ought to be mature enough to realize that the whole world doesn't revolve around you."

Gwen grabbed her Neiman Marcus bag. "I am leaving now," she announced. "And by the time I see you back in Chicago, David," she added haughtily, "I expect an apology."

With that she swept out of the room with an icy smoothness that Grace Kelly would have admired.

"You're not going to go after her?" I asked David.

He shook his head. "No. Not this time. It's time for Gwen to wake up. She should have been more understanding when my work got in the way of that cruise. And she should be more understanding about this, too, Abby. Personally, I think you and my dad will make a terrific couple."

"Seriously? You really don't mind?"

"Abby, come on. You know I love you," he said.

I drew him into a hug and gave him a kiss on the cheek. "Sometimes I wonder if my daughter deserves you," I murmured.

"I love her. That's all that matters."

"I can't leave it like this," I said. "I have to go to her."

I ran out the door without a coat. I had to try to straighten things out. I had to keep the lines of communication open or there was every chance that my relationship with Gwen would turn into the kind of relationship Olivia had with her mother. That, I could never bear.

I caught Gwen while she was still checking her makeup in the lighted mirror behind the visor. If I didn't know for a fact that this was her usual routine, I might have thought she was stalling.

I yanked open the passenger door and slid in.

"Mother, I don't want to talk to you about this right now. I simply can't."

"Well, I can't let you leave without telling you how much I love you and how much I hope you'll think about what you've just learned."

"That's the point in my leaving—the point in my telling you

I don't want to talk about this. I don't *want* to think about it, Mother. In fact, it turns my stomach to think about it. And anyway, you're the one who'd better think about it. I don't know what happened between you and Cole in the space of a week—and I don't want to know," she quickly added. "But I think you'd better try to remember that this is the same man you could barely talk to at my wedding."

"Fair enough. I intend to give this a lot of thought before I make a decision. And here's something you'd better think about. That beautiful young man in there loves you but one of these times you might push him too far. If you want to keep your husband, Gwen, you better think about growing up a little."

She refused to look at me or acknowledge what I'd said. "Gwen, you're acting like a child."

Her chin was starting to quiver. "So I suppose that means you're going to desert me just like Daddy did."

I smoothed her hair back from her troubled face. "Honey, Daddy didn't desert you. Given a choice he'd still be here for you. Just like I'll always be here for you. It's easy to love people when they're at their best and everything is going well, Gwen. But it's more important to keep loving them when things aren't so great. You were right—I'm far from perfect. Nobody's perfect. Not even you."

She covered her face with her hands. "Nothing is ever going to be the same again if you go."

"You're right. Just like nothing was the same for me when you left. Please tell me that you'll try to accept this."

She stared straight ahead and didn't say a word. So I leaned over and kissed her on the cheek. "I love you," I said. "I really do." Then I got out of the car.

She burned rubber without so much as a backward glance.

"Wow," Natalie said from behind me, "I didn't know she could drive like that."

I sighed. "She's pretty upset."

"She'll get over it," Nat offered.

"What about you? How are you taking this? Gwen didn't leave much room for anyone else's reaction."

"My first reaction was *whoa*—I mean, it was pretty much a whopper of a surprise. Gwen's got a point, you know, Ma. You really *didn't* like him."

I laughed softly. "I know. I'm not denying that."

"But the more I thought about it, the more I could see it made some sense. I mean, he is slightly hot for an older guy. And his world would be so new to you—and I think you need that. I know you haven't been happy for awhile now."

I looked at her in surprise. "You knew that?"

"Ma—I've been living with you for almost four months. I'm not stupid."

No, she wasn't. This rebellious daughter of mine was turning out to be a wise, generous and understanding woman.

"Besides, you're too young and beautiful to do without sex for the rest of your life."

Now it was my turn to gasp. And blush. And sputter.

Natalie laughed and put her arm around my shoulders. "Come on. It's freezing out here."

We hurried back to the house, arms around each other for support as much as warmth.

David was getting ready to leave.

"I hope you're not in for too rough a time of it," I said as I put my hand against his cheek. I'd loved him almost from the moment I'd met him, but now that I was in love with his father, he was all the more dear to me.

"I can handle it. What I can't handle is being without her."

I watched from the living room window as David drove away. Still thinking about his last statement, I knew exactly how he felt. Cole wouldn't be easy. I knew that. But not having him in my life would be harder still.

"Don't let her make up your mind for you," Nat said.

I turned away from the window. "It's just so hard to know what to do. I've hurt Gwen. I've hurt Iris. And there's no guarantee that my relationship with Cole will last."

"You want my advice?"

"Of course. I'd value your advice very much."

Natalie beamed and I thought "thank you, Olivia."

"If I had worried about other people's opinions and feelings, I never would have married Jeremy. And you wouldn't have three grandchildren to love."

CHAPTER 12

I was up nearly all night. I filled legal pads with notes. Went over the work Jeremy had done while I was gone. Examined papers that pertained to the house and the business. In the morning, I decided to see my lawyer. I had a plan, but I had to make sure it would work.

John Brillion's offices were located above the dime store, at the opposite end of Willow Creek's tiny downtown from the diner. The day was sunny and crisp so I parked the car in front of Dempsey's figuring I'd walk the two blocks to the lawyer's, then walk back. Thus giving me the perfect excuse to stop in at the diner for coffee and donuts.

John's mother, who was about eighty and looked ninety-five thanks to the dowager's hump on her back and decades of gardening without the benefits of a hat or an SPF, still worked as his secretary.

"Well, if it isn't our world traveler," she said, her watery blue eyes twinkling. She pointed a crooked finger at me. "I always knew you were flighty."

For years it had been a sore point between my mother and Mrs. Brillion that John and I had had a few dates but then I'd broken it off. I'd had a mad crush on the captain of the debate team. Mrs. Brillion had made it a lifetime joke to tease both me and my mother about it. Unfortunately, my mother never had much of a sense of humor about that kind of thing.

"If I were flighty, Mrs. Brillion, I wouldn't have chosen your son to be my lawyer," I told her.

She laughed. "You were always a quick one, too," she said. "I'll tell Johnny you're here."

An hour later I was patting Mrs. Brillion's hump and wishing her a happy new year. Back out on Main Street, I started a leisurely stroll the same way I'd come. As I passed the jewelry store, I heard the sound of tapping on glass and looked up to find Ivan Mueller motioning for me to come inside.

"There she is," he said when I went inside, "my beauty of a bookkeeper. I have something for you."

He toddled off to the back of the shop and I took a look around while I was waiting. There wasn't much to look at. The glass-fronted jewelry counters were nearly empty.

"Looks like you're a little low on stock," I said when Ivan came back.

"And I have you to thank for that. Such a holiday season I've never had! A lot of those reporters did their Christmas shopping here. I saw one of those anchor people on TV the other day wearing a pair of my earrings!" He held out a small, beautifully wrapped present. "This is for you."

"I'm not sure I deserve it this year, Ivan. I'm so sorry I wasn't here when you found out about the audit."

He flapped a heavily veined hand at me. "A woman isn't allowed a vacation? Besides, that son-in-law of yours—he's a good man. He helped me a lot. Even took me out for a beer."

Well, that was certainly one thing I'd never done for Ivan.

"Maybe I should hire him permanently."

Ivan nodded. "You should. You should. He took me over to your office and showed me my records on the computer. My goodness, he can make that thing go fast. He says I should maybe think about getting one."

I just smiled. I'd told Ivan the same thing more than once. But Ivan was of the generation that was more likely to listen to a man than a woman and I wasn't going to hold that against him. Especially not after what I'd just discussed with my lawyer. Knowing Jeremy could be effective with my clients was an important part of my plan.

"Now, open your gift," he said.

I untied the gold ribbon and carefully removed the gold paper to find a small black velvet box. I opened the lid.

I put my fingers to my mouth when I saw what was inside. "Oh—Ivan. I couldn't."

"Too late. It's already yours."

I took the pearl pendant out of the box and put it on. "It's just so perfect," I said as I looked at myself in the footed looking glass on the counter. "You have no idea what a perfect gift this is."

"I am glad I didn't get you pearl earrings," he said, nodding toward one of my ears.

I held up my wrist.

He smiled. "Or a bracelet."

"That's what makes the pendant so perfect."

I was wearing my black Ralph Lauren trousers, cashmere sweater and coat. With my shorter, sleeker hairstyle, the pearls set the look off perfectly.

"You want an old man's advice?" Ivan asked. At first I thought he was talking about the jewelry, but then he said, "Go to him."

"Excuse me?"

"The man who bought you the rest of the pearls. Go to him."

I shook my head. "Small towns. I should have known."

He flapped his hand again. "Listen, so what? People talk. And who doesn't love a romance?"

"So that's one *go to him*," I said, acting as if I were writing it down on an order pad.

"You listen to an old man. I lost my Rita too soon—even though we'd had forty years together. Every day is precious. Don't waste them worrying about what other people think."

I hugged him, promised to remember his advice and thanked him again for the pendant.

When I got to the diner, Jo was making a fresh pot of coffee. I sat at the counter so we could talk while she worked.

"Hear anything from Gwen?" she asked me.

I shook my head. "Not a word since she went back to Chicago."

"Abby, I hate to remind you, but the clock's ticking. Two days until New Year's Eve. You're not going to spoil that wonderfully romantic ending for me, are you?"

"Two days," I repeated.

"Yup," said Jo. "Two days." She leaned on the counter. "You know, you're starting to piss me off. How can you say no to Paris with a foxy, famous architect? I mean, the guy's in love with you. You're in love with him. Plus, there's a challenging new job. What's your problem?"

"But, Gwen—"

"Gwen has her own life, honey," Jo said. "She'll get over it."

"And then there's Iris. She's still angry at me for the last time I left."

"Iris will recover, I promise you. Next thing you know, she'll be planning a trip to France to visit you and poor Cole will have to find her a blind date that she won't eat alive."

I laughed.

"Unless—"

"Unless what?"

Jo hesitated.

"Unless what?" I prompted.

"Unless you're looking for an excuse *not* to go back to Paris," Jo answered.

And there it was. Leave it to a woman's best friend to hit the nail right on the head. It wasn't Gwen's feelings that mattered—or anyone else's. All that mattered was did I have what it took to grab the brass ring and hang on this time? Was I going to be brave at long last?

Jo poured me a cup and cut a big slab of Mike's homemade chocolate layer cake and put it in front of me. I started to eat, washing down the sweet, fluffy frosting with scalding hot coffee.

Jo kept refilling my cup and I kept eating.

"I'll get you another piece," Jo said.

"No!" I cried. "I don't need another piece of cake. I need to go back to Paris!"

"Nothing like chocolate to make someone focus," Jo said.

"Works every time," I agreed.

After I left the diner, I marched across the street and pushed open the door to Iris's House of Beauty.

Iris was just putting a client under the dryer. She looked up when she heard me come in.

"What do you want?" she asked, none too friendly.

"I want you back as my friend, but I can't and won't put

others above myself anymore. I'm going back to Paris. I've got a job waiting for me there and a man I love who loves me. There are phones, there are fax machines, there is the Internet. I see no reason why we can't carry on a long-distance friendship. It's up to you now, Iris," I declared and then I walked out of the shop.

That night, after the kids were in bed and the house was quiet, I called Nat and Jeremy into the living room.

"I have something I want to talk to you about."

"You've made up your mind about Paris," Natalie said.

"Um, yes. I have. I've decided to go."

Natalie grinned. "I knew it! That's awesome, Ma."

"I'm glad at least one of my daughters approves."

"I'm all for it."

"So am I, Abby," Jeremy added.

I reached across the kitchen table and patted their joined hands. "Thanks for your support. It means a lot. But that's not what I want to talk to you both about. I met with John Brillion today."

"Your lawyer?" Nat exclaimed. "Why? What's wrong?"

I smiled at her. "Nothing's wrong. At least I don't think it is. Unless—well, let me tell you what I've been planning."

I laid it out for them. About how I was willing to rent them the house for the princely sum of one dollar a year.

"That way I'm responsible for paying for repairs and property taxes," I explained, "while you two are still getting on your feet."

"Ma—we can't let you do that."

"Yes, you can. It would mean a lot to me to think of you and

Jeremy raising your family here. Especially since you've both always wanted Willow Creek to remain your home."

"I wouldn't want to raise my kids anywhere else," Nat said.

"Me, either," Jeremy agreed.

"Okay, that's settled. Then, I want to hire you, Jeremy, to run my business for me."

"Abby—"

I held up my hand to stop Jeremy from saying any more. "Listen for a minute. From what I've heard and seen, you can do it, Jeremy. You might have to take a few classes and study a little, but you can start slow. We can be in touch through e-mail and online chat. I can help you with whatever you need helping with until you learn enough to be on your own. And then we can talk about you buying the business and house from me on a land contract."

Jeremy didn't say a word, just bowed his head, and I started to wonder if I'd been wrong about him. Would he rather stay rooted on my sofa, letting his wife carry him through, than start a new career that could give him—and his family—a better future? That wasn't the Jeremy I'd known for all these years, but as I'd found out these last few weeks, people—for good or bad— never stopped surprising you. Was Jeremy about to surprise me?

When he looked up again, there were tears in his eyes and I knew I hadn't been wrong about him.

"Abby, you have no idea what this means to me. To have you believe in me like this, after—"

"Hush. You've been going through a rough time. That's what families are for—to stand by each other."

Nat pushed back her chair and got up to come around the table and throw her arms around my neck.

"Oh, Ma—I love you so much. How are we ever going to thank you?"

"By being there for each other—no matter what. By sticking it out and sharing each other's dreams as much as possible. By e-mailing me lots of pictures of my grandchildren."

By now I was crying, too.

"I'm going to miss you, Ma," Natalie said.

Around midnight, I started to wonder if Nat was going to get the chance to miss me. I'd been trying for hours to book a flight to Paris on the Internet. There wasn't anything available—at least not anything that I could afford. I thought of taking up a collection for a first class or business class ticket, but who'd have any extra cash hanging around this time of year?

Well, there was one person.

Cole.

But I could never ask Cole to pay for my ticket to Paris. I wanted to return under my own steam. And, I hadn't spoken to him since Christmas Eve. So for all I knew, he'd had a change of heart and wasn't even planning to meet me at the Eiffel Tower. There was only one way I could be sure he wanted me there as much as I wanted to be there. And that was to show up and find him waiting for me.

Or not.

I grabbed a couple of hours of sleep, setting the alarm for nine in the morning. That's when I started calling travel agents. In Milwaukee. In Chicago. Still, no one had a seat that I could remotely afford.

"I bet that if you called one of those reporters, someone would pay for your ticket in exchange for an exclusive interview," Nat said over tuna salad sandwiches for lunch.

Jeremy was in my office, registering for an online accounting class, and the kids were eating their chicken noodle soup in front of the TV, so we were alone.

"They'd probably want to come along and film the reunion," I told her. A reunion that seemed as if it was never going to happen. Okay, I could wait a few weeks and try to save up some cash. Or I could wait until the holidays were over and hope to find a cheaper seat then. But, damn it, I wanted that romantic reunion beneath the Eiffel Tower on New Year's Eve!

Tomorrow night.

And Paris was seven hours ahead of Willow Creek.

"Ma," Nat said, "you could ask Gwen and David for the money."

"You saw Gwen's reaction to my involvement with Cole. I can't ask her."

"David would give it to you—you know he would."

I shook my head. "Gwen and David are already having problems. I wouldn't want to do anything that might drive them further apart."

"I guess you're right. Too bad we don't have the time to put together a rummage sale," Nat said just as we heard kid commotion erupt from the living room. "I'd better go check that out. I hope there aren't noodles dripping from the Christmas tree."

I laughed, albeit weakly. Frankly, at this moment I didn't really care if the grandkids were decking the halls with chicken noodle soup. I kept thinking about the idea of a rummage sale. Nat was right, there wasn't time for one. But if I could find just one or two things to sell—

My car? Yeah, that might get me a ticket to Milwaukee—on a bus.

The pearls that Cole had given me for Christmas? They were probably the most expensive possession I owned. Also the dearest to my heart. Well, those and my diamond engagement ring.

I held up my hand to look at the one-carat stone mounted on a plain yellow gold band that matched my wedding ring. Madeline had asked me why I still wore it. I'd told her out of loyalty to Charlie's memory. I remembered how Madeline said we take our memories with us wherever we go. Memories didn't reside in objects. They resided in our hearts and in our minds. Charlie would always be part of my past. But Cole was my future.

I pushed aside the rest of my tuna sandwich and headed for the hall closet to get my coat.

"I've got to run an errand," I yelled in the direction of the living room where Nat was lecturing the kids about flinging noodles at each other. "I'll be back soon!"

I roared downtown in my rusty station wagon, heart pounding, mind spinning.

"Charlie," I whispered, "you understand, don't you?"

Just as I turned onto Main Street, a car pulled out of its parking spot in front of Mueller the Jeweler. Like the desperate woman I was, I nonsensically took it as a sign. Charlie knew I'd loved him with all my heart. But Charlie was gone. I'd keep the memory of him with me always. But that was then, this was now. And I was about to sell my engagement ring so I could fly into the future.

I had to parallel park—never one of my strong suits. As soon as I'd maneuvered the wagon into the spot far enough so it wouldn't block traffic, I jumped out and sprinted for Ivan's shop—where I came face-to-face with a sign on the door.

Closed until January 2nd, it read, *have a happy new year!*

"Oh, Ivan." I sighed. "That's exactly what I'm trying to do."

By the time I got home, the soup wars were, thankfully, over and the kids were out in the yard, blowing off steam by stamping snow into geometric shapes. They all waved and yelled out greetings. I waved listlessly back.

Natalie met me at the door.

"You look like hell," she said. "Where did you go?"

Wearily, I slipped out of my coat. "I had a brainstorm but it didn't work out."

She looked as miserable as I felt. "Ma, I'd give anything if Jeremy and I could afford to buy you a first-class ticket."

"I know that, baby. Let's face it, though, I'm too old for fairy tales, anyway. If Cole and I are supposed to be together, we'll find a way to work it out. It just won't be tomorrow night," I added forlornly.

"Life sucks sometimes."

"No shit," I said. "Listen, I'm going upstairs and lay down for a while. I'm beat."

"Okay, Ma," Natalie said.

Now that Gwen was gone, I was sleeping in my old bedroom. I climbed the stairs, went into my room, and shut the door, but I didn't lay down. Instead, I went to the dresser and picked up the velvet box that held Cole's pearls. I'd never called to thank him. I guess, in the back of my mind, I'd pictured myself showing up in Paris on New Year's Eve wearing them. I put the earrings in and slipped on the bracelet. The pearls quickly warmed to my skin.

I should call Cole soon and let him know that I wasn't coming. But, though the situation looked pretty hopeless, I wasn't ready to give up yet. And here I'd always thought I was the practical, down-to-earth one. Instead, I was a crazy *pie in the sky* romantic. Maybe the Pollyanna moniker fit after all.

What miracle did I think was going to happen between this afternoon and tomorrow morning that would send me on my way to Paris?

There was a knock on the door.

"Come in," I said.

It was Natalie. She held the cordless phone out to me. "Phone call for you, Ma," she said.

I had an extension in my bedroom. Funny—I don't remember hearing it ring.

I took the phone from Natalie and put it to my ear. "Hello?"

"There's a first-class ticket waiting for you at O'Hare, Mother," Gwen said. "Your plane for Paris leaves at six tomorrow morning."

"What?"

"I said—"

"I know what you said, but why the change of heart?"

"I didn't say I'd had a change of heart, did I? It's simply that certain parties have managed to convince me that you and Cole deserve a chance to make it just like David and I do."

I looked at Natalie. She had a big grin on her face. No wonder I hadn't heard the phone ring. Natalie had placed the call to Gwen and had somehow convinced her to buy me the ticket.

"Thank you, Gwen. I really appreciate you coming through for me like this."

"You're welcome," she said primly. "However I want to go on record as saying that I still think he's going to make you miserable."

"I'll make a note of that," I said drily. "And if he does make me miserable, I promise to come crawling home and let you say I told you so for the rest of my life."

"That seems fair," she said coolly, then, "Mom, I really do want you to be happy."

"That's all I've ever wanted for you, too, baby. But I didn't always agree with what you thought would make you happy."

"No. I suppose you didn't."

"But I respected your right to go for it anyway."

Gwen sighed heavily. "Mother, I bought you the ticket, didn't I? So can we skip the lecture?"

I laughed. "You've got it. Tell David I said thank you, okay?"

There was silence and then I heard a little sniff.

"Gwen, are you all right?"

"I'm going to miss you, Mom," she said. "You tell that father-in-law of mine that if he isn't good to you, he's going to hear from me."

"That should scare the heck out of him," Nat said after Gwen and I had hung up and I'd related the conversation to her.

I laughed again. "She came through for me, though, didn't she? Thanks to you."

Nat grinned and nodded. "Gwen has her moments. And for once she's put some of David's money into something really, really great."

"How on earth did you manage to convince her to do it?"

"Believe me, Ma, you don't wanna know."

I had this thing about wanting to go to Cole with just my Vuitton pilot's case, exactly the way I'd gone to him the first time. Call me sentimental. Or maybe I just wanted to keep traveling light. This meant that I was pretty much only taking the Ralph Lauren that Cole had bought me and my trusty old flannel pajamas and robe. I would have loved to have shopped for something a little sexier than the flannel, but there was no time.

Nat was in the kitchen putting some kind of dinner together, and I was in my office with Jeremy. We were trying to get him up to speed on my filing system and prepare him for the on-slaught of tax season, when the doorbell rang.

"I'll get it!" Nat yelled from the kitchen.

"And like I said," I was saying to Jeremy when Nat came into the office, "I'll only be an e-mail or phone call away. I can even do some of the work from Paris, if need be, or we could hire someone part-time to help you. I think you're going to do fine. By the time you finish that course on tax preparation, you'll be ready."

"Package for you, Ma," Nat said when I'd stopped talking.

"This time of night?"

"It was one of those express services," she said.

I read the label. "It's from Gwen."

"Uh-oh," Nat said. "Maybe she's changed her mind. Better check to see if it's ticking."

I held it up to my ear. "Sounds safe enough to me," I quipped.

"Well, don't say I didn't warn you."

I shook my head at Nat and opened the package.

Inside the carton was a gift box. I drew it out and opened it. Beneath layers of white tissue paper was a gorgeous gown and matching robe in the palest of pink, each of them dripping with ivory lace.

There was no card, but on plain, expensive cream stationery, Gwen had scrawled,

This way at least I'll approve of your nightwear. Love and luck, Gwen.

"Damn it," Nat said. "Even when she does something nice like this she's gotta be a bitch about it."

But there were tears in Nat's eyes when she said it. She knew her sister was doing her best. I was beginning to think that maybe I'd done a pretty good job with both of my daughters. With me out of the way, who knew what kind of relationship might develop between them?

I picked up the gown again while I imagined the look in Cole's eyes when he saw me in it. The diamond in my engagement ring winked at me as I smoothed my hand across the soft fabric.

It was time.

I folded the gown and placed it back into the box then I slipped off my wedding set and held the engagement ring out to Natalie.

"I want you to have this," I said. "And I think your father would want it, too."

With wide, moist eyes Natalie looked at the ring then at me. "Mom—" she started to protest.

I shook my head to silence her. "I can't go to Cole with another man's ring on my finger. Nat, you wearing this ring— the two of you raising your children in this house. Don't you see? It's perfect. This part of my journey is over—but for you and Jeremy, it's only beginning."

Natalie still hesitated, so Jeremy took the ring from my hand and slipped it on his wife's finger above the plain gold band he'd given her on their wedding day. It loooked exactly right.

Jo was driving me to O'Hare and Jeremy had calculated that we'd need to leave at three in the morning, so no one bothered to go to bed that night. Not even my grandchildren. When Jo came to pick me up, there were plenty of hugs and tears on the front porch. Natalie was crying. Jeremy was trying not to and the grandkids were just charged up with being outside in their pajamas.

Now that the time had come, I couldn't seem to make myself leave. Then suddenly someone yelled, "Will you snap out of it and get your can in the car? You've got a plane to catch, you know!"

It was Iris standing on the sidewalk in leopard print knee boots and a fringed leather jacket. I ran down the steps to throw my arms around her.

"You came!"

"Hey, I didn't get to see you off to Paris the first time. No way was I going to miss the rerun. Besides, you know I'm a better driver than Jo. She'd never get you to O'Hare in time."

I started to laugh and so did Iris.

"Get going, Ma," Natalie called from the front porch. "You're going to miss your plane!"

With one last wave, I got into Iris's car. I could still hear Ashley yelling "Bye, bye, Grandma!" when Jo had turned the corner.

I sniffed and wiped away a couple of tears.

Jo opened a thermos of the diner's coffee and poured me a cup. "Here, hon, you're going to need this."

I gratefully took it and gulped. The heat felt good as it traveled down my throat, nearly melting the unshed tears clogging it.

"I hope you brought donuts to go with this," I said.

Jo produced a white paper bag. "Fresh from the fryer."

"Road food!" Iris yelled as she reached for the bag.

"Hey—I thought you were having trouble zipping your leather jeans."

"Fuck the jeans. I'm fifty-two. I got a right to spread out a little."

Jo and I laughed and we all dug into the bag for a donut. It suddenly occurred to me that it would be a long time before I'd taste one again.

"I have something I have to say," Iris announced.

I squeezed her arm. "No, you don't. I was wrong to leave without telling you. This," I said with emphasis, "is how a woman should leave town—wedged between her two best girl-friends and stuffing herself with donuts."

Iris shook her head. "Thanks for letting me off the hook, but I gotta say this. I'm sorry I've been such a bitch since you got back. I was—well, I was feeling left behind. And you know how I like to be the center of attention. You also know how cavalier I've always been about my independence. About not wanting to be needed."

Jo and I nodded.

"But, damn it, your feet can get pretty damn cold when you're fifty-two and sleeping alone. Lately I've been wondering if being tied down is really such a bad thing."

"You have got to be kidding," Jo commented in disbelief.

"Hey, people change. If Abby can, I figured, why can't I? So, when that guy from Milwaukee didn't ask me out on a third date, I called and asked him instead."

"Pull the car over," Jo squealed. "I need room to faint."

"Sorry, girlfriend," Iris said, "you're going to have to faint sitting up. Abby's got a plane to catch."

"This is huge stuff, Iris," I said. "Huge."

"Yeah, I'm really putting myself out there. And I'm scared shitless about it, too."

"For what it's worth, I'm pretty scared myself. But I'm going back to Paris anyway. I'm going to take that job and I'm going to see if Cole and I can build a life together. One of the things I've learned during all of this is that the only way to overcome fear is to do what your heart tells you to and bravery will always follow."

When we reached O'Hare I insisted they only drop me off. There had been enough goodbyes already.

Iris shook her head as we stood outside in the predawn darkness. "I can't believe you're going to be living in Paris," she said as she put her cigarette out after the second puff.

"You know something? I don't think it would matter where I lived as long as it was with Cole."

She groaned. "Oh, no. Now Jo is going to say the same thing about Mike and I'm going to feel like some kind of pathetic spinster. The hottest girl in the graduating class of 1972 isn't supposed to end up alone."

"Hey, it's not over till it's over," I reminded her. "Who knows what a third date could lead to?"

"True," she agreed. "I mean, who would have thought you'd end up in Paris with a hot, rich architect."

We all laughed, but I suspect it was more to stave off the tears than anything else.

I said, "I'd better go check in."

"Group hug!" Jo yelled.

Iris swore but joined in just the same.

"Listen," she said, wiping the tears from under her eyes with her fingertips, "I want you to go to that perfume place and describe me. See what kind of scent they come up with."

"Something wild and fantastic, I'm sure," I assured her.

"Don't forget who your real friends are," Iris added.

"Never again," I replied, then went into the terminal to find my gate. My trusty Vuitton kept up with me all the way as tears streamed down my face.

The tears didn't last long. The atmosphere on the flight was jubilant. Everyone on the plane was literally flying into the future. We'd reach the New Year seven hours sooner than Chicago. I had my requisite free glass of champagne, but I was mainly an observer—exhausted but unable to sleep. So much had happened in the past week. I'd learned so much about my daughters. They were each strong women in their own way, each loving in their own way, each stubborn in their own way. *Charlie*, I thought as I gazed out the plane's window, *you would be proud of them.*

I think he would be proud of me, too.

We landed at Charles de Gaulle airport at 10:00 p.m., Paris time, on New Year's Eve. As we touched down, I couldn't help but remember the excitement of flying with Cole. Could that have been less than two weeks ago? How can a life change so quickly? Then again, I might have been headed for this very time and place my entire life.

I ended up sharing a taxi into the city with four French college students—none of whom spoke English. I caught a word here and there and managed to convey to them that I wanted to go directly to the Eiffel Tower. They passed the information on to the driver.

When we entered the city, it absurdly felt like coming home. My life was waiting for me here. Cole. A new job. New friends. A brand-new year.

With my suitcase in hand I hopped out of the taxi, as close to the Eiffel Tower as it could get. The streets were clogged with traffic, the air was full of honking horns and blowing whistles and the sound of firecrackers snapping. The sidewalks were alive with people.

I slowed enough to check my watch. It was five minutes to midnight. The Eiffel Tower, ablaze with light, was up ahead.

The closer I got the more nervous I got. What if Cole changed his mind? What if he wasn't there? What if we couldn't find each other and he thought that I'd changed my mind?

What if I'd just done the most ridiculous thing I'd ever done in my life?

No, I thought as I started to run toward the tower. If Cole wasn't there, I'd survive. The same way I'd survived everything else that had ever happened. I was staying in Paris for at least a year, I promised myself, even if I would have to spend that year alone.

Oh, but how I hoped I wouldn't be spending it alone.

Fireworks exploded overhead. Bright sparks against the black sky. People cheered. Church bells chimed. And still I kept running forward.

Then suddenly, the crowd ahead parted and there he was. Handsome and dashing and waiting for me.

I ran toward Cole.

I ran toward my future.

* * * * *

Experience entertaining women's fiction for every woman
who has wondered "what's next?" in her life.
Turn the page for a sneak preview of a new book
from Harlequin NEXT,
WHY IS MURDER ON THE MENU, ANYWAY?
by Stevi Mittman

On sale December 26, wherever books are sold.

"I think maybe what you need to do is give her time."

Design Tip of the Day

Ambience is everything. Imagine eating a foie gras at a luncheonette counter or a side of coleslaw at Le Cirque. It's not a matter of food but one of atmosphere. Remember that when planning your dining room design.

—Tips from *Teddi.com*

"Now that's the kind of man you should be looking for," my mother, the self-appointed keeper of my shelf-life stamp, says. She points with her fork at a man in the corner of the Steak-Out Restaurant, a dive I've just been hired to redecorate. Making this restaurant look four-star will be hard, but not half as hard as getting through lunch without strangling the woman across the table from me. "*He* would make a good husband."

"Oh, you can tell that from across the room?" I ask, wondering how it is she can forget that when we had trouble getting rid of my last husband, she shot him. "Besides being ten minutes away from death if he actually eats all that steak, he's twenty years too old for me and—shallow woman that I am—twenty pounds too heavy. Besides, I am *so* not looking for another husband here. I'm looking to design a new image for this place, looking for some sense of ambience, some feeling, something I can build a proposal on for them."

My mother studies the man in the corner, tilting her head, the better to gauge his age, I suppose. I think she's grimacing, but with all the Botox and Restylane injected into that face, it's hard to tell. She takes another bite of her steak, chews slowly so that I don't miss the fact that the steak is a poor cut and tougher than it should be. "You're concentrating on the wrong kind of proposal," she says finally. "Just look at this place, Teddi. It's a dive. There are hardly any other diners. What does *that* tell you about the food?"

"That they cater to a dinner crowd and it's lunchtime," I tell her.

I don't know what I was thinking bringing her here with me. I suppose I thought it would be better than eating alone. There really are days when my common sense goes on vacation. Clearly, this is one of them. I mean, really, did I not resolve less than three weeks ago that I would not let my mother get to me anymore?

What good are New Year's resolutions, anyway?

Mario approaches the man's table and my mother studies him while they converse. Eventually Mario leaves the table with a huff, after which the diner glances up and meets my mother's gaze. I think she's smiling at him. That or she's got indigestion. They size each other up.

I concentrate on making sketches in my notebook and try to ignore the fact that my mother is flirting. At nearly seventy, she's developed an unhealthy interest in members of the opposite sex to whom she isn't married.

According to my father, who has broken the TMI rule and

given me Too Much Information, she has no interest in sex with him. Better, I suppose, to be clued in on what they aren't doing in the bedroom than have to hear what they might be doing.

"He's not so old," my mother says, noticing that I have barely touched the Chinese chicken salad she warned me not to get. "He's got about as many years on you as you have on your little cop friend."

She does this to make me crazy. I know it, but it works all the same. "Drew Scoones is not my little 'friend.' He's a detective with whom I—"

"Screwed around," my mother says. I must look shocked, because my mother laughs at me and asks if I think she doesn't know the "lingo."

What I thought she didn't know was that Drew and I actually tangled in the sheets. And, since it's possible she's just fishing, I sidestep the issue and tell her that Drew is just a couple of years younger than me and that I don't need reminding. I dig into my salad with renewed vigor, determined to show my mother that Chinese chicken salad in a steak place was not the stupid choice it's proving to be.

After a few more minutes of my picking at the wilted leaves on my plate, the man my mother has me nearly engaged to pays his bill and heads past us toward the back of the restaurant. I watch my mother take in his shoes, his suit and the diamond pinkie ring that seems to be cutting off the circulation in his little finger.

"Such nice hands," she says after the man is out of sight. "Manicured." She and I both stare at my hands. I have two popped acrylics that are being held on at weird angles by bandages. My cuticles are ragged and there's marker decorating my right hand from measuring carelessly when I did a drawing for a customer.

Twenty minutes later she's disappointed that he managed to leave the restaurant without our noticing. He will join the list of the ones I let get away. I will hear about him twenty years from now when—according to my mother—my children will be grown and I will still be single, living pathetically alone with several dogs and cats.

After my ex, that sounds good to me.

The waitress tells us that our meal has been taken care of by the management and, after thanking Mario, the owner, complimenting him on the wonderful meal and assuring him that once I have redecorated his place people will be flocking here in droves (I actually use those words and ignore my mother when she rolls her eyes), my mother and I head for the restroom.

My father—unfortunately not with us today—has the patience of a saint. He got it over the years of living with my mother. She, perhaps as a result, figures he has the patience for both of them, and feels justified having none. For her, no rules apply, and a little thing like a picture of a man on the door to a public restroom is certainly no barrier to using the john. In all fairness, it does seem silly to stand and wait for the ladies' room if no one is using the men's room.

Still, it's the idea that rules don't apply to her, signs don't apply to her, conventions don't apply to her. She knocks on the door to the men's room. When no one answers she gestures to me to go in ahead. I tell her that I can certainly wait for the ladies' room to be free and she shrugs and goes in herself.

Not a minute later there is a bloodcurdling scream from behind the men's room door.

"Mom!" I yell. "Are you all right?"

Mario comes running over, the waitress on his heels. Two customers head our way while my mother continues to scream.

I try the door, but it is locked. I yell for her to open it and she fumbles with the knob. When she finally manages to unlock and open it, she is white behind her two streaks of blush, but she is on her feet and appears shaken but not stirred.

"What happened?" I ask her. So do Mario and the waitress and the few customers who have migrated to the back of the place.

She points toward the bathroom and I go in, thinking it serves her right for using the men's room. But I see nothing amiss.

She gestures toward the stall, and, like any self-respecting and suspicious woman, I poke the door open with one finger, expecting the worst.

What I find is worse than the worst.

The husband my mother picked out for me is sitting on the toilet. His pants are puddled around his ankles, his hands are hanging at his sides. Pinned to his chest is some sort of Health Department certificate.

Oh, and there is a large, round, bloodless bullet hole between his eyes.

Four Nassau County police officers are securing the area, waiting for the detectives and crime scene personnel to show up. They are trying, though not very hard, to comfort my mother, who in another era would be considered to be suffering from the vapors. Less tactful in the twenty-first century, I'd say she was losing it. That is, if I didn't know her better, know she was milking it for everything it was worth.

My mother loves attention. As it begins to flag, she swoons and claims to feel faint. Despite four No Smoking signs, my mother insists it's all right for her to light up because, after all, she's in shock. Not to mention that signs, as we know, don't apply to her.

When asked not to smoke, she collapses mournfully in a chair and lets her head loll to the side, all without mussing her hair.

Eventually, the detectives show up to find the four patrolmen all circled around her, debating whether to administer CPR, smelling salts or simply call the paramedics. I, however, know just what will snap her to attention.

"Detective Scoones," I say loudly. My mother parts the sea of cops.

"We have to stop meeting like this," he says lightly to me, but I can feel him checking me over with his eyes, making sure I'm all right while pretending not to care.

"What have you got in those pants?" my mother asks him, coming to her feet and staring at his crotch accusingly. "*Baydar?* Everywhere we Bayers are, you turn up. You don't expect me to buy that this is a coincidence, I hope."

Drew tells my mother that it's nice to see her, too, and asks if it's his fault that her daughter seems to attract disasters.

Charming to be made to feel like the bearer of a plague.

He asks how I am.

"Just peachy," I tell him. "I seem to be making a habit of finding dead bodies, my mother is driving me crazy and the catering hall I booked two freakin' years ago for Dana's bat mitzvah has just been shut down by the Board of Health!"

"Glad to see your luck's finally changing," he says, giving me a quick squeeze around the shoulders before turning his attention to the patrolmen, asking what they've got, whether they've taken any statements, moved anything, all the sort of stuff you see on TV, without any of the drama. That is, if you don't count my mother's threats to faint every few minutes when she senses no one's paying attention to her.

Mario tells his waitstaff to bring everyone espresso, which I decline because I'm wired enough. Drew pulls him aside and a minute later I'm handed a cup of coffee that smells divinely of Kahlúa.

The man knows me well. Too well.

His partner, whom I've met once or twice, says he'll interview the kitchen staff. Drew asks Mario if he minds if he takes statements from the patrons first and gets to him and the waitstaff afterward.

"No, no," Mario tells him. "Do the patrons first." Drew raises his eyebrow at me like he wants to know if I get the double entendre. I try to look bored.

"What is it with you and murder victims?" he asks me when we sit down at a table in the corner.

I search them out so that I can see you again, I almost say, but I'm afraid it will sound desperate instead of sarcastic.

My mother, lighting up and daring him with a look to tell her not to, reminds him that *she* was the one to find the body.

Drew asks what happened *this time.* My mother tells him how the man in the john was "taken" with me, couldn't take his eyes off me and blatantly flirted with both of us. To his credit, Drew doesn't laugh, but his smirk is undeniable to the trained eye. And I've had my eye trained on him for nearly a year now.

"While he was noticing you," he asks me, "did *you* notice

anything about him? Was he waiting for anyone? Watching for anything?"

I tell him that he didn't appear to be waiting or watching. That he made no phone calls, was fairly intent on eating and did, indeed, flirt with my mother. This last bit Drew takes with a grain of salt, which was the way it was intended.

"And he had a short conversation with Mario," I tell him. "I think he might have been unhappy with the food, though he didn't send it back."

Drew asks what makes me think he was dissatisfied, and I tell him that the discussion seemed acrimonious and that Mario looked distressed when he left the table. Drew makes a note and says he'll look into it and asks about anyone else in the restaurant. Did I see anyone who didn't seem to belong, anyone who was watching the victim, anyone looking suspicious?

"Besides my mother?" I ask him, and Mom huffs and blows her cigarette smoke in my direction.

I tell him that there were several deliveries, the kitchen staff going in and out the back door to grab a smoke. He stops me and asks what I was doing checking out the back door of the restaurant.

Proudly—because, while he was off forgetting me, dropping by only once in a while to say hi to Jesse, my son, or drop something by for one of my daughters that he thought they might like, I was getting on with my life—I tell him that I'm decorating the place.

He looks genuinely impressed. "Commercial customers? That's great," he says. Okay, that's what he *ought* to say. What he actually says is "Whatever pays the bills."

"Howard Rosen, the famous restaurant critic, got her the job," my mother says. "You met him—the good-looking, distinguished gentleman with the *real* job, something to be proud of. I guess you've never read his reviews in *Newsday*."

Drew, without missing a beat, tells her that Howard's reviews are on the top of his list, as soon as he learns how to read.

"I only meant—" my mother starts, but both of us assure her that we know just what she meant.

"So," Drew says. "Deliveries?"

I tell him that Mario would know better than I, but that I saw vegetables come in, maybe fish and linens.

"This is the second restaurant job Howard's got her," my mother tells Drew.

"At least she's getting *something* out of the relationship," he says.

"If he were here," my mother says, ignoring the insinuation, "he'd be comforting her instead of interrogating her. He'd be making sure we're both all right after such an ordeal."

"I'm sure he would," Drew agrees, then looks me in the eyes as if he's measuring my tolerance for shock. Quietly he adds, "But then maybe he doesn't know just what strong stuff your daughter's made of."

It's the closest thing to a tender moment I can expect from Drew Scoones. My mother breaks the spell. "She gets that from me," she says.

Both Drew and I take a minute, probably to pray that's all I inherited from her.

"I'm just trying to save you some time and effort," my mother tells him. "My money's on Howard."

Drew withers her with a look and mutters something that sounds suspiciously like "fool's gold." Then he excuses himself to go back to work.

I catch his sleeve and ask if it's all right for us to leave. He says sure, he knows where we live. I say goodbye to Mario. I assure him that I will have some sketches for him in a few days, all the while hoping that this murder doesn't cancel his redecorating plans. I need the money desperately, the alternative being borrowing from my parents and being strangled by the strings.

My mother is strangely quiet all the way to her house. She doesn't tell me what a loser Drew Scoones is—despite his good looks—and how I was obviously drooling over him. She doesn't ask me where Howard is taking me tonight or warn me not to tell my father about what happened because he will worry about us both and no doubt insist we see our respective psychiatrists.

She fidgets nervously, opening and closing her purse over and over again.

"You okay?" I ask her. After all, she's just found a dead man on the toilet, and tough as she is that's got to be upsetting.

When she doesn't answer me I pull over to the side of the road.

"Mom?" She refuses to meet my eyes. "You want me to take you to see Dr. Cohen?"

She looks out the window as if she's just realized we're on Broadway in Woodmere. "Aren't we near Marvin's Jewelers?" she asks, pulling something out of her purse.

"What have you got, Mother?" I ask, prying open her fingers to find the murdered man's ring.

"It was on the sink," she says in answer to my dropped jaw. "I was going to get his name and address and have you return it to him so that he could ask you out. I thought it was a sign that the two of you were meant to be together."

"He's dead, Mom. You understand that, right?" I ask. You never can tell when my mother is fine and when she's in la-la land.

"Well, I didn't know that," she shouts at me. "Not at the time."

I ask why she didn't give it to Drew, realize that she wouldn't give Drew the time in a clock shop and add, "...or one of the other policemen?"

"For heaven's sake," she tells me. "The man is dead, Teddi, I took his ring. How would that look?"

Before I can tell her it looks just the way it is, she pulls out a cigarette and threatens to light it.

"I mean, really," she says, shaking her head like it's my brains that are loose. "What does he need with it now?"

All women become slightly psychic…eventually!

Lila's psychic ability disappeared the moment her visions led her to a missing heiress tied to the bed of Lila's fiancé. Leaving town to start over, Lila's journey finds her changing in ways she could never have predicted.

Slightly Psychic

by Sandra Steffen

HARLEQUIN®
Next™

HN75
Available January 2007
TheNextNovel.com